Between Love and Honor

BETWEEN LOVE AND HONOR

THE MEN OF THE SECRET SERVICE SERIES

TRACY SOLHEIM

TULE
PUBLISHING

DEDICATION

This one is for my brothers, Kevin and Dave. One's a sailor and the other keeps the hackers away. Any mistakes I made with regard to sailing or the dark web is totally their fault!

PROLOGUE

THE PHOTOGRAPHER PRESSED her back against the hard stone of the building, doing her best to fade into the darkness. Several pairs of boots stomped along the cobblestones in pursuit. She held her breath, willing them to pass her by.

They didn't.

As silently as possible, she released the safety on her handgun and let her training kick in. But just before they rounded the corner, a voice cried out in the distance.

"She went this way," a male shouted in French.

A male who sounded an awful lot like her contact in the palace. As she released the breath she'd been holding, sirens began to wail in the distance. Stowing her gun back into her camera bag, she made her way down the hill to the marketplace. Still occupied by locals and tourists alike, the boisterous crowd was enjoying a warm Saturday night on the North African coast. The scent of saffron and chilies mingled with garlic floated through the air. With a skill born from years of practice, she mixed among the crowd as if she didn't have a care in the world.

Once she had navigated a path to the center of the bazaar, she ducked into one of the stalls to quickly cover her head with a scarf she had tucked into her camera bag. She reversed her jacket for added assurance. Strolling through another stall, she stopped and bought a linen blanket, deliberately paying more than the asking price to ensure the seller's silence. She tied the blanket around her waist before wandering deeper into the market, relieved her sandals had been bought locally the week before. It would be another hour at least before she could make the exchange. If she wanted to remain alive, it would suit her well to blend in.

The wailing sirens grew closer. So did the shouts of soldiers. She took refuge among a group of German tourists, flirting coyly with one who claimed to be a famous football player. His celebrity didn't matter to her as much as his brawn did. The crowd grew restless at the arrival of the soldiers and police. The Germans carried her with them as they swarmed the exit.

Once they had cleared the market, she suggested they all go meet her husband. As expected, the football star and his friends scattered. They were so predictable she might have laughed. But she had something more important to carry out before the night was over.

Keeping to the shadows, she entered one of the few remaining churches in Tunisia. The sanctuary was dark with the exception of the many votive candles in front of the altar. She made her way up front and lit a candle. Then another. And another. Once the signal votives were lit, she slid into the fourth pew on the right side of the church. A stained-glass image of angels watched over her. She took that as a good sign. In her profession, guardian angels were always appreciated. No more than three minutes later, a nun joined her in the pew. She reached a gnarled hand across the wooden bench.

"Do you have it?" the nun asked quietly in French.

"Yes."

She dropped the micro card into the nun's outstretched palm. The older woman squeezed her fingers shut and smiled.

"The Mariner has been foiled again," the nun said. "Well done."

"So it would seem."

"You know what to do from here. Your papers will be waiting for you at the dock. Enjoy your respite."

The woman's knees creaked as she made her way out of the pew.

Enjoy your respite.

Disappearing after an op used to feel like a vacation. A reward for completing a successful mission. But the longer she was in the game, the more the "respites" began to feel like banishment. Still, she had to admit, a few weeks of isolation beat being burned. Gathering up her camera bag, she made her way out of Africa and into the shadows where she vanished yet again.

CHAPTER ONE

B EN SEGAR SWORE in frustration as he tugged at the eighteen inches of silk wrapped tightly around his neck. He was a former army ranger and trained Secret Service agent with advanced degrees from MIT and Stanford, for crying out loud. His fingers could dismantle an IED, fire a kill-shot accurately from fifty meters, and bring a woman to ecstasy in two minutes flat. Yet tonight, they couldn't seem to wrestle a damned bow tie into place.

"Hey, Boy Genius, allow me." Secret Service Agent Christine Groesch tapped him on the shoulder indicating he should turn from the mirror and face her.

The Secret Service lounge, located directly below the Oval Office on the ground floor of the White House, was a frenzy of activity. Agents filled the room changing into either tuxedoes or their battle dress uniforms—or BDUs— depending on their assignment for the evening's state dinner. The event was the finale to the World Economic Summit. With heads of state from twenty different countries attending—not all of whom were on solid diplomatic terms with the US—tensions were running high among the men and women charged with protecting the president of the United States and his family.

"It's like tying your shoes," Christine explained.

Of course, the pesky fabric slid easily through her fingers forming a perfect bow on her first attempt.

"How did you get to be such an expert at bow ties?" Ben asked.

A wistful look settled into Christine's eyes before disappearing behind the professional mask she wore. "My sister has three kids under the age of ten. Which also means her patience isn't what it used to be." She smiled as she straightened Ben's tie. "It fell to me to teach them all how to tie their shoes."

Time spent with loved ones was fleeting for most agents within the president's protective detail. Many families didn't survive the strain. Ben had long ago resolved that a wife and kids were not conducive to a life in law enforcement. He knew firsthand what that type of career could do to a family and he never regretted giving up one for the other. Good friends, a steady diet of willing women to share his bed, and his role as the Mariner, the Secret Service's top cyber asset, gave him all the satisfaction in life he needed.

It appeared Christine might be having regrets of her own, however. *Not another one.* There seemed to be an outbreak of conscious coupling among his friends lately. He shook his head in bewilderment.

"You've been in your 'la-bore-atory' too long, Segar," Lou Caracas called from across the room where he was strapping his service revolver to the leg holster on his BDU. The agent was subbing as a member of the Secret Service's

Counter Assault Tactical (CAT) team tonight. "Since when do they invite the geek squad to a state dinner, anyway?"

"Since the Secretary of Homeland Security issued orders for Segar to be here," a voice boomed behind them.

Agent Adam Lockett, commander of the CAT team stood in the doorway looking like the badass sharpshooter he was. A hush fell over the room with Adam's announcement. Ben would have rather his buddy keep that little bit of intel to himself. The fewer people who knew of his clandestine work for the Secretary of Homeland, the better.

"Just remember to keep your pretty clothes and your tech toys out of the way so the real muscle can do its job tonight, Inspector Gadget," Caracas said with a snicker before picking up his helmet and heading out the door.

"That guy is a hothead," Christine murmured as she pinned the insignia designating her as a member of the Secret Service into the lapel of her sequined pantsuit. The pin was meant to distinguish her from the actual dinner guests—assuming the sensible shoes she wore wouldn't give her away first. "I'm glad Adam will have him dodging raindrops up on the roof all night. I hope it pours."

"Bite your tongue," Adam admonished their friend when he joined them. "It's bad enough my team and I have to spend the evening as human lightning rods. This BDU is heavy as shit when it's wet."

Christine laughed. "I'm sure you'll figure out a way to stay dry. Besides, given how much time you spend canoodling with a certain member of the First Family, I'm sure you already know the best places to hide out in this building." She patted Adam on the shoulder. "See you upstairs, Ben."

"Christine has a point," Ben added. "But instead of hiding out, maybe you should get your fiancée to intervene on your behalf." His buddy had done the unthinkable and fallen in love. In fact, he was set to marry the First Lady's younger sister in a few weeks. "You could escort Josslyn to the dinner and let that smart-ass get drenched up to his balls instead."

"No can do." Adam shook his head. "Joss hates these kinds of events. She's holed up in her office at the zoo working on an op-ed opposing big trophy hunting. The piece will probably have the president's chief of staff spewing his morning coffee tomorrow." A proud grin tugged at the corners of Adam's mouth.

Clearly, he no longer considered his fiancée to be the She-Devil incarnate. A staunch defender of animal rights and hater of all things gun related, Dr. Josslyn Benoit should be an unlikely match for the stoic sniper. Except she wasn't. As much as Ben hated to admit it, the passionate zoologist was, in fact, the perfect match for his friend.

And another one bites the dust. Their third roommate, Griffin Keller, had married the First Lady's goddaughter a few months back. Once upon a time, the three men had sworn a solemn oath to never succumb to the white picket fence in the 'burbs with a wife and two point five kids. Somehow, Ben had become the last man standing.

"They're waiting for you in the Woodshed," Adam said, interrupting Ben's thoughts.

Grabbing the laptop case at his feet, he followed Adam out the door. They strolled down the long hallway to the White House Situation Room, known among senior staff as the Woodshed.

"I'm guessing that whatever got you out of your T-shirt and into the James Bond getup tonight is above my pay grade," Adam remarked quietly.

"More like above your bandwidth," he teased. "This is going to come as a shock, but they want me for my mind." He hefted the laptop case in his hand. "And the beautiful things it creates."

"Try not to bore them with numbers, dude," Adam teased.

His friendship with Adam—and Griffin—dated back to their first summer as plebes at West Point over a dozen years ago. They'd all three found their way to the Secret Service after their tours of duty in the army and even shared a townhouse on Capitol Hill. But as close as the three men were, there was an entire segment of Ben's life that he couldn't share with anyone else. While he assumed his friends suspected there was more to Ben's job than managing the Secret Service's crime lab, it was better for everyone involved that his alter ego be kept exactly where Ben did much of his work, in the dark.

At the end of the hallway, two Marine guards stood at attention on either side of the entry door to the inner sanctum of the White House security. Secret Service Director Worcester was wearing out a hole in the carpet waiting for them. He waved them into the reception area.

"Glad you had evening clothes at the ready, Agent Segar," the director said. "Tonight is crazy enough without having to find you a monkey suit. Nothing seems to be going as it should. Including the damn weather."

Ben shared a look with Adam, hoping the director didn't notice how he'd taped up the cuffs of Adam's tuxedo to accommodate his shorter arms. Since he spent his days tucked away in his lab across town and not on a protective detail, there was no need for Ben to actually own a tux. Luckily, he and Adam were both six-foot-one with a similar muscular frame. Except for their arms. Griffin and Ben teased Adam ruthlessly about his gorilla arms.

Adam slapped Ben on the back before turning to leave. "Enjoy the party, Inspector Gadget."

Ben leveled a withering look at his friend.

Adam shrugged. "Hey, you gotta admit the name fits you."

"Keep the Crown safe tonight, Agent Lockett," the director ordered, referring to the White House by its Secret Service code name.

"Always job number one." Adam saluted them before disappearing.

"The guests will be arriving shortly." The director indicated Ben should precede him down the few steps leading to the briefing room.

Ben hesitated briefly. When he woke up that morning, the only stressful thing on his agenda was making sure his thirty-five-foot sailboat was secure ahead of the line of nasty summer storms predicted to pass through the nation's capital this evening. But then his dark web alias had received a very troubling message. One that required a speedy intervention.

"Make way for the president," Director Worcester murmured sharply, prodding Ben into action.

As the men and women assembled at the table rose to their feet, Ben hurried to one of the two empty chairs lining the walls directly behind his boss, the Secretary of Homeland Security. She nodded toward Ben confidently as the president seated himself at the head of the table. The others followed suit amid a chorus of, "Good evening, Mr. President."

President Conrad Manning acknowledged them with a weary sigh. "Diplomacy is difficult enough without having to battle severe weather and a known terrorist hacker trying to crash dinner." He unbuttoned his tuxedo jacket and leaned back in his chair. "We're taking a huge political risk letting him through the front door. Tell me we have the intelligence to identify this guy before he gets into the State Dining Room."

"We have no idea of this person's actual identity, only his online alias," the Secretary of Homeland responded. "He's been visiting multiple terrorist outposts boasting of his apparent prowess in hacking into various entities' computer systems and holding them for ransom. Our sources indicate he's working with someone here in Washington to perpetrate a cyberattack against the US."

"This is a big country," the president said. "Can't your sources get more specific than that?"

"Only that we believe he is the leader of a ring of cyber hackers who have been taking over banks worldwide. His success would be catastrophic to the US economy, sir."

The Secretary of Homeland's words settled over the room causing most of those assembled to shift uncomfortably in their seats.

President Manning pinched the bridge of his nose. "All of this based on some chatter on the dark web? What the hell is the dark web, anyway? A chat room for a bunch of terrorists and criminals? Can we believe anything that even goes on there?"

The NSA director cleared his throat. "With all due respect, sir, we've been monitoring this individual's activities via multiple channels in addition to the dark web. Based on this, we concur that the intel the Secret Service provided is viable."

Damn right it's viable! Ben tried not to jump out of his chair at the NSA director's snarky tone. The man hated that Ben was always able to put the pieces of the puzzle together quicker than his own staff.

"We'd be committing diplomatic suicide to exclude an entire delegation from the dinner based on our assumptions," the Secretary of State interjected. "It's better to let him through the door as long as we can catch him before he meets his contact."

"And then what?" the president demanded.

"We continue our search for his contact," the Secretary of Homeland replied matter-of-factly.

The CIA director spoke up from the end of the table.

"Our sources indicate our unwanted dinner guest is a member of the prince's entourage. All we have to go on, however, is a dimly lit photo our operative was able to shoot during one of this guy's marketing visits."

Everyone looked toward the screen at the end of the room where a photo popped up. It was dark, but Ben's pulse sped up at the challenge the grainy image presented. He was confident VOYEUR, the facial recognition software he'd spent close to ten million dollars of taxpayers' money refining, would be able to identify the suspect quickly. His fingers twitched around the handle to his laptop case housing the VOYEUR software.

"As you can see, his profile is heavily shadowed," the CIA director continued.

"Our suspect will be enjoying dessert before any artificial intelligence can identify him from that photo," the NSA director announced in disgust.

"Not necessarily."

All eyes turned toward Ben. He'd been impertinent by speaking up, that much was evident by the look on the Secretary of Homeland Security's face. But they didn't have time to get into a turf battle with NSA. The artificial intelligence NSA used would take time to pinpoint the suspect. VOYEUR had passed all the field tests demonstrating it could work more rapidly than the technology other agencies were using. It was time to put the system to work.

"You seem confident you can pull this off, Agent . . ." The president looked at Ben as if he was trying to place him.

"Segar, sir. Special Agent Ben Segar. I'm a friend of Dr. Benoit's."

"Ah," President Manning said, recognition dawning as he motioned for Ben to continue.

"I am confident, Mr. President. I've finessed the program so that it calculates in nanoseconds what other facial recognition programs take minutes, sometimes hours, to calculate. Unlike other artificial intelligence systems, VOYEUR can even recognize a face at any age in the spectrum. In other words, my system can identify a face from a picture taken years prior. And vice versa."

The president arched an eyebrow at him. Ben took it as his cue to continue.

"You see, the patterns used in automated facial recognition algorithms don't correlate to obvious anatomical features such as the eyes, nose or mouth in a one-to-one manner, although they are affected by these features. The algorithms see faces in a way that differs from how we visualize them. VOYEUR is able to use precise mathematical correlations—"

The president held up his hand. "I appreciate your enthusiasm for your work, Agent Segar, but I'm a statesman. I never made it past college calculus. I'm going to have to trust your very capable mathematical mind on this one." His expression grew steely as he met the eyes of each of his advisors surrounding the table. "I'm going to have to trust all of you." The president's gaze landed back on Ben. "See that the person of interest is identified and apprehended for questioning before he gets a finger on a single hors d'oeuvre."

BEN SET UP his laptop just inside the usher's office on the first floor. His fingers moved quickly over the keyboard as he logged into the White House's closed-circuit television feed. He bypassed all the cameras except the two in the makeshift security shed at the bottom of the North Portico steps. With the exception of the heads of state, all the visitors to the dinner would pass through metal detectors at the security checkpoint. Thirty seconds was all he needed to hone in on each image and make a match.

"You realize if this works, you're sitting on millions of dollars' worth of proprietary technology?" a voice said at his shoulder.

He wasn't surprised to see the NSA director breathing down his neck. The director had made his case about artificial intelligence getting into the wrong hands at numerous conferences the two men had attended. The race to perfect and speedup the technology not only existed among countries but between private and public-sector entities within the United States, as well.

"China would likely pay billions for it," the director continued. "Lord knows they like to keep a close eye on their people."

Ben could envision hundreds, if not thousands, of potential uses for VOYEUR, some commercial and others decidedly nefarious. And the director was right; someone would pay a lot for the system, if not just the mathematic equations behind it. But he hadn't been motivated by money when he first starting dabbling with facial recognition software.

He'd been looking for someone.

He'd been looking for *her*.

Tonight, however, he was looking for a potential cyber-terrorist, he quickly reminded himself. And when he found him, they'd shut down a cell of radicals worldwide. Besides, he needed to admit she was the one puzzle he would never be able to solve anyway. She wasn't coming back.

Ben ran his fingers over the mousepad, adjusting the recording angle of the two cameras to ensure the best view. The VOYEUR cover page popped up on the screen.

"Wow. She's quite the looker," the NSA director said from over Ben's shoulder. "It always surprises me how you computer geeks end up with a stunner like her."

The director was assuming Ben *had* ended up with her. He hadn't. He clicked over to the closed-circuit feed again.

"She's just the test face I used to calibrate the software," he explained to the director. It wasn't a lie.

"The first guests are rolling up," Agent Groesch announced via the earpiece Ben wore.

He could hear the rain in the background as thunder rumbled loud enough to nearly drown out the marine band playing in the Cross Hall. The nasty weather wasn't doing Ben any favors. The Uniformed Division officers likely wanted to hurry guests through in order to keep them out of the rain. Ben might not have even thirty seconds with which to work.

The initial contingent of partygoers began to pass through the security checkpoint. Women in evening gowns followed by men in black-tie filtered past the cameras. He measured the amount of time VOYEUR took to execute the facial recognition against the seven databases it searched. *Twenty-one seconds.* His program was exceeding even his own wildest expectations. Too bad the knowledge did very little to calm his nerves. Unlike his other covert ops, his name was on this one. Front and center. If it failed, everyone would know who to blame.

The crowd monitoring him grew as Director Worcester joined them at the usher's desk. Ben reached up and tugged the bow tie loose to keep the sweat from pooling on his neck. He was confident in VOYEUR. But many of the guests passing through the metal detectors were already known entities, their clearance checked and rechecked multiple times before they were even invited to the White House. How long would it take to match a rogue face to the partial photograph the CIA had given him? He sat staring at the screen, his pulse pounding in his ears as he settled in to wait.

"Here comes the prince's delegation now," the NSA director said ten minutes later.

The air in the room seemed to crackle around them as lightning flashed outside the windows. Ben tried to steady his breathing. This was no different than some of the secret projects he ran on the dark web. He would prevail here, too.

A few minutes later, Ben's computer chirped loudly when the final member of the prince's delegation went through the metal detector. The screen confirmed a full facial match to the picture the CIA director had provided.

"That's our guy," Ben announced. His mouth had become so dry that the words were hard to push out. But Director Worcester was already communicating with the Uniformed Division officers manning the checkpoint.

The next few minutes were a blur as the staff for the State Department worked with Secret Service agents outside to escort the suspect to another location. The Secretary of Homeland paraded through the usher's office, drink in hand, and patted Ben on the back.

"I knew you could do it, Agent Segar," she said.

The NSA director was more sanguine. "I'll see you in my office first thing, Segar. There's no reason we all shouldn't be using your technology. Remember, it's government property. And for the time being, *you* are government property, too."

"You really are the Boy Genius." Griffin Keller slipped into the chair next to Ben and handed him a small plate full of appetizers. "I guess all those nights you spent with your fingers caressing your keyboard instead of a woman finally paid off. I hope you'll remember us little people when you leave government service and become a bazillionaire."

Ben shot his friend a questioning look. "I'm sorry, what's your name again?" he teased. "Could it be Asshole, perhaps?"

"And so it begins."

"I'm surprised they still let you in this place." Ben speared a piece of shrimp off the plate. Prior to his marriage, Griffin had transferred to a job with the Department of Treasury, citing the more predictable hours as his reason for deserting the Secret Service. Getting leg-shackled did that to a man.

"I've got a person of interest on the guest list. He caught us off guard by showing up tonight. We suspect he's aware we're building a case against him, but he entered the US anyway. He's the arrogant playboy son of a Russian billionaire. Junior is buying up a lot of local real estate," Griff explained keeping his voice down so as not to be overheard. "Then taking out some serious loans using his newly acquired residences as collateral."

"That's a good way to make dirty money clean again."

"Exactly. And now he's branching out into cybercurrency."

"It's the wave of the future," Ben said.

"So you say. The good old paper stuff still works fine for me." Griff picked up a pastry off his plate and grinned at it foolishly. "Plus, I never pass up an excuse to stop by the Crown and corner the curator on the back stairs."

"Didn't Marin tell you?" Ben teased, referring to Griffin's wife, formerly the White House executive pastry chef and now it's historian. "She's dumping your ass for me. She even promised to save me some of her special cream puffs for later."

Griffin actually growled. Ben would have laughed had

his laptop not chimed at the same moment. In all the excitement of earlier, he'd forgotten to power off VO-YEUR. His heart raced, thinking he'd somehow identified the wrong guy.

"Speak of the devil," Griff said as he glanced at the laptop screen. "There's my Russian friend Alexi Ronoff now. As usual, he has a gorgeous piece of arm candy accompanying him. Although I haven't seen this redhead before. I have to admit Alexi has great taste."

Ben's computer chimed again as VOYEUR zeroed in on the woman with Ronoff. Reaching for his bow tie and pulling it completely off, he struggled to get air into his lungs. *He* had seen that redhead before.

Slamming his laptop shut he dumped it into Griffin's lap. "Don't let this out of your sight!"

"What the hell, Bennett?"

But Ben was already sliding across the slick floor of the North Lobby. He skidded to a halt just as the couple passed through the doors at the top of the steps. The screech of his shoes on the marble floor had everyone turning to stare at him, including the very stunned pair of sea-green eyes belonging to none other than Quinn Darby. The woman he had been waiting thirteen years to confront.

And then, as if to underscore the significance of the moment, lightning crackled viciously overhead. Seconds later, the White House went dark.

CHAPTER TWO

DAWN WAS BREAKING behind the Washington Monument. The sun's fledgling rays bathed the Tidal Basin in hues of pinks and purples. Adding to the beauty, the heavy rainfall from the night before made everything look as though it was dusted with glitter. From her vantage point, leaning against one of the marble columns of the Lincoln Memorial, Quinn Darby glanced through the viewfinder of her camera at the joggers hurrying along the pathways between the two landmarks. All of the runners were seemingly oblivious to the beautiful impressionist vista Mother Nature was in the process of painting.

She drew in a lungful of the sparkling air. Hours from now, the shine would wear off this place when thousands of tourists and heavy humidity descended. But this early in the day, the memorial was tranquil, still holding the promise of the optimism it was erected to memorialize.

Good thing since Quinn was in need of all the optimism she could get right now.

As usual, the scent of her handler's cologne reached her first. Distinctive and unique, it was a warm, homey fragrance an older man might wear. It made her want to lean a shoulder on his and unburden herself.

She didn't dare, though.

Neither could she turn around to see his face. He had been explicit about that particular command. The man explained it was for her own protection, but since she was the one straddling the dark side, she figured her handler's anonymity was more for his security than hers. Still, she appreciated the kindness of him wanting her to think otherwise.

"Did you know I was born here?" she blurted out.

She wasn't sure why she led with that random tidbit except she was feeling a bit nostalgic this morning. *Not to mention off-kilter.* She blamed last night's close encounter with Ben Segar for both moods. Not once in her illustrious career had she felt this unbalanced. She was always the steady one. The confident one. Unfazed and unflappable with any assignment.

But not today.

And all because a boy she tried—and failed—not to fall in love with thirteen years earlier had appeared out of seemingly nowhere.

"I was born three miles away at Georgetown Hospital," she babbled on in hopes of getting her mind to deviate from its present course.

She'd only lived in the United States' capital city on occasion during the past thirty years, however. Her mother's career took her to countless countries before she'd reached her teens. Quinn's own career took her even farther afield, never staying in one place long enough to fill out a change of address card, much less put down roots. The nomadic life was a trade-off for the thrilling challenge of being in the game. The risks she took to clandestinely retrieve lost items of importance delivered a potent adrenaline high she thrived on.

"Why, yes, my dear." Her contact's low, well-worn voice sounded amused by her departure from protocol. "I know everything about you."

Of course he does. The man behind her was the only one in the world who knew the real Quinn Darby. Not to mention every alias she'd ever adopted. Ironic, since she knew nothing about him at all.

"Were you able to retrieve the micro card?" he asked.

She shifted her feet nervously. She'd had some close calls and a few failed first attempts at recovering items she was sent to retrieve before, but nothing as unpredictable as last night. Things got hairy when lightning struck the White House causing a temporary blackout and a mass exodus from the building. While the weather provided the perfect cloak for her to slip away without having to face the person she'd been avoiding for nearly half her life, it also meant she wasn't able to secure the item she had been sent to the dinner to retrieve. And this time, what she was seeking had dire consequences to her personally.

"No, I don't have it. But the good news is Alexi Ronoff doesn't have it either."

Quinn felt his sharp intake of breath behind her. "You know this for a fact?"

She nodded. "Alexi isn't aware I speak Russian."

One of the advantages of growing up all over the world

was she'd developed a flair for linguistics. She spoke seven languages fluently and she understood several more. Her talent proved useful in both her careers.

"He was very upset about being hustled out of the White House before the exchange was made. But the seller has already been in contact with him late last night demanding the final payment. Which leads me to the bad news. I suspect someone else unknowingly has the micro card containing the list."

And she had a good idea who that someone else was. *Ben Segar.* Her heart raced at the thought. Yesterday evening, Ben had been in the wrong place at the right time. Why he had even been at the White House was a mystery. The exchange was scheduled to take place immediately upon arriving at the dinner. In all the confusion of the sudden darkness, two people had bumped against her and Alexi. One of them was Ben. The way he'd softly uttered her name in the dark nearly paralyzed her when a second body bumped them. The seller must have mistakenly dropped the micro card into Ben's pocket thinking it was Alexi's. It was the only scenario that made sense.

It was also the only scenario more catastrophic than Alexi getting his hands on the information contained in that file. Because if she could put the pieces together, so too could Alexi. And he'd already proven he was ruthless enough to kill for it.

Her contact echoed her point. "He won't stop until he gets that card. The Phoenix was integral in blocking many of Ronoff's father's business dealings worldwide. He lost several fortunes at the hands of many of the names on that list. One in particular."

Quinn sighed anxiously. "I know." Her stomach felt as if it was turning inside out. Every op she took on came with its own degree of risk. But this one carried an additional peril to the ones she loved. She mentally added Ben Segar to the list of people she couldn't let down.

"I'm assigning someone else to finish this."

Despite the fact she anticipated this might happen, she still had to force herself to remain calm at his declaration. His decision made sense in one respect; she'd outlasted her cover story. For the past several months, she'd been cozying up to Alexi, photographing his many homes and estates throughout the world. The pompous Russian never suspected she was there in a second capacity as a mole. It was sheer luck she'd been able to convince him to allow her to accompany him to the White House the previous evening, sweetly demanding to be his escort as a bonus for getting his homes multipage spreads in all the famous architectural magazines.

But Quinn had a bigger stake in the game than any other operative. And with the addition of Ben Segar as a player, she wasn't going to meekly sit the rest of it out.

"What if I told you I have an idea where to look for the micro card?"

He was quiet for several long heartbeats and Quinn began to fear he'd already left.

"I have to ask how you know this?" he finally demanded.

She was treading a very a fine line here. Her primary goal was to ensure Ronoff did not get the list. If that meant someone had to take her place, so be it. But sweet Ben Segar with the moral compass that never strayed from true north was an innocent in all of this. She'd hurt him once. She'd do everything in her power to make sure he wasn't hurt a second time because of her.

"As I said, I believe a civilian may have intercepted the micro card inadvertently. It's so small they likely don't even know they have it. I'd like permission to retrieve it."

The silence stretched even longer this time. She could feel the tension practically bristling off the man behind her.

"You'd best do so before Ronoff does," he commanded eventually. "Be careful, my dear, and trust no one. There is a traitor among us. Someone willing to sell out our kind. Often, it is the person we least suspect."

She quashed the shiver threatening to traipse up her spine. Such was the life of a spy. It was a good thing she made it a point never to trust anyone. She preferred it that way. Survival within the game was easier when she only had herself to watch out for.

"You know how to contact me once you've gotten the list. I will await your signal."

And with that, he was gone.

While parts of her did a little celebratory happy dance at the potential of another close encounter with Ben, other parts cringed in fear. *Or shame.* No doubt he already hated her for what she'd done to him over a decade before. But it hadn't been her fault. She had no control over her life then or now. All she could do was send up a silent prayer that she'd get out of this op without him hating her more than he likely already did. With less than steady hands, Quinn lifted her camera to her face again to capture a shot of the spectacular sunrise, but the vibrant scene she'd witnessed moments earlier had already faded.

"DUDE, DID YOU sleep in my tux?" Adam's voice shattered the quiet of Ben's office. The dark room was tucked in the back corner of the cyber security lab at Secret Service headquarters seven blocks from the White House. "Damn, I'll never get those wrinkles out."

It wasn't unusual for Ben to catch a few *Zs* at his desk. He often lost track of time when he was working on a case. Last night, however, he'd been hunting through surveillance camera footage, trying in vain to retrace the path of a certain redhead who had seemingly vanished before his eyes.

Again.

The scent of strong coffee made it easier for him to pry his eyelids open. He sighed with gratitude when he saw his friend holding two cups. Adam set one on the desk. Ben wrapped his fingers around it drawing enough energy from the steaming brew to pull himself into an upright position.

"I'll pay for the dry cleaning, but the bow tie is a goner." He took a long swallow, letting the caffeine work its magic. "What time did you get away from the Crown?"

Adam slid into the opposite chair and propped his booted feet onto the desk. "Twenty minutes ago."

"Wow." Ben glanced at his fitness tracker. Seven fifteen. "It took that long to clear the place out?"

"Yeah, well, while you were getting your beauty sleep, Inspector Gadget, someone had to check every nook and cranny of those eighteen acres for stragglers and for sparks."

"Crazy night."

Adam leaned back in the chair and studied Ben over the rim of his coffee cup.

"I heard your program worked like a champ." He saluted Ben with his coffee. "Props on shutting down a ring of cyberterrorists. Who knew you could be such a badass with a simple computer? Now you know what it's like to take down the bad guys."

As much as he wanted to, Ben couldn't tell his buddy this wasn't the first group of terrorists he'd put out of commission. That the conferences he frequently attended doubled as covert ops. To do his job effectively, he needed to keep his alter ego under wraps. The isolation wore on him sometimes, but the payoff was worth the price.

This morning, he could finally take credit for something. And he couldn't help the burst of pride he felt at VOYEUR's success. The program had worked just as he'd envisioned. Even better, according to his CIA contacts, the suspect was already taking a deal and naming names.

But Ben didn't like the contemplative look on his friend's face. Clearly, the sniper had more on his mind.

"Listen, Adam, thanks for the coffee, but I've got to

back up the VOYEUR program before the NSA director hacks it right off my hard drive. Bro-time is going to have to wait until later."

His friend ignored him. "Christine said the most interesting thing to me earlier."

Ben shuffled some papers on his desk trying to appear circumspect. "She says a lot of things."

"Yeah, but this one seemed very out of character. According to her, at the time of the blackout, you were locking eyes with some guest in the Cross Hall, almost as if you'd seen a ghost."

Ben swore beneath his breath. "Christine talks too much."

Adam's eyebrows jumped up his forehead. "I take that as a confirmation. It's not like you to lose your cool on the job. Who is she, dude?"

"What is this, the ladies' room? I told you, I don't have time to shoot the shit with you this morning. I've got important data to sift through."

"Uh-huh." Adam nodded at the bank of computer screens lining one of the walls of the office, all of which were displaying multiple video images of a certain fiery-haired woman in a skintight emerald-green gown. "Don't tell me Cinderella left the ball before you could get her name and number?"

Ben shook his head. He didn't need Cinderella's name. He already had it. Not to mention her date of birth, her mother's maiden name, and her current address. He'd been tracking the woman for years. Thirteen to be precise. Ever since the night she'd made a fool of him in high school.

"Wait." Adam slammed his boots back to the floor and leaned toward one of the monitors. "She looks very familiar in that picture."

"No. She doesn't. She was the date of Griffin's person of interest. Nothing more. And I've got work to do, so beat it." Ben wanted Adam gone before he figured things out.

"No. I swear I've seen her before," Adam argued. "Whoa! That's the babe on your screen saver. Well I'll be damned. She is a real person and not some fantasy woman you're building in a lab somewhere."

Too late. Ben flipped him off.

Adam laughed. "Methinks you do protest too much."

Ben jumped from his chair and began to circle the room.

"Who is she Bennett?"

Adam's quietly asked question made Ben halt his frantic pacing. Heaving a sigh, he rested a hip on the corner of his desk. His eyes landed on one of the still videos depicting Quinn smiling in wonderment at Alexi Ronoff as they entered the White House. Memories of her gifting him with that same tender smile made his chest constrict.

Had she ever really meant it? Or had he been played in the worst way possible?

Despite being a whiz at unearthing information others couldn't find, everything he'd been able to track down about her was superficial. While every other woman on the planet was flaunting her life on social media, Quinn's electronic footprint consisted of a simple business page for her photography business. No school records. No traffic tickets, hell, he couldn't even find a freaking dental record for her. It was as if she was an apparition.

Except she'd been very real last night. The moment his fingers brushed against her skin he'd felt shock waves reverberate through his body. Her quick gasp at the contact told him she felt it too. Still.

He forced the emotion from his throat. "Her name is Quinn Darby. She's a photographer to the rich and famous. Judging by who she attended last night's dinner with, she doesn't care how clean the money they pay her with is."

"Let me rephrase. Who is she to you?"

A harsh laugh escaped Ben's throat before he could pull it back. "She used to be everything to me." It was the first time he'd ever admitted that out loud. He shook his head. "But I was young and stupid then. I know better now."

"Talk to me, Bennett."

He made his way to the sofa on the other side of the room and slid down into the soft leather. "It's your typical story. Exotic girl moves into a small town. Geeky high-schooler makes a fool out of himself over her. She leads him on before eventually ghosting him the night of the prom. He ends up as the laughingstock of everyone in town."

"You're too smart to let that happen."

Leaning his head against the back of the sofa, Ben closed his eyes. "Just because I have a superior intellect doesn't mean I can't be a fool."

And he had been. From the moment Quinn Darby arrived in Watertown, with her long tan legs, her lush cinnamon lashes, and her sultry British accent, he had been captivated by her. Of course, so had every other male in town between the ages of five and ninety-five.

"We were lab partners in chemistry." He laughed at the irony. "Apparently, I was the only one who thought the chemistry was real."

"Did you ever find out why she stood you up for the prom?"

"Isn't it obvious? She wanted to humiliate me."

And humiliate him she did. By mutual agreement, he and Quinn kept their budding relationship quiet. Ben did so because he didn't want to tempt fate or whatever gods had prompted her to look at him twice. He thought she'd felt the same. That what they shared was unique and fragile and too special to broadcast to anyone else. Then, when she'd agreed to attend the prom with him, his ego took hold and he went caveman, bragging to anyone who'd listen. Right up to the night she'd blindsided him.

For years, he grappled with the particular puzzle of why. Mostly because every time he ventured back home to Watertown some asshole brought it up. Nothing ever blew over in a small town. He wished they'd all forget. He wished he could forget. But, try as he might, he couldn't erase the memory of that fateful night.

When no one answered the door the evening of the prom, he'd called the sheriff's office. His grandfather, a deputy with thirty years on the force, arrived in his cruiser five minutes later. He could still see the pity in the old man's eyes. No one really believed the wealthy beauty would consent to attending the prom with a nerd like Ben.

"Face it, son," his no-nonsense grandfather said after they knocked on every door of the house to no avail. "She got a better offer. They probably jetted off to the islands for the long Memorial Day weekend."

But Ben didn't want to face it. Not after what he and Quinn had shared. He and his bruised ego staked out the Darby house for the entire holiday weekend, ignoring the commands of his mother and aunt to come work at their family's marina. By Monday, he was desperate. So desperate that the straight arrow Boy Scout did the unthinkable. He risked his commission to West Point by breaking and entering Quinn's house.

He had never been inside the stately home. Whenever the two of them worked on homework it was at the library or at his aunt's tackle shop at the marina. He now realized she was likely embarrassed to have anything to do with a townie; the son of a widowed school teacher and slain police officer.

That dark night, he wandered through the rooms of the house not caring about the fact he could be caught at any moment. He just wanted answers. Wherever she and her parents had gone, they'd left in a hurry. And if the empty drawers and closets were any indication, they weren't coming back.

The familiar scent of Quinn's perfume led him to her bedroom. He'd fingered the cheerleader pom-poms hanging from the doorknob. Random photos she'd taken of friends framed the side of the big mirror on her dresser. His heart had stopped when he spied a snapshot of the two of them among the others. He looked like a goofball in the picture with his cheesy smile, but the way she was smiling up at him still made his throat tighten and his chest swell.

Just then, a car had slowed out front. He quickly glanced around the room for more clues. In desperation, he snatched up the photo and shoved it in his pocket before bolting down the back stairs and into the inky darkness of the backyard. He'd spent the rest of that night hypothesizing about all the possible scenarios for her abrupt disappearance. Most of them involving terrorists or mafioso. It wasn't until the next day at school he'd learned the truth.

And Blaine Simpson, captain of the lacrosse team and leader of the snotty rich crowd had taken great glee in delivering the blow. Quinn's father had been recalled to England. According to Blaine the Pain, Quinn had known for weeks it was coming and that she wouldn't be around for the prom. Apparently, the only one who didn't know was the one boy in town who supposedly knew everything. Ben had never been more grateful to report to the Beast Barracks for his plebe summer at West Point five days after graduation.

"Kind of ironic that the one time you're in the White House for an event, she shows up," Adam commented, interrupting Ben's painful stroll down memory lane.

Ben sprang from the sofa. He didn't believe in irony,

coincidence, or anything else that couldn't be explained by fact. And his gut was telling him Quinn Darby showing up after all these years, on the arm of a Russian criminal, meant something. He just needed to figure out what.

The rapid pinging of his computer distracted him from solving the puzzle of Quinn, however. He tapped a couple of keys to open an email from the Secretary of Homeland summoning him to her office. Apparently, the NSA director was serious about wanting VOYEUR as soon as he could get his hands on it.

"Well, alrighty then." Adam got to his feet. "Good chat." He headed for the door. "I really stopped by to see if we're still on for dinner in Watertown tonight. Joss wants to sample some of the seafood appetizers we're serving at the reception. Probably the best part of this wedding planning, if you ask me."

"Yeah," he replied absently. "I'll see you there."

Adam hesitated with his hand on the doorknob. "Look, Bennett, I realize I'm not one to call a guy out on the secrets he keeps close to the vest. But a hotshot from MIT once had to set me straight about the value of friendship. Now I'm gonna return the favor. Griff and I, we're your brothers and we've always got your six. We're here when you want to talk."

"Adam," Ben called out before his friend slipped out the door. "Thanks for the coffee."

Five minutes later, Ben was in a cab headed to South-west, DC and the Department of Homeland. Secretary Lyle was already at her desk. Unlike him, she was showered and, from the looks of it, had slept in an actual bed the night before.

Ben fingered the micro card in his pocket containing a copy of the operating system for VOYEUR. He felt a bit conflicted turning it over to the NSA. But the artificial intelligence program had passed its trial run with flying colors last night—including its original purpose in identifying Quinn, astoundingly. There was no reason it shouldn't be rolled out to the rest of the US intelligence community. It would be a critical tool. Still, it felt a little like giving up a puppy he'd raised from birth.

"One of last night's guests was found murdered," she blindsided him by saying.

He shook his head briefly to regroup. "I just spoke with Agent Lockett. He didn't mention they'd found a homicide victim when they were searching through the White House."

"That's because the Secret Service didn't find him. The Russians did."

Ben swayed slightly trying to process the information. "Who was he?"

"Kir Abramov." She passed him a file folder. "Russia's representative to the board of governors with the World Bank."

"What aren't you telling me?"

She gestured to the folder.

Ben opened it and quickly scanned its contents. "Abramov worked for us?"

"In a manner of speaking," she replied. "There are

times when our two countries need to share intelligence for the greater good. Abramov was often the conduit of sanctioned information from Moscow. And vice versa."

"So, his own country didn't off him?"

Shaking her head, she wandered over to the big window overlooking the harbor. "We were supposed to meet at the White House last night. He had some information to share with me regarding the Phoenix."

"The Phoenix? Isn't he some legendary spymaster?"

"Was. Past tense."

"There are some who say he isn't dead."

"I was at Langley when the Phoenix was active. Trust me when I tell you the spymaster is no more." She headed back to her desk. "There's a rumor circulating that a manifest of all the operatives who served under the Phoenix exists, however. And it's for sale."

"That would be devastating if it fell into the wrong hands."

"Yes." The secretary massaged her brow. "Except I have my doubts such a list even exists. There were only seventeen agents being handled by the Phoenix. More than half were from other intelligence agencies in allied countries. Only the Phoenix knew all seventeen names."

"Then someone's selling false information? Why?"

"If we find the who, we'll discover the why."

"And you think whoever this is may have killed our Russian?"

She sighed wearily. "I think there is enough interest in the Phoenix to warrant chasing down that lead. I've stalled the NSA director's demands for VOYEUR for now. I want you to work your magic with it, the dark web, and whatever else you need to dig up any intel on those individuals most impacted by the Phoenix Project. Start with Vladmir Ronoff. He laundered two billion dollars of rubles into dollars before the Phoenix caught him. The Russian president recently pardoned him. Ronoff would have a big axe to grind against the World Bank and the Phoenix."

Ben stilled at the mention of Ronoff. "He wouldn't happen to be related to Alexi Ronoff, would he?"

"Alexi is his son. And, yes, I saw his name on last night's guest list. It's too strong of a coincidence if you ask me." Secretary Lyle eyed him carefully. "Make sure your search takes place off the grid. Until we know who's out there selling classified intel, I don't want to share my theories with the rest of the intelligence community."

"Understood." The familiar adrenaline rush that always preceded the hunt surged through him. Solving puzzles was his jam. Working to hide his trail would only make the hunt sweeter. And he had just the place to carry out his mission. "I'll get right on this."

He shoved the micro card back into his pocket before tucking the folder beneath his arm and heading for the door.

"Agent Segar," she called after him. "Keep me in the loop."

As he made his way out of the secretary's office, his fingers were already itching to get to a keyboard. The assignment would certainly take his mind off solving the mystery of Quinn Darby's reappearance. Except for the fact that she was somehow involved with Alexi Ronoff. That particular piece of intel fired up a burning sensation deep within his gut.

Adjusting his sunglasses, he strolled out into the bright sunshine and hailed a cab. He gave the driver the address for the marina where his sailboat was docked. No sense wasting time heading home to change. He had clothes aboard the *Seas the Day* and more at his secure cyber getaway he'd dubbed the Think Tank. The sooner he solved this puzzle, the better. He told himself his eagerness was because he wanted to solve a murder. Not because we wanted to have an excuse to delve deeper into the mystery of Quinn Darby.

CHAPTER THREE

Q UINN SAT IN the shaded corner of the marina's deck, sipping her iced coffee. Hiding behind her sunglasses, she pretended to watch the gulls dive-bomb the trash cans along the small dock surrounding the restaurant when, in fact, her gaze was riveted several yards farther in the distance. Standing aboard an impressive sailboat docked in one of the slips closest to the marina, a sandy-haired, shirtless man was vigorously polishing the chrome railing. The bronzed muscles in his back bunched and flexed seductively with every pass of the cloth.

She remembered those capable hands. Their warmth and their innate strength. So much like the careful, confident boy they belonged to. Except, as she'd discovered last night, he wasn't a boy any longer. Ben Segar was all grown up. She sucked on a piece of ice to try to cool her body's reaction to the sexy adult version of her high school lab partner.

It wasn't working.

"Ah, I see you've spotted one of Watertown's natural wonders."

The waitress's words startled Quinn.

"We probably should charge extra for the view when

Ben's in town," the other woman remarked as she placed a crab salad on the table in front of Quinn. The waitress's gaze lingered on Ben a bit longer than necessary before a soft sigh escaped her lips. "If only I was twenty years younger."

"Does he come here often?"

Quinn was both relieved and surprised when she'd received the intel Ben had gone directly from the Department of Homeland to his sailboat still wearing his tuxedo. She'd been even more surprised to find out the destination of his morning sail was his hometown, Watertown, Maryland.

"His family owns this marina," the waitress replied, not telling Quinn anything she didn't already know. "He lives in DC, but he sails over for the weekend pretty regularly. Dotes on his mom. Kind of sweet, really." She then drifted off to wait on another table.

Quinn wasn't sure why she expected Ben to have left Watertown in his rearview mirror years ago. Or that he would be living in some exotic locale running his own billion-dollar company by now. Except he'd been a gifted kid with a brilliant mind. Unlike her, whose path had been set since the cradle, the world held endless possibilities for him.

Instead, he was a computer analyst for the Secret Service. Not even a gun-toting agent. Well respected, but a bit tame for the boy who'd once dreamed of being the next Bill Gates.

Her feelings were jumbled about being back in the

quaint bayside town after all this time. Not much had changed, a fact for which she was glad. Watertown was always her safe haven even if only in her mind. The past years spent shifting from identity to identity had gone from exhilarating to isolating. The oddity of her existence becoming more pronounced the longer she remained in the game. During those dark times, her mind often drifted back to the folksy town where she would fantasize about what might have been. The memory of the water and the slower pace always calmed her down.

"Everything okay with your salad?" the waitress asked.

"It's wonderful," Quinn lied. Her thoughts were so consumed with the past, she'd yet to take a bite. She stabbed some crab with her fork.

The waitress laughed. "Ben has that effect on women. Just a word of warning though, he's a confirmed bachelor. He frequently entertains"—she made air quotes with her fingers—"women aboard his boat. But no one has been able to get a commitment out of him. Rumor has it he's still nursing a broken heart from the one that got away."

The other woman's words had Quinn nearly choking on her lunch. She reached for her water glass and gulped down its contents despite her throat constricting with something feeling a lot like guilt. No doubt he'd been hurt when she didn't show up for their senior prom. Especially after what they'd shared. But the knowledge that yet another woman had damaged his heart made her own ache. If she couldn't have a happily ever after of her own, she wanted sweet, honorable Ben to have one.

Closing her eyes, she allowed herself to do something she rarely permitted, to drift back thirteen years. She kept the memories of her days spent exploring the bay aboard Ben's Sunfish sailboat buried deep. They always painfully reminded her of what might have been. She and her parents lived in Watertown for only a brief period. But they were the best ten months of Quinn's then teenage life. Popular and pretty, she was quickly accepted among the historic town's elite—the entitled kids whose parents held well connected appointments and jobs in DC, commuting out to the trendy little hamlet on the Chesapeake Bay.

Ben hadn't been a part of her circle of popular, wealthy friends. He was a townie whose family didn't belong to the nearby Annapolis Yacht Club. Instead, he was the president of the robotics club, a star of the cross-country team, and class valedictorian.

They'd been assigned as lab partners in AP chemistry. Quinn had no business taking the class, but her mother had a bad case of "keeping up with the Joneses" despite her only child's less than stellar science capabilities. Appearances mattered to Quinn's parents. Particularly in the role they were playing in Watertown. And if the other kids were taking advanced classes, so too would their daughter.

Ben realized Quinn was a fish out of water that first day. But he'd never patronized or embarrassed her. Instead, he quietly encouraged her as he easily carried them both through the rigorous coursework. Before long, she was relying on the boy with the quicksilver grin and soulful eyes to help her with calculus. He was relaxed and easy to be around. She found she preferred his company over the handsy boys with fat wallets and fast cars.

With Ben, she could relax and be herself.

At least the self she wanted to be. A typical teenage girl with an adoring boyfriend. She'd gotten so caught up in the make believe of the role she was playing, she'd agreed to go to the prom with him despite the fact she knew her time in the small town was drawing to an end. She told herself it was because she wanted to create a lasting memory of a normal childhood that she could carry with her for the rest of her life. But the truth was she'd fallen for the studious townie. And she wanted everyone in Watertown to know it, even if it was for only one night.

Unfortunately, her mother's handlers had other plans. Circumstances required a hasty retreat out of the country. She never got a chance to wear the beautiful gown she'd picked out. Even worse, she never got the chance to say goodbye to Ben. Nursing a broken heart she blamed her mother for causing, she stepped into her mother's shoes with a zeal unrivaled by any other operative within the service. Ironically, she'd learned a valuable lesson while here in Watertown. Never let anyone close enough to know the real Quinn. There would only be heartache if she did. It was a lesson that helped her survive life in the game.

"Care for anything else?" The waitress was back interrupting Quinn's rehashing of her greatest mistake. "We've got a chocolate cake that is bound to be just as satisfying as the view." The woman winked conspiratorially.

As much as she would prefer to indulge in the healing

powers of chocolate, she had a job to do. And if she hurried, she just might be able to retrieve the micro card with Ben being none the wiser.

"Just a check," she murmured, keeping her gaze trained on Ben.

He climbed onto the dock and was headed into town.

"Sure." The waitress handed her the handwritten tab. "Enjoy the rest of your day."

Quinn left several bills on the table, securing them with the tin of Old Bay so the bills didn't become a casualty to the afternoon breeze. She made her way into the air-conditioned storefront of the marina, recognizing that not everything in Watertown had remained the same. What once had been a bait and tackle shop was now a gourmet takeout restaurant selling everything from worms to wine. There was an impressive deli counter with an array of ready-made foods for boaters and fishermen alike. Even with the changes, the family-owned shop still reverberated with the hominess she'd always loved when she and Ben studied together here.

Forcing herself to focus on her task, she hurried out onto the dock and made her way to Ben's sailboat. She glanced into the reflection of the chrome railings on the bow of a speedboat to make sure no one was watching from the restaurant deck behind her. The deck was blessedly empty. Quinn lengthened her stride toward Ben's boat. She was just about to climb aboard when the name painted on its side stopped her in her tracks.

Seas the Day.

The moniker was an homage to their carefree spring break senior year when they'd dreamt up a future together. A future that included a sail around the world aboard a boat with a name they'd come up with while huddled around a campfire—*Seas the Day*. She'd been playing a dangerous game then, spinning a fantasy of a life she could never have. Not with her family background. Ben had nurtured a lot more faith in their future, apparently. The ever-present shame that had been clinging to her for years suddenly made her eyes sting and her mouth dry. He'd never know how she wished all their dreams could have come true.

"I thought you were dead."

The sound of his voice behind her startled her. Not only that, but the words he uttered made her stomach drop. She was glad for her dark sunglasses that hid the astonishment surely reflected in her eyes.

Had anyone ever worried about her?

Her parents loved her. But they loved each other more. For much of her life, Quinn was just a project to them. Someone to groom to be an even bigger player in the game. But sweet Ben, the boy whose heart she'd apparently dented if not broken, had actually worried about her. His revelation shook her to her core.

She pivoted slowly so they were facing one another. He stood with his arms crossed over his impressive chest. Just for a moment, she wondered what it would be like to have his strong body wrapped around her again. To be the one who was being protected instead of the one who was forced by circumstances beyond her control to do the protecting.

Except her life wasn't a fairy tale. Ben Segar wasn't going to ride in and rescue her. He had no idea what she'd become. And it was better this way. Because if she let him in, he'd hate her even more than he likely already did. And that just might destroy the shred of integrity she still possessed.

"Still alive and kicking," she managed to say without her voice cracking.

I THOUGHT YOU were dead.

Not exactly the line he imagined he'd lead with after all these years. It revealed too much. The last thing he wanted was for her to think he had actually missed her.

But for once in his life, Ben knew what it was like to have his brain scrambled. Probably because she was standing before him, wearing a pair of shorts displaying her long, lean legs to perfection. She no longer exuded the innocence she once wore like armor. Instead, she had matured in all the right places, looking a hell of a lot more exotic than she ever had. And he hated how much the sight of her was turning him on right now.

He managed to bob his chin up and down in response, but he couldn't seem to move anything else. That was probably a good thing because were his limbs not frozen, he wasn't sure if he'd be able to stop himself from throttling her.

Or kissing her.

And that thought made him even angrier.

"What are you doing here?" he demanded instead.

Quinn traced her lower lip with the tip of her tongue. He recognized the tell from their days in chemistry when she claimed she understood even if she didn't. She was going to lie to him. He didn't know why the realization felt like a sucker punch to the gut, but it did.

"I'm visiting the area," she said. "And I thought I'd stop by and say hello."

He was incredulous. She could say hello but the hell with *good-bye*? Or *I'm sorry*? Thankfully, his anger propelled him into motion. Not trusting himself to respond, he stepped around her and climbed aboard the *Seas the Day*.

"Ben."

His name slipped through her lips almost as an exhale, the sound of it so erotic, he couldn't help himself. He turned around to face her.

"It's been thirteen years with no contact, Quinn," he said. "You said your hello. I don't know what else there is to say."

He grabbed at the lines securing the *Seas the Day* to the dock.

"You're leaving?"

"Yep. That ought to be something you're very familiar with." He scrambled to the bow to untie the lines there.

"Wait. I came here to explain. I'm sure you don't believe me, but I am sorry."

Her admission was so unexpected, he turned to glance

back at her standing on the dock. Too bad her sunglasses prevented him from gauging the sincerity of her confession.

"I wanted you to know I regret I couldn't be the girl you wanted me to be," she continued softly. "I thought maybe we could talk for a few minutes. You know, start over and try to make things right between us."

Come again? Was this one of those twelve-step programs where a person had to ask forgiveness of everyone they wronged? Adam's father had recently done the same, right before he passed away. Ben's heart suddenly constricted.

Was Quinn dying? Was he to lose her again so quickly after just finding her? He mentally shook himself.

She's just playing you again. Don't buy it.

"You're under the false impression there's anything to talk about. That was high school, Quinn. We're not the same people."

"You named your boat *Seas the Day!*"

"I wouldn't read anything into that," he replied trying to appear nonchalant. "I'm not creative. I'm a numbers guy, remember? It's just a boat. And that's just a name. Doesn't mean a thing."

She jerked her shoulders back as though he'd slapped her. Still, Ben didn't take any joy in landing a verbal blow.

"I don't believe you," she challenged. "Now who's running away?"

He studied her for a long moment. *Since when had Quinn Darby developed a backbone?* In high school, she used to sway with whatever wind the rich kids blew. Yet here she was spinning some yarn that had them rehashing history. She was up to something. And given her relationship with Alexi Ronoff, Ben's interest was piqued. What the hell? He could spend some time hearing her out for the good of the case. But only under his terms.

"All right. I'll be back this evening. I'm having dinner here at seven. If you want to make peace, it will have to be then."

Her shoulders relaxed. "I'm staying at the B and B in town, but you don't have to pick me up. I can just meet you back here."

"Well then, isn't that just like old times," he said as he tossed the line at her feet.

QUINN STOOD ON the dock and watched Ben deftly navigate the large sailboat out of the slip and into the bay as if it were second nature. He'd always been confident, but even more so on the water. Probably because he'd learned to sail practically after he'd learned to walk.

It's just a boat.

He was lying. The boy she once knew and loved had dreamt of that sailboat since kindergarten. And as for the name having no significance, she was calling BS on that, as well.

Except this wasn't the boy she once knew. She only had to replay their last exchange as evidence. Grown up Ben Segar was harder. And not just physically. He'd always exuded sureness, but this was something else. All the more reason to keep Alexi away from him. Ben was just brash enough to play the white knight. But a self-proclaimed computer geek would be no match for the ruthless Russian.

She sighed heavily. If only she'd been able to grab the stupid micro card and leave without confronting him. It was one thing to go through life carrying around the guilt that he hated her. But having to face the loathing head-on was an entirely different heartache altogether. Even worse, he didn't sound as though he had any intention of forgiving her. Not that she blamed him. Tonight, she'd find a way aboard his sailboat, seize the list, and slip away before her heart was in tatters.

As she made her way back to the B and B to wait for him to return, her phone rang deep in her handbag.

She glanced at the caller ID and groaned. "Alexi. How are you?"

"The more important question would be where are you, my princess?"

The back of Quinn's neck began to tingle. The location settings on her phone were deactivated, but that didn't mean he couldn't track her signal while she spoke to him.

"Did we have plans for today?"

"No," he drawled. "But you left so quickly last night. I was worried about you."

She bristled at the lie. Alexi never worried about anyone other than himself.

"You seemed upset to have your visit to the White House cut short," she hedged. "I thought it best to head to my hotel room and let you brood in peace."

His laugh rang a bit hollow. "You still haven't answered my question."

"I'm on the Eastern Shore photographing some old homes for another client." It was a plausible alibi and one he couldn't discredit. "That dress I wore last night didn't pay for itself, you know."

He was silent for a long moment. Quinn mentally calculated the time it would take for him to ping her location.

"Do I not pay you enough?"

"You pay me handsomely, Alexi. But, like you, this client is a friend and I couldn't say no." She prayed he bought her excuse. "But we can always talk about a fee increase when I return on Monday."

"Yes. We will have a candid conversation when we see each other again," he said cryptically. "I'll look forward to it."

Quinn quickly disconnected and turned off her phone. Glancing over her shoulder, she watched as Ben's sailboat disappeared on the horizon. Alexi suspected something. And that meant she needed to act quickly. She needed that micro card. More than that, she needed to protect Ben.

CHAPTER FOUR

B EN LEANED IN, allowing the scanner to probe his eye. The beam flickered before the lock on the door clicked open. Securing the door behind him, he took the metal stairs built into the interior of the lighthouse two at a time. He bypassed both floors of living space, instead climbing to what once had been the torch room when the beacon was active over a hundred years ago. The glow of multiple computer monitors made up the room's light source today.

Sliding into the leather desk chair, he skimmed the monitors without really registering what was on them. He needed to focus on the task at hand, but his damn mind only wanted to focus on the seductive woman he'd left standing on the dock. She was up to something. No doubt about it. Despite her being back in Watertown, he was even further away from solving the puzzle of Quinn. Heaving a sigh, he leaned his head against the chair back and closed his eyes. He needed sleep. But every time he drifted off, she was there to haunt him with her hypnotizing green eyes and traitorous lips. *Damn it.* He rose from the chair and headed downstairs for a shower.

A lot had changed inside since his high school days

when Ben used the old lighthouse as a hideout from his female-dominated family. Thanks to the sale of a few apps he'd developed while in grad school at MIT, he had been able to renovate the entire place, turning it into a geek's refuge and a safe house for his secret work. The first floor was no longer dark with wood paneling. Whitewashed shiplap boards gave the space an airy, open appearance. Instead of a beat-up old futon, the room featured two oversized sofas strategically placed to capture all the warmth from the fireplace as well as the panoramic views outside. Off to the side was a little game room housing both a foosball table and an air hockey game. A sleek galley kitchen now stood where he once had an old dorm room refrigerator and nothing else.

He'd dubbed the place the Think Tank and it was where he retreated for those assignments when he needed to bypass the government's servers and lurk on the dark web. He was proud of the secure space he'd created. Too bad no one else could ever know about it. Thanks to his deep cover, his buddies would never enjoy the game room. Marin would never cook one of her gourmet feasts in the kitchen. He would never seduce a woman in front of the lighthouse's stone fireplace.

Except he had seduced a female in front of that fireplace.

Thirteen years ago.

It was ironic that Quinn was the only person he would ever share this space with. That particular memory irked him more than any other involving her. Swearing violently, he headed for the bedroom and a shower.

A long, cold one.

Once he was showered and changed, he returned to the torch room to research the Phoenix. Three hours later, he was no closer to having any definitive proof the elusive spymaster was dead or alive. But he did have a fairly good picture of why the Ronoff family would want him murdered. Time to do some digging on Alexi Ronoff. And he knew just where to start.

Griffin answered the FaceTime call on the second ring.

"I thought you were sailing today?"

"Change in plans."

"Don't tell me some chick handcuffed herself to your berth again?"

Marin's laughing face appeared alongside Griffin's. "Oh, my gosh," she cried. "This sounds like a story I've got to hear."

"One time, asshole," Ben said. "That happened one time!"

The couple exchanged an amused look, silently communicating to each other judging by the quirk of Marin's eyebrow. The intimacy of the moment had him feeling like the odd man out.

Again.

"I need to talk shop with you, Griff," he said. "What can you tell me about your person of interest from last night? Alexi Ronoff?"

Griffin eyed him curiously. "Is this about the redhead?"

"What redhead?" Marin asked.

"The one who was at the White House last night on the arm of a wealthy Russian criminal," Griffin replied smugly. "Turns out she's also the woman who ghosted him at his senior prom."

Ben bit back a few choice words about Adam and his big mouth. "Don't you people have enough to do besides sitting around and gossiping about me like a bunch of hens?"

"I imagine that once we have kids, our attention on you will wane," his friend quipped. "Speaking of which. . ." He began to nuzzle his wife's neck.

"Well, whoever she is, I don't like her." Marin swatted at her husband. "Not only because she dates criminals, but any girl would have been thrilled to go to the prom with you, Ben."

He shot her an appreciative grin. "You're going to make a great mother one day."

"Yeah, about that, we were just getting ready to work on her potential motherhood when you rudely interrupted us," Griffin said.

Marin slapped his shoulder. "You wish." She vanished from the screen but her voice remained. "I'm busy making sample wedding cakes for Adam and Josslyn to taste test tomorrow. Do you want me to save you some, Ben?"

"Yeah, sure," he replied half-heartedly.

"Huh," Griffin joked. "This must be serious if you're not jumping at the chance for free food."

"When you were working counterfeit crimes, did you ever hear of the Phoenix?"

Griffin immediately sobered up. "He was before my time, but definitely a legend. His team took down some very prolific and dangerous money launderers. No one knows who was pulling the strings as the Phoenix. Even his death is shrouded in mystery. He died in a fiery car crash that's still a cold case. Why do you ask?"

"The rumors of his death may have been greatly exaggerated."

His friend was all ears now. "And you know this how, exactly?"

Ben shook his head. "I'm not at liberty to say. But I understand the Ronoff family was one of the Phoenix's more prominent convictions. I'd love to get whatever intel you have concerning junior."

"Sure thing. How quickly do you need it?"

"An hour ago."

"Why did I know you'd say that? I'll head over to the bureau and see what I can pull together for you." Griffin stood up and stretched. "And what about the redhead? What's she got to do with all of this?"

That was the million-dollar question if there was one.

"I don't know," he replied. "I guess I'll find out tonight."

"You found her?"

"More like she found me."

"That's a very interesting coincidence," Griffin said. "And you know how I feel about those."

Ben had to agree with his buddy there. Marin appeared on the screen again.

"Well, just so you know, if this woman hurts you, she'll have to answer to me. And I'm very handy with a knife when it comes to the people I love."

Touched by her words, he blew her a kiss. A few months earlier, the pretty blonde was forced to kill a man in order to save Griffin's life. The episode still haunted her deeply.

"Thank you, Marin. But it won't come to that. She can't hurt me. I have a heart of stone, remember?"

She shook her head. "You just think you do. And something tells me this woman is the one who put the idea in your head."

Rather than offer any comment, he just gave her what he hoped was an appeasing grin. Because she was wrong. Quinn Darby would never get another shot at Ben's heart.

After agreeing to catch up with Griffin in the morning, he signed off on the call. He then texted Adam likely at the same time Griffin was texting him. But he wanted his buddy to play it cool where Quinn was concerned tonight. Not to let on he knew who she was or how she knew Ben. It would be easier to question her that way. At least that was what he wanted Adam to believe. He wanted her to believe her disappearance hadn't affected him.

Even if it had.

"What doesn't kill you makes you stronger." He recited his mother's favorite mantra aloud, but the computers in the room ignored him. Ben activated the alarm and made his way out the door. He had stalled long enough. It was time to face his past.

Q̲uinn strolled along the marina dock trying not to appear as anxious as she felt. It had been five hours since Alexi's phone call. If he was going to track her down, he could have done so by now. Still, she would feel better once she had her hands on the micro card and Ben was no longer embroiled in this mess.

She peered at the horizon, watching as the *Seas the Day* grew larger. He was coming from the direction of the cove where the decommissioned lighthouse was located. Blushing at the memory, she wondered if he still ventured inside the old place.

There was a great deal she wondered about Ben, if she was being honest. Starting with who was the one that got away? Did he still like to reread *Harry Potter*? Was he still obsessed with puzzles? Did he still dream of sailing around the world? What had happened to the brilliant, confident, driven boy who craved adventure to turn him into a computer-geek bureaucrat?

More importantly, she wondered if his kisses still had the power to make her weak at the knees.

None of those questions would be answered, however. Particularly that last one. If she was going to keep him safe, she needed to get the micro card and vanish as quickly as possible.

Ben steered the *Seas the Day* into the slip, the bow gently bumping against the rubber lining the dock. Ignoring the disappointment that he'd donned a shirt, she made herself useful by grabbing the lines at the bow and tying them off on the cleat bolted to the dock.

"Glad to see you haven't forgotten everything from our time together," he remarked as he edged his way to the stern of the boat.

"I haven't forgotten anything about our time together."

Her flirtatious reply had his head snapping up from where he was securing the sail. It was hard to decipher his expression from behind his sunglasses, but she could feel the heat when he tilted his head to take in the sleeveless teal sundress she'd worn and the way it clung to certain areas of her body more than others. A single pearl dangling on a thin silver chain between her breasts shimmered in the evening sunlight.

Perhaps he wasn't as immune to her as she thought.

"Permission to come aboard?" she asked.

When he didn't immediately respond, she stepped off the dock. Before she could climb aboard, however, his hands were suddenly spanning her waist. He lifted her easily, swinging her off the dock and letting her body slowly slide against the hard muscles of his torso before gently placing her into the boat. She sucked in a ragged breath. It was either that or faint. She might never know for sure if his kisses still affected her, but judging by the heat pooling in her belly, it was a safe bet they would do more than just make her knees weak.

The moment stretched. His fingers lingered at her waist. The deck rocked lazily from side to side. Neither one of them seemed in a hurry to move. Instead, they stood there for several long heartbeats just letting the evening breeze wash over them.

It was magical.

Right up until he ruined it by speaking.

"What kind of game are you playing?" he demanded, his warm breath fanning her ear.

Somehow, her hands had found their way to his shoulders. She quickly dragged them to her sides. He wasn't as quick to release her, giving her body a little shake when he finally did so.

"I'm not playing anything," she lied. "I told you why I came."

Quinn wasn't proud of the role she'd been forced to play. She'd often lied and cheated to accomplish her mission. But that was so good could prevail over evil. Somehow, lying to Ben made her feel cheap and deceitful.

"Then let's get this over with," he said. "Tell me what I need to say so you can feel better about things and move on to happily ever after with your Russian boyfriend."

His accusation caught her off guard. "Russian boyfriend?" she sputtered. "Alexi is not my boyfriend."

He shoved his sunglasses on top of his head and studied her quizzically with those solemn hazel eyes of his. The look of astonishment she'd seen at the White House the night before had been replaced with a look of vexation. Something stirred within her. Suddenly, she desperately needed him to believe her on this particular truth.

"Alexi likes women as arm candy," she explained softly. "But he prefers men for everything else."

"Huh." He took a step back. "That doesn't come up when you google the guy."

"You googled him? Why?"

He slipped his sunglasses back over his eyes. "Because I was curious about what you saw in him."

A warm glow spread over her cheeks. *He did still care.* The thought both thrilled and terrified her. She needed to keep him safe.

She needed to keep everyone safe.

"So, then, what are you to him?" he asked.

"I take photos of his properties and sell them to magazines," she replied, glad she could be honest about at least one part of her life. "I'm a professional photographer."

"Who's a professional photographer?" a female voice called from the dock beside the *Seas the Day.*

She looked over to see a stunning, dark-haired woman climbing aboard. A tall, military-looking man followed her. Quinn immediately recognized the couple from the cover of tabloid magazines. The woman was the exotic half-sister of the First Lady. And the man accompanying her was her Secret Service agent fiancé. That explained his presence at the White House last night. Ben might be a run-of-the-mill computer analyst within the Secret Service, but he ran with some impressive friends.

Ben grabbed the woman's hand when she teetered on her ridiculously high heels and guided her to one of the bench seats.

"Stilettos, Josslyn. Really?"

"I have to wear them to have any hope of reaching Adam's chin much less his lips," she quipped. "Now what's this about a photographer? Because I've been interviewing them all week and I still don't have one for our wedding."

"I told you, Joss, we can just use one of the White House photographers," Adam said. "And if you want to reach my lips, just tell me. I can work something out."

Josslyn tsked. "I don't want a portraitist to chronicle our wedding. I want an artist."

"Please excuse her." Adam winked at Quinn. "She's still peevish because the president nixed holding the ceremony on the Serengeti."

"And *I'm* peevish because this was a private conversation," Ben announced. "I thought we were meeting at the restaurant?"

"Bennett." Josslyn donned a cat-ate-the-canary grin. "I have very fond memories of this boat. You know that."

Quinn wasn't sure but she thought Adam might be blushing. For his part, Ben simply groaned.

"Besides," the other woman continued. "We saw you here and we wanted to meet your friend."

She smiled expectantly in Quinn's direction.

Ben sighed. "You would have met her at dinner if you'd been even a little patient."

"She's joining us for dinner? Awesome."

"I'm joining you for dinner?" Quinn asked at the same time.

Adam chuckled loudly. "Wow, Ben. We need to work on your dating skills." He turned to Quinn. "You have to excuse him, most of his dates take place in virtual reality."

"Hey!" Ben shoved his friend in the shoulder.

It was Quinn's turn to smile. She extended her hand. "Since I have the advantage of knowing who you are, allow me to introduce myself. I'm Quinn Darby. Pleased to meet you."

Josslyn's gray eyes went wide. "You're Quinn Darby? The Quinn Darby who photographed Princess Eleanor's wedding in Cape Town? Those pictures were absolutely stunning."

"Thank you."

She was particularly proud of the job she'd done shooting the princess's wedding. The photographs had turned out to be some of her best work. Not only that, but she'd managed to nab the evidence to indict a British MP for his involvement with an African drug cartel. All in all, it was quite a weekend endeavor.

"That's exactly the type of pictures I want of our wedding," Josslyn gushed. "I mean, the White House rose garden isn't much of a backdrop. It's pretty tame compared to the compound in South Africa."

Adam laughed again. "There are no guarantees about how tame the guests will be, though."

Josslyn elbowed him in the ribs. "Hush. You'll scare her off just when I'm trying to talk her into the job. As I mentioned, we're getting married at the White House in two weeks. And we desperately need a photographer. The woman I hired has been put on bedrest for a high-risk pregnancy. And you, well, you're exactly what I'm looking for."

Quinn swallowed roughly. As much as she'd love the artistic challenge of photographing a wedding in the White House, her life wasn't her own. It never had been. After she secured the list, Quinn would need to make herself scarce. Once she fulfilled this mission, there would be another one waiting. Then another several weeks of laying low. Alone. Her life was a carousel of role playing and isolation. But it was the only one she knew. And it worked for her.

At least that was what she kept telling herself.

She swiped the tip of her tongue along her bottom lip. "I'm already booked completely for the rest of the summer. I'm so sorry."

Another lie. She hated how they suddenly felt painful leaving her lips. Out of the corner of her eye, she saw Ben's mouth frown in what looked like disgust.

Josslyn visibly deflated before her. Adam wrapped an arm around her waist and nuzzled the top of her head. "We'll find someone. I promise."

His fiancée smiled up at him. "At the end of the day, it doesn't matter. As long as you're waiting for me at the end of the aisle."

"I'm happy to ask around to see who else is available," Quinn offered.

And she was genuinely happy to do so. These were Ben's friends. Despite the teasing, they all seemed to be fond of each other. She would do something nice for Josslyn and Adam because Ben cared for them.

What would it be like to have friends like that?

She quashed the envy rolling in her stomach. She'd

made her own choices, following in the path she'd been set upon at a young age. That path didn't allow for long-lasting friendships. Or any relationship for that matter. Why was it the only time the situation bothered her was when Ben was around?

"That would be wonderful, Quinn," Josslyn said. "But, really, I don't mean to be a bridezilla about it. Adam is right. The White House photographers will do a lovely job."

Quinn reached out and squeezed the other woman's hand. "We'll find you someone who will do more than just lovely."

A stunning smile lit up Josslyn's face. "Thank you. And now we get to taste test the hors d'oeuvres we're serving at the reception. Come on. This is going to be fun."

Adam helped his fiancée to the dock as Quinn tried to think of a plausible excuse to remain behind and search for the micro card. But then Ben was extending his hand to her.

"Come on, Brit, let's go fill up on appetizers."

Her stomach did a little stutter-step at his use of the nickname he'd given her all those years ago. Even better, the corners of his mouth had actually turned up in a slight smile. She looked longingly at his outstretched hand. Once they were occupied taste testing appetizers, she could double back to the sailboat and grab the list. But in the meantime, it would be nice to take a break from the game and enjoy the company of her first love. Memories of these next couple of hours would have to sustain her for a lifetime.

Without a second thought, she slipped her fingers into his and followed him off the boat.

CHAPTER FIVE

THE IRONY WASN'T lost on Ben that after all these years, he was finally holding Quinn Darby's hand in public. Parading two blocks up Watertown's Main Street, to be precise. He half expected her to yank her fingers free once they left the marina, but she kept them there, wrapped in his, relaxed and soft against his skin.

Too bad those assholes who still teased him about being left holding a corsage at the prom couldn't see him now. They wouldn't be so quick to dispute his relationship with the beautiful redhead. Unfortunately, the onlookers and paparazzi were too busy focusing their attention on Josslyn, the more famous member of their entourage that included not only the four of them, but Josslyn's detail of Christine and another agent.

Quinn adjusted their grip, lacing her fingers more firmly—*more intimately*—through his. A surge of desire roared through him before he beat it back. He shouldn't have touched her aboard the *Seas the Day* much less be holding her hand right now. But perhaps things were just as she said and she was simply an innocent photographer mixed up with the wrong crowd. Apparently, she had entre to the world's beautiful people, documenting their extravagant lives for magazines and social media. Maybe if he heard her out, she'd have a good excuse for deserting him. Maybe they could start over.

He mentally shook himself. *Stop being such a damn sucker.* Based on the lie she'd told Josslyn about photographing their wedding, Quinn had no intention of sticking around for long. He needed to keep reminding certain parts of his body she was a means to an end, just as he had been to her all those years ago. This, their stroll and dinner, constituted nothing more than a simple op. Quinn was a person of interest.

End of story.

He didn't realize he'd tightened his grip on her hand until she shot him a confused look. He quickly released her fingers and shoved his hand in his pocket.

She sighed beside him. "Where are we going?"

"Ben's sister has a fabulous place right here along the water," Josslyn answered for him.

"Your sister left New York?"

He was surprised Quinn remembered he had a sister much less that Rebecca once managed a famous restaurant in Manhattan. It was her first job out of college and, back then, she vowed to never live anywhere else. But marriage had a way of altering plans, as Ben was finding out watching his friends succumb to the ball and chain.

"The shine wore off the Big Apple pretty quickly," was all he said.

The sun was sliding toward the horizon when they arrived at the lively dockside restaurant. What once was a small fishing wholesale warehouse had been turned into a trendy eatery complete with an open-air bar and double-tier deck for dining alfresco. Situated as it was at the end of the Water Street, the view consisted of nothing but glistening water and the occasional dolphin. The restaurant always drew a steady clientele, especially on summer weekends. Every time he entered, Ben felt a little burst of pride at the success his sister had made of the place.

The young hostess led them to a table tucked away in the corner of the lower deck giving them a perfect view of the bay. Quinn pulled a camera from her purse and immediately began snapping pictures of the water, now a deep purple as twilight descended.

"This place is fantastic," she said as she continued to shoot. "Your sister is right. This is much better than New York, if you ask me."

Ben thought so, too. One of the things he'd most loved about Quinn was her appreciation of Watertown. Despite her international upbringing, she took pleasure in the natural beauty of the town and surrounding area.

At least, she had always appeared to.

Christine and the other agent took the table beside them, essentially cutting them off from the other diners. As Adam and Josslyn seated themselves at the table, Ben pulled out a chair for Quinn. She was sliding into her seat when he was nearly taken down at the knees by two imps slamming into the back of his legs.

"Daddy! You came home!"

"Momma said you weren't ever going to come get us!

We missed you, Daddy!"

He swore as he tried to untangle the little beasts from his lower body. Quinn rose from the table, he hoped to help him out, but her startled expression said otherwise. She looked like she was poised for flight. Adam and Josslyn were laughing too hard to be of any help, damn them.

His aunt's laughter added to the chaos of the moment. "Still gets me every time," she said between guffaws.

"Still *not* funny, Aunt Marnie." He grabbed his nephew by the ear and yanked him off.

"Ow!" Liam released his wrestler's hold on Ben's leg to massage his tender lobe.

"Next time, whatever Aunt Marnie pays you to pull this prank, I'll pay you double *not* to do it. Understand?"

He looked into the seven-year-old's coffee-colored eyes, so shrewd for his age.

"She said she'd pay me a hundred dollars," Liam announced boldly.

Adam laughed loudly. Ben shot him a look.

"Don't lie to your uncle, young man." Aunt Marnie cuffed Liam lightly on the shoulder. "You know I was paying you *five* hundred."

Ben heaved a sigh at his crazy aunt and her little coconspirators. His four-year-old niece, Brianna, took pity on him. She gently wrapped his hand in both of hers.

"Uncle Ben," she whispered loudly. "She was only paying us a dollar."

He couldn't hold back the indulgent smile the little girl always seemed to innocently coax from him. Ben scooped her up so they were eye-to-eye. She had the caramel skin of her father's African-American family but the moss-green eyes of Ben's sister. It was a good thing his brother-in-law was a former military policeman turned sheriff. Rich would likely need all his training to keep the boys at bay in a few years.

"You're worth much more than that amount, little Bri." He touched his nose to hers. "And if you're going to commit a crime, always make sure it's worth the money."

"Did we commit a crime?" Bri's face fell. "Daddy is going to be so mad at us."

"Here come the water works," Liam announced to the rest of the diners on the deck.

Aunt Marnie grabbed the boy by the forearm. "Abort the mission, rug rat. Abort!" The two of them scurried around the tables and back toward the kitchen.

True to Liam's prediction, Bri was crying in earnest, her entire body shaking with sobs.

"Shh." Ben pulled her in for a hug. "That was a bad choice of words on my part."

When he glanced over the little girl's shoulder at Quinn, he was taken aback by the look of astonishment on her face. She seemed transfixed by his interactions with his niece.

"My mother usually watches them at night, but she's out of town," he explained. "It's probably child endangerment to have Aunt Marnie watch after them, but we do what we can for each other."

"I love Aunt Marnie," Bri blubbered, soaking his shirt

in the process.

"That's because she's a big kid herself. That's her favorite prank, by the way," he said to Quinn.

"It usually ends with Ben's date in tears, though," Adam joked.

A slow smile formed on Quinn's lips. She reached into her big bag and pulled out a bright yellow piece of paper. In less than a minute, she'd transformed it into a bird.

"Will this make things a little better?" she asked as she slid the origami figure across the table.

Ben swallowed roughly at the sweet gesture.

"That's beautiful," Josslyn exclaimed.

"A woman of many talents," Adam added with a cheeky grin.

Bri gulped a sob before shyly glancing side-eyed at Quinn. One look at the bird and the child's tears ended almost as abruptly as they'd begun. She clamored out of Ben's arms to carefully wrap her tiny fingers around the origami artwork.

"Look, Uncle Ben, he's just like the one you have." She held it up for Ben's inspection.

Shit. He sucked in a panicked breath. Quinn once made him a similar bird that now occupied a place of honor aboard the *Seas the Day*. Frantically trying to distract the child before she said more, he waved at the waitress. "How about some chicken tenders, Bri?"

His niece climbed into Josslyn's lap, carefully cradling the paper bird in her hands. "I already had mac and cheese for dinner."

The waitress indicated she'd be a minute. Ben bit back a curse.

"Uncle Ben has a bird just like this on his boat," Bri told Quinn. "But we're not supposed to touch it."

Defeated, Ben slid into his chair.

Josslyn leaned toward Bri conspiratorially. "He won't let you play with it? That's not nice of him." She shot Ben a sly smile.

Ben glared at the waitress, willing her to hurry up. It didn't work.

"It's 'cause his bird is special," Bri explained, her little voice earnest. "He's keeping it safe for someone important. She lost it and Uncle Ben is looking everywhere for her so he can give it back."

Quinn's face was solemn as her glance shifted from Bri to Ben. "That's very sweet of him."

"And then he's gonna marry her," his niece proclaimed.

Of course, the waitress picked that moment to make her way to their table. Adam mocked him with a shit-eating grin. Josslyn's expression wasn't much better. For her part, Quinn thankfully remained subdued.

"What can I get you to drink?" the waitress asked.

Suddenly Ben just wanted to get this evening over with before all of his secrets were exposed. "We'll start with a pitcher of whatever sangria is the special tonight."

"I'll take some lemonade," Bri chirped.

"Only if it's in a shot glass." His brother-in-law came up behind the waitress, still dressed in his sheriff's uniform. "It's too close to bedtime."

As usual, Rich had impeccable timing, arriving five minutes too late to stop his daughter from embarrassing the crap out of him.

"Daddy!"

Rich hauled his daughter up for a kiss.

"Look what I got! Uncle Ben's friend made it for me."

"That's beautiful, sweetie." He smiled at his daughter adoringly. "Okay, let's go wrangle up your brother so you kids can get home and your uncle and his friends can eat their dinner in peace. Say good night, Bri."

"Good night, Bri," his niece repeated with a giggle. "See you later, Uncle Bennett!"

"I want a little girl just like her." Josslyn batted her eyes at her fiancé.

"Unfortunately, she has a vivid imagination," Ben said mostly for Quinn's benefit. Hopefully she'd get the message that he never harbored dreams of marrying her. *At least not recently.* "Liam, on the other hand, spends too much time with Aunt Marnie. I'm afraid he's destined for a life in crime."

"They're both adorable," Quinn remarked wistfully. "You're very lucky to have a close family."

The waitress arrived with the sangria, giving him a minute to gather his wits. He knew she was an only child. Her parents had been doting, if not a little distant. Her mother was a visiting professor at St. Mary's University and her dad worked at the British Embassy. But had something happened to them since he'd seen her last?

Despite the fact he had to keep much of his work life a

secret, he still had his relatives and friends to rely on. Granted, Aunt Marnie and the rest of his crazy family could be intrusive, but he wasn't lying when he said they looked out for one another. He'd do anything for them. And they would do anything for him.

Who looked out for Quinn?

The sudden thought plowed through him, making his rib cage grow tight. He opened his mouth to ask about her parents, but Josslyn was quicker.

"So, how did you two kids meet?" she asked despite the fact he was pretty sure his friend's fiancée already knew the answer.

"Quinn lived in Watertown my senior year," he answered before she could. "We were lab partners." He'd had a change of heart in the last fifteen minutes.

If they were going to rehash their relationship, he would rather the two of them do so without an audience. A look of sadness flashed in Quinn's eyes before she masked her expression and took a sip from her sangria. Was she upset he didn't tell his friends they were a lot more than lab partners? He felt another twinge deep in his gut. Fortunately, his sister arrived at that moment, preventing Josslyn from doing any more digging.

"Evening folks," Rebecca said. "Milo is preparing the first round of appetizers and they'll be out shortly. Have I mentioned how honored we are that you chose our restaurant to prepare some of the food for your wedding?"

"The chefs at the White House are fabulous," Josslyn said. "But they love to bring in outside chefs to give local restaurants exposure. And Adam and I adore Milo's food. So, really, it's a win for all of us."

Rebecca fixed her gaze on Quinn for a second before landing on Ben. "Would you mind if I stole my brother away for a few minutes. We're having trouble with the dishwasher again. And he's the only one who seems to be able to coax it back to life."

The dishwasher was on its last legs, but he suspected this was his sister's way of getting him alone so she could question him about his companion. It wasn't lost on him that she hadn't even acknowledged Quinn. It likely wasn't lost on Quinn, either.

"Ben does have a way with machines," Adam joked. "We'll add dishwasher whisperer to the long list of his talents. Go. We can hold down the fort. But I can't promise Christine won't eat your share of the food."

He looked anxiously at Quinn. She waved him off with a smile as fake as Aunt Marnie's hair color. He was suddenly conflicted, wanting to clear the air with her now rather than later. It had been a stupid idea not to hear her out when she first approached him at the marina. He'd been a jerk, rushing to judgment without basis. Now he had the sinking feeling he might be too late.

He shook himself again. She was safely ensconced with his friends. He'd take care of the dishwasher minus any interrogation by his sister and hurry back to the table. Later, he would take Quinn back to the *Seas the Day* where they could talk privately.

And to see what came next.

"Be back in ten," he said before following his sister to the kitchen.

QUINN NEEDED TO get out of the restaurant. Away from Ben. *Far away.* Seeing him around his friends and his family was doing things to her. Children weren't something she ever imagined for her life. At least not while she was in the game. But watching him interact with his beautiful little niece brought on an ache so heavy she could barely breathe from the weight of it.

It was need at its purest and simplest form. She wanted the boy she'd given her heart and the rest of her body to all those years ago. And she wanted the man he'd become. Not only that, she realized with a shock, but she wanted everything that went with it.

Except she could never have him.

That particular reality hurt the most.

She needed to face facts. The more time she spent around him, the harder it would be to leave him again. Not to mention the risk she put him in. It was time to retrieve the list and disappear from Ben's life once and for all.

Mustering her courage, she rose from the table. "I think I'll go freshen up while you two wait for the food to arrive," she announced, gesturing for Josslyn to remain seated. The last thing she needed was for Ben's friend to want to chat it up in the loo. "I'll be right back."

Without waiting for a response, she hurried inside being careful to avoid not only the kitchen, but the watchful eyes of the two Secret Service agents accompanying Josslyn. She bypassed the loo, instead discreetly slipping into a crowd of guests leaving the restaurant. Once safely outside, she quickly headed the two blocks back to the marina. With luck, she'd be able to snatch the micro card from Ben's tuxedo pocket before he had the dishwasher fixed.

The *Seas the Day* quietly bobbed with the tide when Quinn climbed aboard. She tried the door to the galley, but it was locked. No surprise there. She dug into her bag and grabbed the set of lockpicks from her makeup pouch. Subtly, she glanced around at the other boats moored in the slips beside Ben's. They were all empty. She crouched down so she was eye level with the lock. Thirty seconds later, she had the door open. After one last look around, she entered Ben's private lair and closed the door behind her.

The interior of the sailboat was equally as impressive as the outside. She made her way down the four steps into a fully equipped galley complete with a banquette seating for six. The kitchen was state of the art. Trailing a finger along the stainless-steel countertop, she couldn't resist a peek inside the cabinets. Her lips turned up at the corners when she saw the boxes of Teddy Grahams stored there. The cookies had always been his crack.

"Oh, Ben," she whispered. "I'm glad some things haven't changed that much."

Forcing herself not to linger, she searched the two aft cabins, each one housing a double murphy bed and a desk.

The head was next. She was pleased to see it was a decent sized lavatory complete with a shower. They'd had many lively discussions of the size of the shower when they were planning their trip around the world. Of course, she'd been living a fantasy. But, Ben . . . He hadn't been dreaming at all.

The forward cabin was clearly Ben's domain. She closed her eyes to breathe in the faint trace of the scent that was uniquely him. A huge triangular shaped bed took up most of the cabin, nestled into the bow of the boat. Surrounding it on two sides was a gorgeous teak shelf lined with photos and knickknacks he'd collected during his travels. Among them, a purple origami bird just like the one she'd made for Bri minutes ago.

Tears burned the back of her eyes.

And then he's going to marry her.

If only.

A noise on the dock pulled her from her pity party. Quickly, she rifled through the closet looking for the tuxedo he'd been wearing when he boarded that morning. It wasn't there.

Damn.

She searched the desk drawer for any sign of the card, but the only things there were loose change and condoms. Apparently, the waitress wasn't exaggerating about Ben's frequent onboard entertainment. Ignoring the stab of jealousy, she headed back through the galley, carefully checking the few drawers there. Nothing. He must have gotten rid of the tux this afternoon. But where?

Quinn had no choice but to head back to the restaurant and continue with the charade of dinner. It was her only hope of discovering the whereabouts of the micro card. She'd just have to spend a few more hours torturing herself with what could have been. It would be fine, she tried to convince herself. After all, there were worse kinds of torture she could be faced with in her profession. Gathering up her handbag, along with her resolve, she headed back up the steps to the aft deck. When she opened the door, however, her heart leapt to her throat at the familiar face waiting to greet her.

"Did you find what you were looking for, my princess?"

CHAPTER SIX

T HE DISHWASHER ENDED up taking Ben closer to fifteen minutes to fix. He was wiping his hands on a towel when his sister ambushed him.

"Tell me that isn't Quinn Darby at your table?"

Rather than answer, he snagged a crab puff from the tray of a passing waiter and popped it in his mouth. With a shrug of his shoulders, he headed back toward the dining room.

"What is she doing here after all these years?" Rebecca called after him.

"No idea. But when I find out, I'll be sure and let you know."

She followed him to the deck. "Don't you dare let her break your heart again."

Her plea had him stopping in his tracks and turning to face his older sister. Only two years separated them, but since the death of their father nearly twenty years ago, Rebecca had been as much of a mother to him as their actual mom. It seemed she wasn't ready to relinquish the role despite the fact he had reached the ripe-old-age of thirty-one.

He brushed a kiss over her forehead. "So many women

concerned over the safety of my heart. I'm a very lucky man."

"Must you be such an obtuse ass?"

"Hey, this obtuse ass just fixed your dishwasher. Again. You're welcome, by the way."

She pulled him in for a hug. "Thank you. For always being there for me. I'm so glad you settled into a career where the greatest injury you can suffer is carpal tunnel. I have enough stress worrying about Rich every day."

He gave her a reassuring pat on the back. Sometimes what his family didn't know couldn't hurt them. "You can take me off your list of people to worry about, then. I can take care of myself."

Wearing an expression full of doubt, she released him. "I'll be the judge of that." The bartender waved her down. "Go back to your friends and enjoy Milo's fabulous food."

"Rebecca," he called after her. His sister glanced back over her shoulder. "I love you, too."

She replied with a smile before shooing him away and heading in the direction of the bar. Ben weaved through the maze of diners, arriving at the table he'd left fifteen minutes earlier to find Christine and her partner on Josslyn's detail making their way through a plate of beef Wellington while Adam was feeding oysters to his fiancée. It was the absence of one of their party that had the back of his neck tingling, however.

"Where's Quinn?"

Adam looked past him. "She's not with you?"

The tingling felt like a full-fledge vise grip now. "No. I

left her here." He glared at Adam. "With you."

"Whoa there, Bennett, if you intended for me to keep tabs on her, you should have given me a damn heads-up," Adam snapped as he shot to his feet.

Josslyn jumped between them. "Boys! She said she was going to freshen up."

"When was that exactly?"

The four exchanged uneasy looks. "Right after you left," Josslyn finally answered. "Agent Groesch checked out the ladies' room a few minutes ago, but she wasn't there."

Ben swore violently.

"We assumed she was with you, though," Josslyn continued. "I figured I'd made her uncomfortable with the pressure to photograph our wedding somehow and she didn't want to be left alone with us."

"She wasn't with me," he said.

Anger squeezed his chest. How could he have been so stupid? She'd been playing him.

Again.

His phone rang, startling him. He checked the caller ID.

"Aunt Marnie, I don't have time right—"

"You better get down to the marina, Bennett. Someone's trashing your boat. I've already called Rich."

"Shit!" He shoved his phone into his pocket and made a beeline for the door.

"Stay with Josslyn," he heard Adam command the agents in her detail.

The two of them sprinted out the door, circumventing

a couple on a tandem bike, and headed toward the docks. The siren from Rich's squad car blared, but it was still some distance away.

"What are we looking at?" Adam asked.

"Someone's vandalizing my boat."

"Quinn?"

Ben didn't bother answering. Of course, it was Quinn. She'd been lurking beside the *Seas the Day* when he'd first encountered her earlier today. Her bullshit about seeking him out to make amends was just that—bullshit. But what was her game? Once again, she had sucker-punched him and he with the superior IQ hadn't seen it coming. Adam had put the pieces together faster than he had. His anger at being duped made him run faster.

They took the stairs down to the dock single file. He could just make out movement on the back deck of his boat. But it wasn't Quinn. Instead, it was a trio of men. All of them chattering in Russian. Ben suddenly had a really bad feeling. Adam already had his gun in his hand when they turned down the row housing the *Seas the Day*. Rich's siren was now much closer.

But still not close enough.

A woman's muffled scream was followed a few seconds later by a loud splash.

Quinn!

The men disembarked and were headed toward the end of the dock. Adam and Ben took cover behind one of the boats.

"Stay right where you are, gentlemen," Rich called out

over the loudspeaker in his squad car.

Apparently, the Russian's didn't understand English or they were just brazening it out because they continued walking. Adam fired a shot over their heads to get their attention. The two men at the back quickly returned fire while the man at the front carried on as if oblivious, calmly walking to the edge of the dock before jumping off. Rich fired off a few rounds from his rifle but the other two men followed their friend over the side. An outboard engine roared to life and suddenly the three were hurtling over the bay in two Jet Skis at a breakneck speed.

"Well, that was interesting," Adam said.

But Ben was already heading toward his boat. He leaped onto the back deck.

"Quinn!"

Her purse was on its side on the deck.

"She's not down here," Adam said from the galley behind him.

Ben frantically clicked on the running lights, illuminating the water around the stern.

"There!" Adam pointed to a ripple along the surface.

Adam was still shrugging out of his boots when Ben dove in. He kicked his legs out with enough force to propel him deeper toward the sandy bottom. The lights only illuminated the water behind the boat a couple of feet. It was another three meters or so to reach the bottom. Blindly flailing his arms, he tried in vain to search the area in front of him.

She had to be there.

Another body sluiced through the water. It was Adam carrying an underwater flashlight. He arched the beam in a slow circle beneath them. Too slowly for Ben, though. His lungs were already on fire. Quinn had been under water a good two minutes longer than him. They didn't have a moment to lose. He grabbed at the lantern just as its beam reflected off something shiny below. He kicked down deeper. A third body swam past him, following the same reflection.

Rich was already skimming the sandy bottom when he saw her.

The necklace she was wearing danced eerily above her neck as the pearl caught the lantern light. A halo of red hair spread out from her still body. Her hands and feet were tied together with the auxiliary stern anchor from the *Seas the Day* secured to her ankles, its weight easily pressing her to the floor of the bay. Duct tape covered her mouth. Rich was already sawing at the anchor's ropes when Ben lifted her body and began rapidly kicking them both to the surface. Adam grabbed Ben by the midsection and within seconds, they were above the water gasping for air.

A crowd had gathered along the dock and suddenly there was a swell of voices among the outstretched hands trying to pull them out of the bay. Rich shot out of the water and grabbed onto the deck gulping lungsful of air. The EMTs reached for Quinn, but Ben was reluctant to let her go. He anxiously searched her neck for a pulse.

"Bennett, let them do their job." Adam reached around him and hauled Quinn's body up onto the dock where the two EMTs ripped the tape off her mouth and began resuscitating her.

A hush fell over the crowd as Ben crawled up onto the dock. Aunt Marnie wrapped a towel over his shoulders but he didn't dare take his eyes off Quinn long enough to even wipe his face.

Breathe, he silently urged. Everyone around him seemed to be collectively holding their breath. Time stood still. When suddenly she began to choke and cough, it was almost as if the dock itself sighed with relief. He scrambled closer helping the EMTs to reassure her as she struggled against their attempts to get oxygen to her lungs.

"Ben." She gasped his name between violent coughing spasms.

"I'm here." He squeezed her hand. "Just relax. Leave the mask on and breathe."

She shook her head agitatedly. "No," she cried, yanking at the mask. "Need to. . . get out of here."

"Shh," he tried to reassure her. "It's okay. You're safe. I'm not going to let anything happen to you."

The EMT was inserting a line into her arm. "Her BP is through the roof. This will help keep her calm," he murmured. "The IV fluids will stabilize her body temp."

Ben attempted to place the mask back over her nose and mouth, but she swatted it away.

Her eyes pleaded with him, but her labored words were difficult to make out. "Must. . . disappear. Can't know. . . I'm alive!" Her eyelids drooped as the medicine began to take effect. Her words were slurred slightly now. "Make sure he doesn't get it. Please, Ben."

"Who, Quinn?" Ben demanded. "Who are you afraid of?"

"She's out," the EMT explained when she didn't answer.

"Make sure who doesn't get what?" Adam asked from where he had crouched down beside him.

"Damned if I know," Ben said. "But I'm sure as hell going to find out."

"My guess is she has something those guys want badly enough to kill for," Rich announced from his perch on the *Seas the Day*. "From the looks of it, those goons believed it was on your boat. Any ideas?"

"No clue."

Could she have planted something on his boat earlier? *Damn it.* He'd been too busy lusting over her like a horny teenager to notice if she had.

The EMTs carefully loaded her onto a gurney and wrapped a thermal blanket around her body. She looked so innocent. Minutes before, she'd looked just as peaceful floating to the bottom of the bay. Nausea rolled through his belly. Those men thought nothing of dumping her in the water and leaving her to die. No matter how angry he was with her right now, he never wanted that for her.

Never.

And, right now, he desperately wanted her safe and alive because he had questions for her. Lots of them.

"How do we know those guys got what they were looking for?" he asked. "Or that they won't come back and finish her off. We need to get her someplace we can secure."

Adam eyed him warily. "Dude, you may not be thinking with the correct body part here. She's clearly not as innocent as she appears. She ghosted you, remember? Are you sure you want to involve yourself in her shit storm?"

"I gave her my word," he snapped.

His asshole buddy was wrong. Ben needed Quinn safe so he could question her about her "friend" Alexi Ronoff. That was all. He hadn't been able to get a good look at any of the men, but his gut was telling him that Ronoff was among them.

Adam heaved a sigh. "Fine. POTUS and FLOTUS are headed to California. I can get Joss to agree to have a guest sleep over. No one can get to your runaway prom date there. But she's under escort the entire time she's in the Crown. Understood?"

Ben nodded.

"Hey, this woman is lucky we were right here when you pulled her out, but she's still a victim of a near drowning," one of the EMT's objected. "She needs further medical attention, just in case."

"Good thing the Crown has its own medical staff, then." Adam pinned the paramedic with his no-nonsense sniper's gaze.

"That's not within our standard protocol." The EMT refused to back down.

Ben shot his brother-in-law a beleaguered look.

Rich sighed heavily. "The feds outrank us, boys. I'm

overriding protocol tonight. She goes with them."

Adam pulled out his cell phone and began making the necessary arrangements.

"Before you take off, Ben, you might want to come up here and see if anything is missing," Rich said.

"I got her," Adam reassured him.

Ben climbed aboard the *Seas the Day*. He hadn't been paying too much attention earlier; he was so laser-focused on finding Quinn. But Rich was correct. His boat had been thoroughly tossed. He bent down to retrieve the contents of Quinn's purse scattered on the back deck. Growing up in a house full of females, he knew enough not to separate a woman from her purse.

"Whoa there, Bennett," Rich said. "I'm not skipping every protocol. This is still the scene of an attempted murder. I'll make sure that gets bagged up and returned to her."

There was the queasiness again. Every time he thought of Quinn dying. Ben was in the process of getting to his feet when something just inside her bag caught his eye.

"Do you have evidence gloves?" he asked his brother in law.

Rich handed him a pair of latex gloves. Ben pulled them on and reached for a silver tube that looked a lot like a lipstick container, only longer. Inside was a sophisticated set of lock picks.

What does a photographer need with those?

His pulse pounded harder when he dug a little deeper and pulled out a small, but lethal, Ruger twenty-two caliber handgun. He checked the barrel. It was fully loaded. Any lingering guilt about invading her privacy disappeared. He picked up her camera and discovered the SIM card had been removed. Her cell phone was switched to the off position. Unusual for most people unless she didn't want to be easily located.

He inspected her wallet next. It contained one credit card, a smattering of cash and a British driver's license, but nothing else. No coupons, or discount cards. Not even a damn postage stamp. None of the things most women stuffed into their wallets.

"Who are you, Quinn Darby," he asked quietly.

"Hey, Bennett," Adam called from the dock. "We're ready to move out."

"Be right down. I just need to grab something from my cabin."

He headed belowdecks pulling up to an abrupt halt at the bottom of the steps. The Russians were thorough. Every drawer and cabinet had been opened; the contents strewn on the floor. Wading through the mess, he headed for the front cabin. No surprise; it had been ransacked as well. He made a beeline for the fake Rubik's Cube he kept at his bedside, frantically digging his fingers inside.

It was empty.

Fuck.

Those assholes took the copy of VOYEUR he'd stowed there earlier that day.

QUINN WAS FLOATING. A sea of dense fog enveloped her. Beyond the curtain of gray, she heard voices. Familiar ones. Her dad was singing, his deep baritone familiar and comforting. But try as she might, Quinn couldn't make out the words of the song. Frustrated, she struggled to get closer, but was stopped by the warm weight that descended every time she tried to move.

Moments or hours later, she wasn't sure, the haze grew thinner and she was on the water. The sun was warm on her exposed skin and the breeze gently tousled her hair. She was sailing Ben's little Sun Fish out in the middle of the bay. He was behind her. Quinn couldn't see him, but she heard him.

"You're doing great, Brit," he encouraged her. "Don't worry, I'm right here with you."

The agitation seeped from her weary limbs replaced by pure joy. She was free. And she was with Ben. But then her head began to pound. She could see her parents standing on the shore waving to her. Except the closer she got to the sand, the further her mum and dad moved away. There was something she needed to tell them, but she couldn't remember what. Panic seized her chest, she looked back hoping Ben would calm her.

But he wasn't there.

Alexi Ronoff was behind her instead.

With a malevolent smile, Alexi draped the anchor around her neck, laughing as he pushed her overboard. A silent scream escaped her lips before she was swallowed up by the darkness again. She tried in vain to move her arms and legs, but the warm weight descended as before, instantly soothing her. Something soft brushed against her forehead. Ben's voice was back, so close, but still unreachable.

It's okay, Brit. I've got you. And I'm not going to let you go.

She let the warmth surround her as she settled into a deep slumber.

QUINN RAISED HER eyelids just far enough so she could assess her situation without appearing to be awake should someone be watching. Through the fringe of her eyelashes, she could make out a fabric canopy hanging above her. To her right were three windows, adorned in matching fabric draperies, but devoid of iron bars. Always a good sign.

She relaxed as she realized she wasn't in a dank prison cell. Of course, that didn't mean she wasn't being held against her will. The sluggishness of her body told her she'd been drugged with something. She spied a secretary desk several feet beyond the end of the bed. Two upholstered chairs were placed on either side of the desk. Sitting in one of them was the pretty blonde Secret Service agent who'd accompanied Josslyn Benoit to dinner last night.

Obviously, the cotton in her head was as thick as the cotton lining her mouth because she was having a tough time recalling how she'd gotten from the dockside restaurant to wherever she was now. She closed her eyes and willed her memory to return. Images of Ben with his family and friends danced before her stirring up the now familiar yearning deep in her belly. It was quickly swallowed up by fear.

She needed to protect him.

Suddenly, it all came back to her. She'd gone back to Ben's beautiful boat to retrieve the card before Alexi figured out where it was. But she was too late. Her heart began to pound as she realized her nightmare was real, he had tied the anchor to her and thrown her overboard. Gasping for air, she shot up to a sitting position.

"Easy." The Secret Service agent murmured something into her sleeve as she jumped to her feet. "You're safe here."

She wanted to ask where exactly "here" was, but she was having trouble getting air into her lungs, much less forming words.

"Try a couple of deep breaths," the agent urged. "The doctor is on his way."

A door on the other end of the room opened. A middle-aged woman entered, carrying a tray with a pitcher of water and, blessedly, a teakettle with saucers and cups.

"Well, good morning." The woman bristled with efficiency as she set the tray on the bedside table. "I'm so glad to see you're awake. I'm Terrie Bloodworth, the head housekeeper. I thought you might be getting thirsty by now. Agent Segar suggested a cup of tea might be just the thing for you."

Ben was nearby.

And still watching out for her, apparently. The thought

eased the tightness in her chest.

"Where is he?" she croaked.

"He was a little worse for wear after worrying about you all night," Terrie explained. "I sent him downstairs to the Secret Service lounge for a shower and a rest. Not that he'll heed my instructions about the latter."

It suddenly dawned on Quinn where she was. "Wait. Are you telling me I'm at the White House?" She quickly glanced around.

"This isn't the Lincoln bedroom if that's what you're thinking," the housekeeper said with a smile. "But, yes, Josslyn insisted you recover here rather than a hospital."

Quinn rubbed her temple. Her memory remained fuzzy on all the details, but she was relieved Ben hadn't come to any harm. Alexi remained out there looking for the micro card, however, which meant Ben was still in danger. Her, too, if the Russian found out she was still alive. Somehow, he'd figured her out. She needed to get that dashed thing before anyone else got hurt.

Or worse.

"I need to get out of here." As she dragged her legs from beneath the covers, she was alarmed to discover she wasn't wearing anything but an oversized T-shirt. Looking down, she saw the Secret Service emblem emblazoned across the chest.

"I'm afraid it was necessary to cut you from your wet clothing," Terrie explained. "Agent Groesch here, was nice enough to loan you something from her locker."

Unfortunately, the agent hadn't bothered to include a

pair of underwear. It seemed that if she wanted to leave, she'd be making her walk of shame out of the White House going commando. She had to hand it to Ben and his fellow agents, the only thing more effective in holding her captive in this room would be actual physical restraints.

"Any chance I can borrow some clothes so I can leave?"

The housekeeper handed Quinn a cup of tea. "We'll see what we can round up, *after* the doctor has cleared you to go. For now, let's get some fluids in you. Then perhaps a shower. I'm sure you want to wash the Chesapeake off your body."

Taking a few resigned sips from the hot tea, she silently pondered her situation. Even if she could distract the housekeeper, Agent Groesch didn't look as if she was about to let down her guard enough for her to escape. Never mind the dozens of agents and uniformed officers likely manning the White House, all of whom were bound to stop her from getting away. Not only that, but the stench from her hair was offending even Quinn. The idea of a warm shower was too good to pass up.

Besides, both she and Ben were safe where they were at the moment. The fact that Alexi thought she was dead certainly gave her an advantage. And she fully intended to use it. All she needed now was to find out where Ben stashed his tuxedo before Alexi did. The idea of spending more time with Ben while trying to coax it out of him wouldn't exactly be torture, either.

"A shower sounds wonderful," she said.

CHAPTER SEVEN

"DID SHE SAY anything at all last night?" Griffin asked.

Ben shook his head before taking a long pull from his coffee. He, Adam, and Griff were camped out in the director's office on the ground floor of the White House. The fact that it was a Saturday, combined with POTUS being out of town, meant the office was experiencing a rare couple of hours of quiet.

"The doctor gave her something so she'd sleep."

Not that Quinn's sleep was exactly peaceful. Ben spent the previous night lying beside her in the bed and doing his best to comfort her during her frequent bouts of restlessness. At times she'd been so agitated that it was all he could do to calm her. Eventually, she'd settled into a deep slumber, her body clinging to his like a barnacle.

Not that he minded.

Much.

The torture of having her in his arms again and not being able to do anything wasn't quite as painful as the idea that the girl he once loved was now involved with a criminal who didn't give a second thought to killing her. There was something he was missing here. He was pretty sure he'd find the answer he was looking for if he could unlock the complicated puzzle that was Quinn Darby. But he was lying if he didn't admit to being a bit apprehensive of what he might uncover.

"When she first came to, she mentioned something about not letting 'him' get it," Adam said. "I think that's where you need to start."

Ben already had a good idea of who the him was. "Fill me in on her friend, Alexi Ronoff," he said to Griffin.

"I don't have much more than what I told you yesterday." Griffin opened a folder and spread the contents out on the coffee table. "Although, I did some digging to figure out how he was invited to the White House in the first place. Turns out he was a last-minute substitution to the Russian delegation when someone else had to bow out."

"Do you have a name for the guest who canceled?" Ben had an ugly hunch he already knew the answer to his own question.

Griffin consulted his notes. "A banker by the name of Kir Abramov."

Ben gripped the back of his neck before blowing out a breath.

"Interesting," Adam commented. "You don't seem surprised. Care to share?"

"Abramov is dead."

His buddies exchanged a look. Ben held up his hand.

"That's all the sharing I can do right now. At least until I can get some answers out of Quinn."

Mainly, what the "it" was she didn't want Ronoff to

find. Although, he was beginning to have a good idea about that, as well. Just how she fit into the picture still eluded him though. Not to mention how Ronoff knew about VOYEUR.

Adam shifted in his chair. "We can't hide her here much longer, Bennett. POTUS and FLOTUS are due back tomorrow night."

"Clearly, Ronoff is one bad dude," Griffin added. "He's bound to figure out she's not dead. Then what?"

He didn't know.

For once in his life, his agile brain couldn't compute the correct answer. Fortunately for him, his phone was buzzing with a text from the one woman who could help. Assuming the Secretary of Homeland didn't serve up his balls in a paper bag for allowing a copy of VOYEUR to slip into the wrong hands.

"I've got to run out for a little bit."

"Seriously, dude?" Griffin stood along with Ben. "What are we supposed to do with your runaway prom date in the meantime?"

Ben looked between his best friends. "Didn't Marin mention something about wedding cakes? Every woman loves wedding cake."

Adam snarled something profane.

"Look, she's probably going to sleep until noon. I'll be back well before then."

"Actually, she's already awake," the head housekeeper said from the hallway. "In fact, she's taking a shower right now. I was just going to round her up some clothing."

Shit. His buddies were shooting him death glares. No way could he escape without confronting Quinn first. He needed to let her know she wasn't leaving the Crown just yet. Not until he had the full story.

"Just get me a robe or something," he said. "I'll take it to her."

Terrie arched an eyebrow at him. "The White House is *not* a fraternity house, Agent Segar."

Adam snickered behind him. Terrie smiled at him indulgently. "You're not one to talk, Agent Lockett."

Griffin wisely kept his gaze trained on the floor. Both men had seen action in the Queen's bedroom a time or two. But Ben's situation was different. He was just trying to keep Quinn safe from herself. To do that, he needed to keep her secluded on the third floor until he could make alternative arrangements.

"I'm sure Josslyn has something she can borrow." He decided to shoot straight with the housekeeper. "But I do need to speak with her right away. It's a matter of national security."

Thankfully, his buddies remained stoic behind him. For her part, Terrie narrowed her eyes and scrutinized him as if he was a scuff on the marble floor in the Cross Hall.

"Of the three of you, I had you pegged as the most responsible," she finally said. "Don't let me down."

She turned on her heel and headed toward the kitchen.

Griffin snorted as soon as her footsteps faded on the marble. "You brought a damn stranger with questionable connections into the Crown and spent the night in bed with her. How does that make you more responsible than us?"

"Because she was unconscious?" Adam quipped.

Ben ignored them. "Look, can you just keep an eye on her while I check out a lead?"

Both men reluctantly agreed. He made his way to the stairs and jogged up the three flights to the top floor of the residence. As he rounded the corner into the Center Hall, he was greeted by the frantic yipping of Fergus, the Scottish terrier belonging to the First Lady's ailing father. The little dog made a beeline for the laces of Ben's boat shoes.

"Don't even think about it, you little monster."

He scooped up a knotted sock and tossed it across the room. Fergus took the bait and dashed down the hall. Before the dog could return, Ben hurried into the room where he'd left Quinn sleeping a couple of hours ago.

"Hey! Have you ever heard of knocking?" Christine chided him.

But he didn't hear a word the other agent said. All of his attention was instantly laser-focused on the second woman in the room. The one wrapped in nothing but a fluffy white towel; her cheeks rosy from the warm water. The long, tan legs he'd dreamt of having wrapped around him again were still slick with moisture. Just like that, the erotic image she posed had him hard as a rock.

As if she was aware of the potency of her allure, she raised her chin a notch, meeting his stare with a challenging one of her own. Suddenly, it was all he could do to keep from reaching beneath the turban on her head and tangling his fingers in silky strands of her hair. Or, better yet, sliding his tongue along the soft skin covering her collarbone.

Damn it. This would never do. He needed to get his head—*the one housing his brain*—in the game and get some answers.

"Christine, can you give us a minute?" He didn't bother breaking eye contact with Quinn.

"Leave you two unchaperoned and risk the wrath of Terrie? I don't think so."

When he didn't answer, Christine huffed a beleaguered sigh. "The things I do for you idiots," she mumbled.

With a little more force than was necessary, she shut the door behind her. For a long moment the only sound in the room was the hum of tension radiating between him and Quinn.

"We need to talk," he began.

"Thank you," she murmured softly at the same time.

Her husky tone nearly took him out at the knees. He shook his head to refocus. "What?"

She inched forward giving Ben a bird's-eye view of her dewy cleavage. He swallowed roughly.

"I said thank you. For saving my life." She gestured toward the canopied bed. "And for . . . comforting me last night. Agent Groesch said you stayed with me."

"Yeah, well, I wasn't going to let you drown without finding out why the hell you trashed my boat."

He wouldn't regret his harsh tone, even when she took a step back. Although he did regret losing the enticing view.

"I didn't trash your boat."

He waited for the telltale signal she was lying, but there wasn't one. Only annoyance. Both surprised him.

"Then who did?"

She looked away, but he was in no mood to put up with any more duplicity from her. He was tired and horny and both afflictions seemed to be forcing him into making rash decisions. Closing the distance between them, he wrapped his fingers around her chin and tilted it so they were once again eye to eye. He would make her talk.

But the alarm he saw shadowing her face had his gut clenching with guilt. She was afraid. Of who? Of him?

Wrapping his arms around her, Ben pulled her body flush against his. He brushed his lips over her forehead.

"He tried to kill you," he murmured against her soft skin. "Don't you dare try to protect him."

"I'm not protecting him," she whispered.

She was protecting someone. Every fiber of his body was telling him so.

"Talk to me, Quinn. Let me help you."

Gripping the towel wrapped around her with one hand, she reached up with the other to trace her fingers along his jaw. "This is something I need to handle myself."

Unable to tame his frustration, he gave her body a little shake. *Who the hell did she think she was, Wonder Woman?*

She caressed his cheek with her palm. "Please, Ben. It's best for everyone. Let me go."

Let me go.

Those three little words seemed to unleash something

within him. The roaring in his ears was brought on by years of pent-up emotions wondering why she'd left and what had become of her. And agonizing over 'what if?' No way was he letting her go again. Not until he had answers.

And maybe not even after that.

"I didn't pull you out of the damn Chesapeake Bay to let you go," he growled.

And before either of them knew what was happening, he captured her mouth in a fierce kiss. He was tired of waiting. Now he was taking. And take he did. Shoving the towel from her head, he buried his fingers in her wet hair. He tipped her head so he had a better angle to more thoroughly ravage her mouth.

Thankfully, Quinn didn't put up any resistance. When he opened her lips with his own, she welcomed him in with a sexy moan from deep in the back of her throat. Her fingers scored the back of his head as though she was trying to fuse their bodies together. He let his own hands roam beneath the towel covering her body, skimming over the globes of her ass. She nipped at his tongue when he squeezed gently.

His brain was yelling at him to slow things down, but the rest of his body parts weren't listening. He deepened the kiss, tangling his tongue with hers while his fingers traced the sensuous curves of her body. Her pleasure-filled sighs spurred him on even more. He needed to get her to the bed.

Now.

"National Security my ass!"

Terrie's words were like a bomb dropping in the room. Ben swore savagely when Quinn broke off their kiss. She was flushed head-to-toe. Clutching her towel to her chest she glanced around the room, looking for likely escape routes if he had to guess. Fergus added to the commotion by yipping and dancing between their legs.

"Out!" Terrie commanded. "And take the little dog with you."

Jesus.

Ben gave his head a little shake to try to restore some rational thought. Thank goodness Terrie had come along when she had. He needed to stop reacting to Quinn as if she was the girl from his youth. That girl was gone. He had no idea who the woman he'd just been locking lips with was. Or whether or not her heated response was real. And that pissed him off. He needed to put some distance between them and sort out his next move.

But he couldn't leave Quinn yet. Not until she'd agreed to stay put. She was his only connection to Ronoff and he still needed answers about the Russian.

"Promise me you'll be here when I get back."

Her eyes were shining with equal parts apprehension and frustration. She looked as if she was going to argue. But then she nodded solemnly.

"Can I trust you?" he whispered, not sure if he would even believe her answer.

"Yes." She nodded again, this time with determination.

The temptation to brush the backs of his knuckles along her cheek was strong. He resisted. "Then trust me.

And stay put."

Fergus was having a field day with Ben's shoelaces. Terrie cleared her throat angrily. Quinn stepped away. He picked up the pesky dog and left the room just as the door slammed behind him.

Christine waited outside, an I-told-you-so look pasted firmly on her face.

"Can you keep an eye on her?" he asked. "Please."

The other agent crossed her arms over her chest. "Are you sure she's who you think she is?"

No.

He wasn't sure about anything. "Actually, I sincerely hope she's not the person I think she is right now."

With that, he handed her the dog and headed out to confront the Secretary of Homeland.

TRUST ME.

Ben's words ricocheted around inside Quinn's head all morning. Trust wasn't exactly in her wheelhouse. Mainly because, in her profession, trusting someone often came with the possibility she might end up dead. But given her current situation, she had no choice. Until she figured out a way to slip out from beneath the watchful eyes of Ben's friends, she was forced to trust him with her life.

Too bad it was his life she was more worried about. As long as Ronoff believed he had the micro card, Ben was in danger. He'd obviously left the safety of the White House, but where had he gone? She said a silent prayer he'd taken his sniper friend with him.

"Did Ben say when he'd be back?" she asked for what had to be the third time already.

Josslyn looked up from the stack of wedding response cards she was sorting with the First Lady's secretary. They were seated at a table on the Truman Balcony overlooking the south lawn of the White House. The late morning breeze carried with it the muffled sounds of traffic and tourists.

"He didn't." Her indulgent smile was beginning to look strained.

No doubt Ben's friends were a little apprehensive about welcoming into their midst a woman who Russian thugs had left for dead. Not that she could blame them. Given the chilly reception from the other woman in the room— Marin, the wife of another agent—she suspected he had shared with his friends the salient details of their past.

Still, she was grateful for the clothing Josslyn had loaned her. She was pretty sure the woman had done so at Ben's request. But at least she didn't have to hide in one of the bedrooms with a towel as her only covering. Once again, she found herself wondering what it would be like to have close friends who would do anything for her. Ben was a lucky guy. The sooner she diverted the danger away from him—and his friends—the better.

But how? Her tech gear and the other equipment she needed were three miles away in a storage cabinet within the British Embassy. Not only that, but she needed to get word to her handler that her identity had been compromised. She sighed as she walked over to the railing of the balcony. The little terrier followed her, letting out a woeful whimper in an effort to get attention. She bent down and scratched him between the ears, trying in vain to come up with a solution.

"Perhaps I could borrow your phone," she asked Josslyn. "That way I can start reaching out to my colleagues to see who might be available to shoot your wedding."

Agent Groesch didn't bother being discreet as she shook her head no. Marin snorted her own disapproval. Josslyn looked uncomfortable as she wiped her hands along her jeans.

"Personal cell phones are not allowed inside the White House," she explained. "Claire can help us make those calls later."

The secretary nodded.

"Why don't we go downstairs and meet with the florist," Josslyn suggested. "I can't wait to see what Marilyn has dreamed up for the centerpieces." She jumped up from the sofa and the other ladies rose like lemmings to follow her.

Quinn wanted to scream. The very idea of spending the rest of the morning debating the merits of tea roses, nosegay, and peonies was making her head pound. She was a woman of action. And right now, she needed to find a tiny piece of plastic containing very sensitive information.

Except she'd promised Ben she'd stay until he got back. And she hadn't done a very good job of keeping her promises to him thus far. The last thing she wanted to do was let him down again. Pasting on a false smile, she followed the other women out of the Yellow Oval.

They strolled across the Center Hall, exiting through a pair of double pocket doors mounted beneath a stunning fan-light window. The thick carpeting on the stairs muffled their steps as they made their way down to the lower floors of the White House. Owing to the fact it was the weekend, the mansion was quiet, almost reverent, as if the walls were aware of the historical distinction they held as the center-piece of a nation's identity.

Quinn's visit to the White House was so brief the other evening, she didn't get the chance to glimpse any of the rooms or artwork. When they reached the first floor, she slowed her steps so she could sneak a peek into the Green Room before they continued down to the ground floor.

"I'm sure if you ask nicely, Ben will give you a tour later." Agent Groesch indicated she should hurry to keep up with the other women.

There was nothing Quinn's artistic eye would enjoy more than time to explore the famed paintings and architecture of the White House. Especially if she got to spend time with Ben while doing so. Although, given how she had responded to his kiss earlier, she suspected what both of them most wanted to explore was each other's body. Parts of her were growing warm just thinking about the possibility. Always a fast study, he had clearly learned a few moves since the last time he'd had his hands and mouth on her naked body.

Really good moves.

But getting involved with him would only end in more heartache. Despite his brilliance, he was still just a computer nerd who spent his days behind a keyboard. The trustworthy boy-next-door would never understand or condone the decisions she'd made. In her line of work, she was the polar opposite of Ben, living a life of deception. She was darkness where he was light. As much as she wanted to rekindle the attraction between them, she had to keep her distance. She needed to keep her eye on the mission. Get the list and disappear.

Once they reached the ground floor, they took a sharp right and rounded the corner to the hallway between the curator's office and the Secret Service director's office. Adam and another man sporting a pair of fabulous dimples looked up from the baseball game they were watching on a laptop.

"And where are you beautiful ladies off to?" Dimples asked.

Marin smiled for the first time that morning before sashaying over to him. "We're going to pick out flowers for the wedding. Want to join us?"

He looked like he'd likely agree to a root canal if Marin asked to give him one, but Adam spoke up before Dimples could answer her.

"Joss has carte blanche on floral arrangements. She has better taste for that than I do. But when it's time for cake, we're all in."

Josslyn leaned down to give him a sexy kiss on the lips

just as the other man wrapped his arms around Marin and pulled her into him. Agent Groesch made gagging noises behind Quinn.

"Really? Is there something in the water making you three boys behave like sex-crazed middle schoolers today?" The agent jabbed a thumb in Quinn's direction. "It's bad enough Ben got caught by Terrie unwrapping the little mermaid here. But Adam and Griffin, you should know enough to have some decorum within the Crown."

Fabulous.

Four pairs of eyes homed in on Quinn. She willed her cheeks not to flush without much success. As if Ben's friends didn't trust her already, Agent Groesch had given them one more reason not to like her. There wasn't much she could do except meet their glares head-on. Griffin's dimples disappeared and his smoky eyes grew hard. She jerked her chin up in response.

"Do you think it's wise to allow her free range of the House?" Griffin asked, not bothering to hide his disdain.

Agent Groesch scoffed. "I haven't left her alone for a single minute since Ben left. I don't need you to tell me how to do my job, Griffin. Which, I'd like to point out for the record, is not technically my job because she's not even supposed to be in the residence."

Quinn bristled. "I'm happy to leave at any time."

"Stop it. All of you," Josslyn demanded before linking an arm through Quinn's. "Quinn is my guest. We promised Ben we'd keep her company. And that's what we are going to do. First the centerpieces. Then the cake."

Quinn allowed Josslyn to propel her down the hall and around the corner to the flower shop. The earthy aroma of plants had Quinn's nose twitching while the airiness of the workshop helped to calm her nerves a bit. Sunlight beamed through several windows opening into a courtyard. The rooms were separated by walls of glass blocks helping to keep the shop bright and cheery.

An older woman who looked as though she should have retired long ago greeted them with a wide smile and twinkle in her eye. She hung a set of keys on a hook beside her desk.

"I must thank you, Miss Josslyn, for arranging for me to park in the courtyard. I stand most of the day and not having to make that long walk to the parking lot at the end of the day helps." She winked at them. "I might have outdone myself with these arrangements, Miss Josslyn, if I do say so myself."

"I have no doubt." Josslyn smiled fondly at the woman. "Quinn, this wonderful lady is Marilyn Johnson, the fairy godmother of the White House floral shop. She spent years as the mastermind of all the floral arrangements within the mansion. It took a little coaxing, but I convinced her to come out of retirement for a few weeks to plan the arrangements for our wedding. If I couldn't go to the Serengeti, then I wanted Marilyn to bring it to Washington."

The florist beamed as she stepped away from her worktable to reveal a breathtaking centerpiece comprised of beige and gold colored flowers, tall shocks of river grass and roses seemingly dipped in bronze. A chorus of *oohs* and *ahhs* echoed throughout the workshop.

"Those roses are amazing," Quinn couldn't help but say. "I've never seen them before. What kind are they?"

"They're Kahala roses," the florist replied. "I thought the beige color with the bronze elements perfectly captured the feel of the desert's colors. Especially when using the Vermeil candelabras to showcase them."

"They're perfect," Quinn and Josslyn responded at the same time.

When Josslyn grinned at her, Quinn relaxed, and got into the spirit of things.

"What color are your bridesmaids wearing?" Quinn asked, her mind whirring at the potential of complementary colors. *How much fun would it be to actually photograph this wedding?* The thought stunned her in its randomness. She pushed it aside, reminding herself she was playing a role. She was always playing a role.

"No bridesmaids. We're trying to keep it as intimate as possible. My sister, the First Lady, is my maid of honor and my niece is the flower girl," Josslyn explained. "Harriett and I haven't picked out a color for her dress yet. She has designers pretty much at her disposal, but we'll need to make a decision this week."

"Peach. The color of sunset on the Serengeti." Quinn glanced over at the florist. "Maybe with bouquets of Oceana roses mixed with some off-white lilies and one or two of these Kahala roses?"

The older woman nodded. "With the cream and moss-green accents of the Truman china on the table, that would be perfect. You have a very good eye for color."

"Quinn is a photographer. She's shot quite a few celebrity weddings." Josslyn grinned at Marin. "Thank goodness I know two people with impeccable eyes for art or this wedding would be a simple safari theme."

The First Lady's secretary coughed discreetly into her hand. The florist shook her head. For her part, Marin seemed to grimace as if she didn't like being placed in the same friend category as Quinn.

"I once photographed a wedding with a cake that had strings of topaz beads wrapped around the layers," Quinn said, trying anything to win the other woman over. "With low lighting it allowed for some pretty shots. Topaz would fit into the color scheme perfectly. And with the candelabras as the light source—"

"Don't tell me how to decorate a wedding cake," Marin interrupted her. "I'm not sure why you're interjecting yourself into this wedding, anyway. Not with your track record of disappearing without a trace. I'd stick with the White House photographer, Josslyn. At least that way you'll know they'll show up when they say they will."

With that, Marin turned on her heel and left the floral shop. Quinn's stomach rolled. She'd brought that on herself. And she was angry that the approval of Ben's friends meant so much to her. Marin was right, however. Quinn would be disappearing. And the sooner the better. She had no business trying to forge relationships with these people.

But what if?

There was that thought again. Just for a moment, Quinn let it take hold. What if she was no longer in the game and these could be her friends? What if she could help Josslyn with her wedding? How much fun would it be to dance with Ben at the reception. Or to create the artistic photos the bride desired. She was suddenly overcome with a longing more painful than the sting of Marin's words. A yearning for a life different from the only one she'd ever known. A life that up until yesterday, had fulfilled her, challenged her. Only now, she knew what she was missing. And the realization hurt.

The room was suddenly quiet as everyone looked everywhere else but at Quinn.

"She's very protective of Ben," Agent Groesch said quietly. "We all are."

"I'm sure you don't believe me, but I'm glad you all are protective of him. So very glad." Quinn somehow managed to get the words out despite a thick throat. "Griffin is right. I think it's best if I wait upstairs for Ben to return."

Agent Groesch nodded and Quinn followed her to the lift.

CHAPTER EIGHT

S TILL REELING FROM the conflicting emotions brought on by his encounter with Quinn, Ben didn't bother to temper his frustration when he knocked on the front door of the Secretary of Homeland's residence. A long moment later, Agent Caracas pulled the door open with a smirk.

Damn. He'd forgotten the idiot was on the secretary's personal detail.

"No need to be so ferocious, Inspector Gadget. We hear you."

"Stuff it, Caracas." He shoved past him. "Where is she?"

"In the backyard, communing with nature."

He was through the narrow row house in an instant. When he emerged out onto the flagstone patio, the secretary didn't bother looking up from the flowers she was dead-heading.

"Your urgent text interrupted a perfect Saturday morning, Agent Segar."

He heard Caracas snort behind him, the unprofessional jerk.

"This needs to be discussed inside."

No way was Ben going to cop to his mistake in front of

Caracas, the service's biggest gossip. Not only that, but he had no idea who might be on the other side of the privacy fence listening in with a Stingray. The secretary's detail was supposed to be monitoring for those types of issues, but Caracas wasn't known for taking those routine measures too seriously.

Secretary Lyle straightened at his words. He was relieved to see her drop the shears in the bucket beside her. The family jewels were safe for now. She pulled off her gardening gloves and tossed them in the bucket as well.

"Very well, then," she remarked when she trudged past him. "Inside it is."

She led the way to her study, which was actually a secure, sound-proof room, outfitted for her to conduct business from home when necessary. Ben took great pleasure in shutting the door in Caracas's face.

"I was actually going to send him for coffee," she said with a cocked eyebrow. "He'll remind me the task is way below his skill level, but I enjoy messing with his ego."

He might have laughed had he not been so uptight right now. "You might want something stronger to drink."

"I take it I have bigger problems than beetles in my garden?"

She removed the wide-brimmed hat covering her jet-black hair and tossed it on the sofa with a sigh. Green eyes collided with his and Ben was momentarily taken aback by the fortitude shining within them. They reminded him of another pair of strong-minded green eyes.

"Does this mean you've found something on Ronoff?"

she asked.

"More like Ronoff found me. Or rather his son did."

That got her attention. "Explain."

"A trio of Russians tossed my sailboat last night. Video from the surrounding boats and the marina IDed one of them as Alexi Ronoff. He made no attempt to disguise himself."

"How did they make the connection to you?"

"That's the million-dollar question."

She swiped at her brow as she plopped into her desk chair. "I assume their visit was timed while you were ashore and no one was hurt?"

"Actually, Ronoff took the opportunity to drown a woman."

Her head snapped up in shock.

He held up a hand. "We were able to get to her in time."

"She's alive?"

"Yes, but I'd rather the world thinks she's dead." His heart was racing again at the thought of Quinn actually dying. He needed to work harder to compartmentalize his feelings for her. "It will help keep her safe. I believe Ronoff tracked her to my boat with the intention of killing her."

"Who is she and why was she on your sailboat?" the secretary demanded.

Too bad Ben couldn't fully answer either of those questions. As much as he hated to admit it, his gut was telling him he never knew the real Quinn Darby. His brain was telling him she was up to something more than just innocent photography. All these years he'd been trying to answer the question of *where* she'd gone. Not *why*. A tactical oversight on his part, he now realized. He needed to put those pieces to the puzzle together before she got into more trouble. Not because he was protecting her, he lied to himself. But because she might hold the keys to the rest of the case.

"Still trying to sort that out, ma'am. But I need your help in keeping her hidden."

"If she can provide a link to Ronoff, of course. I'll make the necessary phone calls," she said. "You have carte blanche in this case."

The tightness in his chest eased for the first time since Quinn was thrown overboard. He'd keep her safe and ferret out her secrets. And he had just the place to do so. Of course, he hadn't delivered his bad news to the secretary. He braced himself for the possibility of her changing her mind about Quinn.

Ben dragged his fingers through his hair. "There's one other thing."

She arched an eyebrow at him.

"When Ronoff was on my boat, he made off with a copy of VOYEUR."

"What?" She shot from her chair. "What was it doing there? It's not like you to be so careless."

"I know, ma'am. There's no excuse. I should have returned it to my office yesterday when you said I could keep it. But in my defense, I didn't expect the guy to come looking for it. I have no idea how he even knew it existed much less that it was on board."

"How much damage can he do with it?"

"Well, once he figures out what the program consists of, he could easily sell it to a foreign entity for a fortune. But given Ronoff's background mining cryptocurrency, the equations embedded in the software would be very useful to someone wanting to manipulate the world market. It would take someone a while to unencrypt them, though, but it can be done."

"Define 'a while,'" she demanded through a tight jaw.

"It would take the average coder a week. Maybe more."

"And you? How long would it take someone with your skill level?"

Ben shifted sheepishly. He doubted anyone else with his skill level existed. Given the secretary's agitated state, he didn't bother mentioning that theory, though.

"I could do it in a day."

A string of unladylike words escaped her lips and he tried not to cringe.

"Find out whatever this woman knows about Ronoff and use it to get that program back," she snapped. "In the meantime, I'll try and flush out whoever leaked the intel to Ronoff that the program even existed." She sighed heavily. "I still need you looking into this mess with the Phoenix. There's no one else with the expertise to sift through the dark web. I need to know who's masquerading as the spymaster trying to sell classified intelligence. Not to mention who is seeking the intel. Ronoff still tops my list as a potential buyer."

"With all due respect, ma'am, you said yourself the list of operatives doesn't exist. Ronoff had no reason to search my sailboat for any possible intel related to the Phoenix. Perhaps it was all a ruse to throw us off the trail of what he really wanted?"

"Either way, someone within the national security community is selling secrets. I want them found." She pinned him with a hard glare. "Now, go work your magic on this mystery woman and get Ronoff."

With the exception of the magic that sparked between them when he had kissed her earlier, Ben couldn't imagine it was going to be easy to unlock Quinn's secrets. As much as he'd like to continue with the seduction method to unveil her mysteries—not to mention her body—he was smart enough to know that way would only lead to disaster. There was so much he didn't know about her.

Starting with whose side she was on.

Twenty minutes later, he arrived back at the White House. He bounded up the stairs to the second floor of the residence. Following the laughter, he made his way to the private family dining room at the end of the hall. His friends were seated around the table spearing pieces of wedding cake with their forks.

"Ben!" Marin jumped up. "You're back. Just in time to break the tie. We're debating which flavor wedding cake tastes best." She grabbed a plate and fork from the sideboard before shushing the others. "No one says a word. We need this to be objective."

But he wasn't interested in the cake. His heart stuttered

as he glanced around the table. "Where's Quinn?"

The four occupants of the room looked away awkward-ly and his panic piqued.

Had she disappeared again? *Damn.* She wasn't strong enough to be out on her own. Not after what she'd been through the night before. The idea of losing her again so soon suddenly made his throat unbearably tight. And not because he needed her to sort out this case. He had a scary feeling he just plain needed her.

And he swore never to let that happen again.

"I said, where is Quinn?" he demanded when his friends remained close-mouthed.

"She's upstairs," Marin finally offered up. "I . . . I might have made her feel uncomfortable earlier."

He had to work to keep the snarl from his voice. "Un-comfortable how?"

Griffin shot him a steely-eyed glare from where he was now standing behind his wife with his hands resting protectively on her shoulders.

"We were doing wedding stuff and, well, it's not like she is going to be around at the end of the month." She crossed her arms over her chest. "The only thing we know about the woman is that she hurt you. Badly. And I, for one, am not going to stand around and let her hurt you again."

"She's got a point, Bennett," Griffin added.

Ben couldn't believe it. He could give a rat's ass about whether Marin had a point or not. He didn't appreciate her going mama bear on him. Didn't anyone think he could take care of himself? Didn't anyone believe he had the brains to not let Quinn close enough to score his heart again? These were his friends. *His brothers.* They had promised to watch her, not shame her, damn it. His fingers clenched into fists.

"Forgive me for not seeing her point," he snapped. "You don't have to know anything at all about that woman upstairs except that someone tried to kill her last night. All I asked was for you to keep her company. To make her feel safe. Not to judge her. I would have done the same for any of you. I *have* done the same for each of you." He leveled a hard stare at Adam and Griff. "So much for that bullshit about being brothers," he added before storming out of the room and up the stairs to the third floor.

Once again, he didn't bother knocking when he entered the bedroom startling both women. Quinn was staring out the window, her shoulder propped up against the frame when she pivoted to face him. Something about her pose made him think she was ready to do battle. Christine looked up from her phone, but before she could chastise him about bursting in without knocking again, he shot out a question.

"Did the doctor examine her?"

"Umm, yeah, he did," Christine said as she got to her feet. "He said it was a miracle she was doing so well. She just needs to take it easy for another day or two and she'll be fully recovered."

Ben searched Quinn's eyes. She kept her expression masked, once again donning her protective armor.

"Excellent," he said. "You're dismissed, Christine. Let's go, Quinn."

"Wait, what?" Christine looked from one to the other. "Didn't you hear what I just said? She needs to take it easy for another couple of days."

"I heard you. And thanks for looking after my friend, but we're leaving now."

He wasn't sure, but he thought he detected a momentary shiver from Quinn before she took a step away from the window.

"Is that wise?" Christine protested. "What if those guys figure out she isn't dead?"

"Obviously, she can't stay here forever," he said. "But I know a place where she'll be safe."

Quinn eyed him warily as she made her way across the room. Clearly, she still didn't trust him completely. He couldn't decide if he was miffed or proud of her caution.

"Shouldn't you bring someone with you?" Christine asked.

Great. Even Christine didn't think he had the willpower to resist the temptation of Quinn. If he hadn't already declared her body off-limits, he'd keep his hands and lips off her just to spite his nosy friends who didn't think he had more common sense than a randy thirteen-year-old boy.

"Thanks, Christine, but contrary to the opinions of the rest of the squad, I've got this."

The other agent opened her mouth to speak before wisely closing it again. Ben gestured for Quinn to precede him out of the room. She stopped short at the sight of Adam and Griff standing in the Center Hall like two sentries.

"Don't worry. We're getting out of your hair," he announced. "Go back to your wedding planning."

"And how are you going to get wherever it is you are going?" Adam asked. "Metro? Not very clandestine."

Ben dragged his fingers through his hair. He was planning on taking a cab, but that would require them to walk to the end of the drive. While he didn't expect Ronoff to know she was alive, he didn't want to take the chance.

"I've got my car here," Griffin added. "Let us drive you."

He looked between his two so-called friends who still thought they were protecting him from himself.

"It's not what you think," Adam said as if reading his mind. "We want to help. Quinn is important to you and that makes her important to us."

Quinn *was* important to him. Not in the way his friends thought, however. Not anymore. She was a means of getting intel on Ronoff and perhaps finding the link to the Phoenix. That was all. Let everyone else believe what they wanted.

"You're the only little brother I've got," Griffin said with his dimpled grin. "And you've always been there when we needed you. Let us return the favor."

Adam shook his head. "He's always lording it over you that he's a few months older."

Ben's tension eased a bit. They were both morons, but

he appreciated their efforts. Still, this was his case. And he couldn't risk involving his friends any longer. He held his hand out palm up.

"Keys."

Griffin hesitated only briefly before pulling his keys from the pocket of his jeans and dropping them in Ben's hand. "You sure you don't need backup?"

"Nah." Ben glanced back at Christine. "You guys have done enough. Thanks. I've got this now."

Adam and Griff exchanged a look, but they backed down without an argument.

"Okay, but remember we're just a phone call away in case you need some fire power," Adam said. "There's nothing I like more than putting the bad guys in their place."

Ben didn't bother telling them he put bad guys in their place daily because neither one of them would understand his other line of work. They took the stairs headed to the first floor where they could exit the West Wing. Marin stood waiting on the landing of the second floor holding several plastic containers. She cleared her throat.

"You haven't eaten much today." She handed the containers to Quinn. "It's just some cake and scones, but I've always found baked goods to be decent sustenance."

Touched by Marin's peace offering, he leaned in to kiss her on the cheek. "Those aren't laced with anything, are they?"

Marin smacked him on the arm. "Please accept my apology," she said to Quinn, her words making his heart swell. "I was rude before and I have absolutely no excuse. I hope we meet again so I can make it up to you."

Quinn wore a deer-in-the-headlights expression. "I'd like that," she stammered.

Too bad she traced her tongue over her lip after she said it.

"WHERE ARE WE going?" Quinn asked when they pulled out of the White House parking lot.

"Somewhere we can finally have that talk you were so eager to have yesterday."

Funny, she wasn't so keen to have that talk any longer. Ben navigated the little SUV through the line of cars slowly cruising past the White House, passenger arms stretched out the windows so the occupants could take photos with their cell phones. She unabashedly studied his profile. He'd donned his sunglasses again making it hard to discern his expression. But if the tightness of his jaw was any indication, he was in full take-no-prisoners mode.

"I'd like to go back to Watertown to retrieve my camera and the rest of my things."

That was not exactly the truth. Everything in her possession was a cover and replaceable with the exception of her lockpicks. Those were the second pair of picks she'd lost this year. Her supply officer wouldn't be happy at having to procure those again. She wouldn't mind having the images of Watertown she'd photographed yesterday, however. Although, it was probably for the best they were lost to her. She didn't need any more painful reminders of the life she might have lived had her mother's career not taken her away from Ben.

"Rich is keeping it all safe for you at the sheriff's office."

He didn't elaborate further, continuing to stare straight ahead as he drove down Pennsylvania Avenue in the direction of the Capitol building. When they turned right on Third Street just past the Smithsonian Museums, Quinn's heart began to speed up. If the information she'd been given about him was correct, they were headed toward his row house on Capitol Hill. Could he have somehow made a pit-stop at his place the other day, stashing his tuxedo there? Her informant was insistent Ben was wearing it when he boarded the *Seas the Day*. But that didn't mean he couldn't have stopped by his home to empty out his pockets. Or sent the darn thing back with someone.

She'd just play along with his knight-in-shining-armor routine long enough to search his place. And then she'd do what she had to and disappear. These past two days had taken a toll on her. The near drowning notwithstanding, being around Ben and his close group of friends awakened something inside of her. An ache for community. For closeness. For unconditional love. Not to mention the wild desires his steamy kiss had conjured up. That made her want so much more. The sooner she could get back to her life, the sooner she could extinguish those feelings.

"I hope wherever you are taking me serves tea because

I'd love a cuppa to go with a piece of this cake."

"We won't be staying long enough for that."

They turned left on the other side of the Capitol taking Independence Avenue past the congressional office buildings before veering back onto Pennsylvania Avenue again. Victorian row houses sitting back behind iron fences and established trees lined the streets. With their dynamic palette of colors, no two were alike.

Ordinarily, her artistic eyes would be drinking in the beauty of the neighborhood. Instead, her brain whirred as she tried to come up with a way to stall him once they arrived. Most likely, what she was looking for was in his bedroom. Her body simmered at the thought. She'd used her feminine wiles many times to get inside a target's bedroom. But her stomach rolled at the thought of deceiving Ben any more than she already was. Seduction was off the table with him. Mainly because the toe-curling lip-lock they'd shared earlier had turned her brain to mush in an instant. She needed to keep her wits about her.

Three blocks later, he turned onto Sixth Street before steering the car into a narrow alley between two houses where he cut the engine.

"We're just going in, grabbing something, and coming right back out," he announced.

"I have to go to the toilet." Better to go with an old standby instead.

His fingers squeezed the steering wheel before letting go. "Fine."

They entered through a back door leading into a wide-open kitchen complete with an island, stainless steel appliances, and a brick fireplace next to a round table and chairs. She was taken aback at the hominess of the room. For a brief moment, Quinn found herself actually thirsting for a cup of tea shared with friends around the table.

If she had friends, of course.

"Bathroom's down this hall." He indicated an area to the front of the house. He was poised to make his way upstairs.

"Is there another one up there?" she asked doing her best to look forlorn. "I'd rather not be alone in a strange place."

His face softened instantly and she felt a twinge of guilt.

"Of course," he said. "I wasn't thinking. You can use the one in my room."

He led the way up the steep staircase. There were three bedrooms on this level and an open loft area up another flight.

"Through here." He indicated a bedroom at the back. "I've just got to get something from the office upstairs. It will only take a minute."

"Take your time," she told him.

Her fantasy of tripping over the tuxedo evaporated once she stepped inside his bedroom. It looked a lot like she imagined a military barracks would look. Neat. Orderly. Boring. The double bed was made up as if a hotel maid had done it. The floor wasn't littered with dirty socks or discarded shoes like most guys' rooms. Not even a container to drop his change or car keys into. In fact, unlike the *Seas the Day*, there was very little to identify who lived in the room. A copy of a John Grisham novel sat on the nightstand next to a phone charger. A few computer magazines were in a wicker basket beside the bed, but other than that, the room was very utilitarian.

Ben's footsteps sounded above her and she made a bee-line for his closet. Quickly, she rifled through the clothes hanging within it. Disappointment washed over her. No tuxedo. She needed to think fast because she was running out of time.

Figuring the nightstand would be the most likely place he'd store personal items from his pockets, she pulled the drawer open. The only things inside were a weathered address book and a stack of photos. Her heart stopped when she caught a glimpse of the one on top of the pile. It was the picture she'd taken of the two of them years ago. She'd propped her camera on top of a rock and used the self-time to capture several images of them. She recognized this one as the photo she'd had hanging on her bedroom mirror. She had a similar one tucked away in a journal in her safe house. How had Ben gotten hold of this one? Her eyes burned as she reverently fingered the picture before nearly dropping it when she heard a loud thump overhead.

Crap! She'd wasted too much time and Ben was on his way down. She quickly closed the door and ran into the loo to flush the toilet. With one last frustrated glance around the room, she headed to the door. A crash sounded from the loft above. Quinn hurried to the stairs.

"Ben?" she called.

The only answer was a grunt and a sharp intake of breath. Cautiously, she hurried up the stairs only to freeze at the sight greeting her once she reached the top. One of Alexi's henchmen had Ben in a choke hold.

CHAPTER NINE

THE GUY CAME out of nowhere. His stealth identified him as a professional. Fortunately, Ben caught the assassin's reflection in the computer monitor just as he was raising his gun outfitted with a silencer. Ben spun his right leg around in a Jiu Jitsu kick and knocked the Beretta from the guy's hand before he had time to react. The gun slid beneath an end table next to the stairs.

Ben was frantically grabbing for anything on the desk he could use as a weapon when the other guy snarled and charged him. A second later, he landed another kick to the guy's shoulder momentarily stunning him. Ben shifted his body around so he wasn't pinned against the desk. The assassin reached beneath his pant leg and pulled a lethal looking knife out of his boot. Ben raised his hand to ward off the knife when he heard Quinn's voice.

Shit!

He'd hoped she'd stay safe in the bedroom. His heart sped up just knowing she was still alive. But he'd hesitated too long. The other guy was on him quickly. Ben managed to get in a nasty strike to the assassin's wrist dislodging the knife, but not before the guy slashed through Ben's T-shirt, ripping the skin on his right shoulder. Between the sting of the wound and the sound of Quinn's footsteps on the stairs, he got distracted long enough for the other guy to get him in a choke hold. Ben was moving the other guy back toward the low ceiling in hopes of getting in a headbutt and a kick to his instep when Quinn appeared on the landing.

The guy choking him seemed surprised to see her before he chuckled.

"You're next."

With the ease of someone comfortable with firearms, Quinn retrieved the gun from beneath the table and pointed it at them. Ben continued to claw at the hands around his neck, praying she wouldn't fire the gun. The only one he'd trust with a shot that tricky was Adam.

"Let him go," she demanded, coolly.

The fingers on his carotid artery tightened. Wheezing, Ben angled his head to slam into the guy's jaw, but he never got a chance. In an instant, the fingers around his neck loosened and the guy behind him slumped against him. Ben gasped in several breaths before shoving the guy backward. When he turned around, the assassin was a heap against the wall, a single bullet hole in the center of the forehead.

Incredulous, he glanced back at Quinn but she had her fingers to her lips.

"He has a partner," she mouthed.

Ben grabbed the knife and made his way over to the stairs. He was a bit stunned to realize she was unfazed and all business after shooting another human being with the cold calculation of a trained killer. Months back, Josslyn had shot a man trying to kidnap a little boy in her care. She'd been shaken for weeks.

Who was this woman seated beside him?

He didn't have time to ponder the question because she was already headed downstairs.

"Wait!" he hissed.

Grabbing her arm, he went to take the gun away, but she just rolled her eyes. He swallowed a savage curse and jumped ahead of her, the knife in his fist as he led the way down.

"Which room has a window that looks out front?" she whispered against his ear.

He nodded to the door directly in front of them that used to be Griff's room. Quietly, they made their way inside. She gestured for him to keep an eye on the door while she edged around the perimeter toward the window. Her fingers separated two slats in the blinds a fraction and then her body relaxed.

"He's out front." She turned to Ben. "But he'll only give his friend another minute. You left the back door unlocked?"

Shit. He didn't appreciate her accusing tone. "We weren't staying long."

Ben wasn't sure but he thought he heard her mumble something that sounded a lot like 'rookie mistake' before she checked the window again.

"He's on the move out back. We'll have to jump him."

There she went again with the Wonder Woman shit.

"Like hell."

No way could she get lucky with a shot like that twice in a row. He grabbed her hand and pulled her toward his room. They entered the bathroom where he locked the door.

"Oh, right." She scowled at him. "Like that's gonna stop the guy, genius."

Ignoring her, he threw open the latch to the window. "How are you at heights?"

Her eyebrows shot up. "Not a problem."

Ben went first, climbing out onto the roof to make sure it wasn't too slippery. The cut on his shoulder burned forcing a groan from his lips. Fortunately, the assassin's partner was already too far away to hear him. The guy was just rounding the end of the row of houses headed toward the alley when Quinn climbed out. She'd stashed the gun into the waist of her jeans.

"Is the damn safety on?"

"Of course," she fired back.

Nodding, he grabbed hold of a branch from the maple tree out front. Stifling another groan at the pain, he swung down and landed on another branch. He then crouched down to grab that branch before swinging down to the ground. He looked up at Quinn.

"Now you do the same thing."

She was beside him before he could finish the sentence.

"Yeah, like that."

The blood was beginning to soak the shoulder of his dark T-shirt. Fortunately, she hadn't noticed yet. But somehow he doubted she was the type who fainted at a drop of blood. He grabbed her wrist and pulled her in the opposite direction the assassin's partner had gone. She dragged her feet when they were beside the thugs' car. Glancing around, she recklessly pulled the gun from her jeans and shot the back tire. The silencer on the gun muffled the sound of the shot.

"What the fuck?" Ben dragged her along. "We need to get out of sight."

"It may buy us some time."

They rounded the other end of the row of houses and he pulled her to a stop so he could peer around the corner. He didn't have long to wait before the other guy was out of the house frantically checking the alley. Fortunately, he retreated the way he'd come. Once he'd turned the corner, Ben quickly raced with Quinn to Griff's car, grateful the other guy didn't have the same maniacal thought as Quinn.

"Stay down," he ordered as he started the ignition.

The second guy jumped in front of the car, his gun drawn, just as they reached the end of the alley.

"Hold on!" he yelled at her.

Ben was about to gun the engine when the guy suddenly crumpled to the ground.

"Let's go!" She dragged the gun back inside the car.

But he couldn't push the gas. He turned to stare at Quinn in stunned silence.

"Ben," she said softly using that same sweet voice that had gotten him off all those years ago. "We have to go."

He knew that. He just needed a few deep breaths to

right his world. She'd just shot a second man to death with pinpoint accuracy and no apparent remorse. "I never pegged you for being so bloodthirsty."

She sighed but didn't offer up any excuses.

"That wasn't a damn compliment."

She placed her hand on his thigh as if to say "I know." The gesture only served to irritate him more. He didn't want reassurance, he wanted answers. Aiming a gun well enough to take down a guy with a single shot took a hell of a lot more skill than aiming a camera. It took years of training. Training no mild-mannered wedding photographer needed to undergo. If he had any lingering doubt she wasn't who she said she was, they were obliterated when she pulled the trigger. Nobody got that lucky twice.

Right now, however, he couldn't afford to speculate on who or what Quinn was. He needed to get them out of there before Ronoff sent another team in to finish the job. Steering the car around the dead body, he headed toward the Washington waterfront.

With one hand he punched in a code to unlock the center console. Inside was a burner phone and a Glock. He was relieved Griff still traveled with backup. He dug out the burner phone and turned it on.

Beside him, Quinn huffed out an appreciative breath. "That would have been handy a few minutes ago."

"You did fine with what you have," he bit out.

"Don't tell me your male ego is feeling threatened?"

He ignored her while he dialed a number on the phone, wondering if the woman on the other end would be as ornery as the one beside him.

"I saved your life," Quinn said. "That makes us even."

They pulled up to a stoplight right before the highway and he risked a glance over at her. She wasn't gloating. Instead, the look she met him with was full of melancholy. His chest contracted sharply.

"This is the second time you're disturbing me on my day off, Agent Segar," the Secretary of Homeland answered. "I was taking a nap."

Ben was pretty sure the woman didn't sleep but he didn't bother contradicting her.

"My apologies," he said as they pulled onto the highway. "But it seems I'm going to have to put my carte blanche authority into action."

"Meaning?"

"Ronoff's friends visited me at my home."

He heard her sharp intake of breath.

"I'm going to need a quiet crime scene cleanup."

"How many bodies?"

"Two. One is outside so this needs to happen fast."

He could hear her typing. "Done. Anything else?"

"Yeah. I need a ride to the Think Tank."

"Is the woman still with you?"

He glanced out of the corner of his eye at Quinn. She didn't bother disguising the fact she was listening to his conversation intently.

"Yep," he replied.

He expected his boss to raise a red flag about taking a civilian—who by now, he very much doubted Quinn was—to a secure, top-secret location. But the secretary didn't hesitate. Evidently, she knew as well as he did it was the best place to keep Quinn safe and secure.

"Done."

"I'll pick it up at the marina on Fort McNair in ten minutes."

"There will be a coast guard cutter waiting for you."

"Thank you."

"I'll be in touch."

With that, the secretary hung up.

"You sounded a little like James Bond there calling Miss Moneypenny. More friends in high places, I presume?"

He punched another number into the phone. "Something like that."

"Miss me already?" Adam joked when he answered.

Ben's chuckle was a bit hollow. Apparently, he was on the run with someone whose skills with guns were comparable to his friend's. The fact that Adam was renowned to be the best sharpshooter in the world had Ben a little on edge. Hell, everything about the woman made him edgy.

"Avoid the townhouse," he warned. "We had company."

Adam bristled through the phone. "Everyone alright?"

"Everyone on our side is," Ben replied, hoping like hell Quinn actually was on their side.

"Where are you? What can we do?"

"Nothing. I've got this."

"Bennett—"

He ended the call. His purpose was to keep Adam from walking into something that wasn't of his making. Not to involve him in whatever game Ronoff was playing. The assassin had been surprised Quinn was alive. It was probably better she'd shot both of them so that information didn't get back to Ronoff. Still, the question of what Ronoff wanted from Ben remained. Not to mention how Quinn fit into the puzzle.

"Annie Oakley, perhaps you could slide the gun under the seat and check the back for a jacket or something."

She did as he asked and handed him one of Griff's hockey jerseys. The damn thing smelled like it hadn't been washed in months. It was large enough to pull over his head easily, though, so Ben really couldn't complain. Just outside the main gate, he pulled over to the curb and began to cautiously maneuver the jersey over his head, grunting as he did so.

"Oh, my gosh," Quinn cried. "That's not sweat, that's blood. He stabbed you!"

He swore as he pulled the jersey over his injured shoulder. "Yeah, but lucky for you, I'll live. I've had wounds that were much worse."

She seemed genuinely surprised at that.

Ben snorted in annoyance. "Let's hope this thing doesn't soak through this jersey in the next three minutes so we can get past the MPs."

Pulling his ID from his wallet he drove to the gate. The military policeman leaned in through the window to get a better look at his ID before he caught sight of Quinn and gave her the once over.

"Where are you two headed?" the MP asked, his eyes still drinking her in.

"Over to the marina to meet a friend," Ben replied, grateful the guy was so focused on the passenger seat. The blood was already leeching through the white jersey. Quinn gave the MP one of her dazzling smiles.

"Lucky friend," he said before backing away and waving them through.

"Is there a hospital on this base?" she asked once they'd cleared the gate area.

"Don't need one. I'll be fine." Griff's jersey, not so much.

She huffed beside him. "Why must men be such boobies?"

He laughed and then instantly regretted it when his shoulder began to burn more intensely. The marina came into view none too soon. He steered the car toward the coast guard cutter berthed in the last slip, its engines already fired up. When he parked, he grabbed the burner phone and the Glock. Quinn reached beneath the seat for the Berretta.

"Leave it," he commanded.

She looked as if she was going to ignore him before thinking better of it. Wisely she grabbed the containers of food instead. When they got out of the car, Ben immediately felt woozy. He ended up leaning on the hood for balance. It was that or faceplant on the asphalt. Quinn raced around to grab him, still delivering a dissertation on the idiocy of men, but Ben was too busy concentrating on keeping himself upright to listen. They hurried up the gangplank where they were greeted by the first officer.

"Is there a medic on board?" Quinn asked before Ben could get a word in.

"I'm fine," he argued. "I just need a bandage and clean shirt."

The first officer exchanged a bemused look with her before they both hauled him off to sickbay just as the cutter was pulling away from the dock.

QUINN WINCED RIGHT along with Ben when the doctor shoved a needle in his shoulder.

"You're lucky," the doctor said. "The knife didn't penetrate deeply at all. It's a long gash which accounted for all the blood. But once we clean it up and glue the ends together just for giggles, you won't even realize it's there, Agent Segar. I'll even add a sympathy bandage as your souvenir of your ride aboard the *Pickering*."

"Are you sure he's okay?" she asked, her stomach still a mass of knots.

She couldn't explain why she felt so helpless. There'd been many occasions when a colleague had been injured in the line of duty—several of them much worse. The distress she'd felt seeing the bloodstain spread on Ben's chest had discombobulated her. It didn't help that the doctor seemed intent on practicing his comedy routine. "He could barely stand up a few minutes ago."

"When was the last time you had something to eat?" the doctor asked.

Right on cue, Ben's stomach growled.

"I don't remember," he answered.

Given the events of the last twenty-four hours, she doubted he'd eaten at all. She reached into the container of goodies Marin had given her and pulled out a scone. The doctor sent his aide off to get a protein shake. Quinn carried the scone over to the exam table where Ben was sitting. His beautiful chest was now marred by an ugly red streak from his shoulder to the opposite corner of his pectoral. *So close to his heart.* She swallowed roughly at the sight.

Forcing her gaze up, her eyes collided with his. The desire she saw reflected in them nearly knocked her off her feet. The heat was quickly replaced by confusion, as if he didn't trust himself completely. Or her. She could relate. Quinn felt the same way.

"Eat this," she commanded softly, lifting the scone to his lips.

He kept his eyes locked with hers as he bit into the flaky pastry. Heat surged through her fingers where his lips brushed against them. His pupils dilated at the contact. She drew in an unsteady breath.

The doctor returned to Ben's side, his presence breaking the trance between them. Ben snatched the rest of the scone from her and popped it in his mouth. He closed his eyes reverently as he chewed and swallowed.

"Mmm. God bless Marin."

The doctor adjusted the bandage causing Ben to flinch. His eyes flew up just as Quinn was licking the sugar off her fingers. She quickly turned away at his pained hiss.

"You're all set," the doctor said. "The captain says we'll be at the drop-off point in another twenty minutes."

Ben was shrugging into a T-shirt with the cutter's name emblazoned on the chest when she turned back to face him.

"Where are we going?"

He didn't answer. Instead, he reached for the container of scones and tucked into them. The doctor disappeared into a glass-walled office at the end of the bay. Ben downed the bottle of water the crew had given each of them on arrival. Just as he was reaching for the last scone, he hesitated, then offered it to her. She shook her head.

"I have a right to know where you're taking me."

Her words were met with a sinister sounding chuckle as he slid off the exam table and thrust the Glock into a holster that had magically appeared from one of the crew members.

"You just killed two men, Brit. I wouldn't push your case about your rights at this moment."

She glanced back at the office to see whether the doctor had overheard him. Thankfully, the man was on the phone.

"I killed both of them to save *your arse*," she whispered harshly.

He took a menacing step forward. "Yeah. About that. Where'd you learn to shoot with such skill?"

This was the problem with dealing with a man of superior intellect. Ben connected the dots a lot quicker than others. Most people were probably intimidated by his brain power. But she found it sexy.

Except for right now.

She'd had no choice but to fire that shot back at the row house. Whatever it took to keep Ben safe, she would do. But in doing so, she'd revealed too much of herself.

What would he say if she blurted out that she'd honed her skills at Fort Monctron in Portsmouth? Or the Joint Services Intelligence school in Scotland? Would he find her skill set as sexy as she found his? Hardly. He was a man after all. One who put a great deal of stock in doing the right thing. Quinn had spent her adult life blurring the lines between right and wrong more often than not.

"I was on the marksmanship team at university," she recited the well-rehearsed fib.

She held his gaze for several long heartbeats, daring him to contradict her. His left eyebrow slowly made its way up to his hairline in question, but, thankfully, he didn't offer up a response. Still, she doubted he believed her.

"Okay," he said finally. "Next question. Why is Ronoff trying to kill me?"

This part of the conversation was a lot trickier to navigate. Quinn was quickly beginning to realize there was more to mild-mannered Ben Segar than he let on. He would be safer knowing the truth. Better able to protect himself from Ronoff. Every fiber of her being was screaming at her to tell him. To share her burden with him.

But she couldn't.

Trust no one, her handler had commanded.

Even if she hadn't been warned against confiding in anyone, it had been her mantra for too long now to ignore. Not that she believed Ben, a computer analyst with friends in high places, was the traitor. But there was too much at risk to take on a sidekick right now. Not even a sexy one who made her long for a life she'd given up. Until she had what she came for, she'd just have to be more diligent in protecting him.

She didn't like what she had to do any more than he was going to like it, but she clenched her jaw firmly shut and gave her shoulders a shrug.

"That's what I thought." He took another step closer so that their bodies were nearly touching.

Idiot that she was, Quinn welcomed the shiver of excitement his nearness always stirred up within her. His fingers glided against her cheek until he was gently caressing her jaw in his palm.

"One way or another, Quinn Darby," he whispered. "I'm going to unlock your secrets. All of them."

Her eyelids were drifting shut in anticipation of his kiss, when his hand fell from her face. Disappointment flared and that made her angry. Angry at Ben for what he could do to her. But mostly angry at herself for allowing it.

"Let's go find the mess." He made his way to the door. "Suddenly, I'm starving."

CHAPTER TEN

B EN HAD TO hand it to her, despite the British refine-
ment and the smoking hot body, Quinn adapted
quickly to every situation without complaint. She'd calmly
climbed over the side of the cutter like she'd done it a
thousand times before, but not without thanking the
captain and the crew for their hospitality first.

They were taken by dinghy to a private dock a mile
south of Watertown. Waiting there for them was Rich's
fishing boat. His brother-in-law had followed Ben's
instructions to the letter. Rich had retrieved Quinn's
luggage from the B and B and stowed them on board along
with her purse, including the damn lockpicks, but not the
little revolver. Ben had had enough of her flaunting her
prowess with a gun for one day. The other bag contained
her camera and some food for the night.

"Everything accounted for?" he asked her as he started
up the engine, hoping she'd check for the lockpicks or the
gun so he could question her about them.

But she blithely sorted through her belongings, suddenly not as concerned about her things as she had been a
couple of hours ago. "I believe so."

Definitely an enigma that woman. She never did the

expected. He'd been serious aboard the ship, however. She was coming clean tonight whether she liked it or not.

A summer storm was forming off in the distance decorating the skyline with deep blues and purples. In order to make sure they'd outrun it, Ben pushed the throttle so the boat was skimming the water. Quinn stood beside him, staring at the bay in wonderment. Conversation was nearly impossible over the roar of the engines. She turned to him, a generous smile on her face.

"I've missed this," she shouted.

Something about her expression told him it was one of the few truthful statements she'd made since their paths had crossed again. He smiled back, glad to have even a small glimpse of the old Quinn. Her face lit up again when he pointed the bow toward the cove housing the Think Tank. The engines quieted when he throttled down, allowing them to drift into the small slip concealed by overgrown bushes.

"It's still standing," she marveled.

A flurry of expressions passed over her face. Surprise. Bashfulness. And finally, unadulterated joy. He hadn't expected that. Throughout the past two days, he'd been searching for the girl he once knew. Hoping to reconnect with the one he'd loved with all his heart. The grownup version of Quinn Darby had kept that girl under lock and key, however.

Until now.

"Tell me we're staying here?" she practically begged, surprising him yet again.

"We are. And you'll be happy to know, I've made some improvements over the years."

They each grabbed a line as the boat idled.

"You actually own it?"

"Yeah. They were going to tear it down." He shrugged, deliberately avoiding the truth. "I had nothing else to do with my money." He cut the engine and reached for her suitcase.

"I can't wait to see it." She grabbed her purse, her camera bag, and the food before gingerly climbing out of the boat.

"Careful," he warned when she slipped on one of the weathered planks leading up the hill. "The terrain is still a bit rough."

All the better to keep the general public away.

She reached the door first, bouncing up and down on her toes in her eagerness to get inside. Ben hesitated a few feet away. He was taking a huge risk bringing her here. Not only was this his private sanctuary, it was also a secret government facility. He wasn't even sure what or who Quinn was. But with its unique location and high-tech security, this was the most secure place to keep her safe while he sorted out her connection to Ronoff. Hell, had he known being back here would unleash the younger version of Quinn, he would have gone all caveman and made off with her the minute he caught her snooping around the *Seas the Day* yesterday. It would have saved them both a great deal of drama.

He walked over to her side and lifted one of the cedar

shingles. When he leaned in and scanned his retina, the locks on the door clicked open automatically. She stopped bouncing and simply gaped at him.

"You *are* James Bond." There was definitely awe in her voice.

"Or a psycho mad scientist." He winked. "Now you have to decide whether or not it's worth the risk to come inside. But beware, you only get to leave when you tell me the truth. The *whole* truth."

She considered him a long moment. There was no trace of insecurity in her expression. No fear. In fact, she looked pretty damn confident that she could beat him at his own game. And damned if he wasn't turned on by her poise.

"I guess I'll take my chances," she called over her shoulder when she stepped inside.

The lights flickered on with every stop she took. Ben followed her to the great room. She dropped her bags on the sofa and walked to the middle of the room where she began slowly pivoting in a circle, taking everything in. Suddenly, he was wary about her opinion of the place. He hadn't realized until just now he'd restored it in hopes of preserving the memory of what they once had.

The memory of her.

And now that he'd glimpsed the Quinn of the past, he didn't want to let her go. If only he could create a scenario where time stood still. Where Ronoff and the Phoenix didn't exist. Where they could go back to being the two people they once were and have the life they'd dreamed of all those years ago.

Lightning flashed beyond the panoramic windows drawing her attention to the view of the ocean just off the deck.

"My God, Ben, this is spectacular." She turned to face him, her eyes shining. "What you've done here is . . ." She shook her head in bewilderment. "It's perfect."

Air rushed through his lungs once again. He gave his head a shake hoping logic would return and chase out the screwed-up scenario he was spinning inside it. They couldn't go back to who they were. Hell, he had no idea if the Quinn he knew back then was even real. He'd refurbished this place based on a fantasy.

Too bad that didn't make him want her any less.

Unsure of how to deal with his newfound revelation, he made his way to the spare bedroom off the great room and placed her suitcase just inside the door.

"You can sleep in here."

She didn't follow him, but went to explore the kitchen instead.

"And where are you going to sleep?"

There was nothing coy about her question. Remembering her plea not to be left alone at the townhouse, he ignored his raging libido.

"There's another bedroom upstairs. Don't worry. This place is secure. No one goes in or out without a code. You're perfectly safe here," he reassured her.

She nodded.

"One of those bags from the boat should have some provisions in them."

They collided into one another as they both reached for the bag. Ben winced when Quinn's palms landed on his chest.

"Oh, I've hurt you! I'm so sorry."

She tried to pull her hands away but he quickly covered them with his own. Their gazes locked and neither of them moved. Thunder rumbled outside but the pulse pounding in his ears was louder. He blamed the intoxicating scent of her because the next thing he knew his hands were on her waist pulling her in closer. She tucked her chin and gently rested her forehead against the uninjured side of his chest.

"Thank you for bringing me here," she murmured.

"I never thought I'd get to show it to you. Yet, here you are." The admission slipped past his lips before he could stop it.

Her eyes were dewy when she finally lifted her head. It was his undoing. Leaning down, he gently traced the seam of her lips with his tongue. She opened her mouth for him without hesitation, inviting him in with a sweet sigh. Slowly, reverently, he explored her hot, silky mouth, savoring every taste and sensation. Their kiss earlier today had been frenzied and explosive. Right now, he just wanted to reacquaint himself with the feel of her again after all these years.

Quinn was doing some reacquainting of her own as she slid her hands down along his belly seeming to trace every muscle. When she moaned with satisfaction, his jeans grew unbearably tight.

"You like what you're finding there, Brit?" he murmured against her lips before playfully nipping the bottom one.

She answered by slipping her hands beneath his T-shirt and spreading her fingers out over his belly. The sensation of being skin-to-skin sent a wild jolt through him. *The hell with going slow.* He captured her mouth in a deep, searing kiss. The keening sound of need coming from the back of her throat spurred him on. He delved deeper with his tongue, kissing her as if he could make up for all the lost years since the last time they were here. Her fingers were now digging into his sides, maneuvering him against her so she was flush with his erection. She rocked her hips into him every time he thrust his tongue. Any residual pain from his wound disappeared as all the blood rushed to his crotch.

He backed her up to a barstool at the counter, lifting her so she could wrap her legs around his waist. She grazed her teeth along his jaw and dug her fingers into his scalp in an effort to take control. As much as he liked a woman who knew what she wanted, something made him hold back from relinquishing any power to her. Instead, he took the opportunity to explore the sensitive column of her neck.

Her lusty sigh nearly had him rethinking his strategy.

"Put your hands up," he instructed.

"Why?" The sultry tone of her voice sent another jolt to his groin.

"Just do it, Brit."

As soon as her hands were raised, he had her shirt and bra off in less than five seconds. A personal best.

She cocked an eyebrow at him. "Definitely a Bond move."

Ben wasn't listening to her. He was too busy studying the sight before him. They were perfection. *She* was perfection. Flat stomach. Round breasts. Dusky pink nipples. He didn't remember them being so dark. But then again, he'd been too nervous back then to spend a lot of time committing her physique to memory. He wrongly thought he'd have more time for that later.

"Now who likes what they're finding?" she teased.

She was unabashedly leaning back with her elbows on the counter behind her. A strand of her hair clung to her cheek. The rest of it was a riot of red waves from where he'd been dragging his fingers through it. Hell, yeah, he liked what he'd found.

He skimmed his fingers up her taut stomach. Her muscles flinched at his initial touch but she boldly kept her gaze locked with his. A quiet gasp escaped her lips when he traced the underside of her breasts. It was the only indication that she wasn't as unaffected as she wanted him to believe. He used it to his advantage, brushing his thumb over her hard nipples. She arched her back at his touch.

"You want me," he said smugly.

"Nothing has changed from before."

Her admission caught him by surprise, dousing his cockiness and nearly stealing his breath.

"I'm here now. With you," she whispered.

Shit. Why did it feel like he was being played?

Using her legs, she squirmed against him. Her urgent

movements scattered whatever coherent thoughts and questions remained in his oversized brain. He bent her over his arm and took what she was offering. The sound of her delighted sighs filled the room as he feasted on her breasts.

"I want you, Quinn," he confessed when he came up for air. "Even though I don't fucking know you."

"You do know me, Ben," she whispered. "You're the only one who's ever known me."

"No!" He pulled her up so they were face-to-face, their noses nearly touching. "I don't know you. Not the real you. I want the truth. All of it. I want to know you inside and out."

Bewilderment lurked in those big green eyes of hers. And sadness. His gut clenched at the realization. She drew in several ragged breaths before her eyes came back into focus and that elegant mask she wore shuttered her face.

"Ben," she began before placing her hands on his chest to push him away.

He gritted his teeth when her fingers grazed his cut.

"Crap. What am I doing?" She jerked out of his embrace. "We can't do this. For many reasons. Not the least of which is you'll get hurt."

She dropped her feet to the floor and began frantically searching around for her clothing.

"Damn it, Quinn, stop." He grabbed her shoulders and turned her to face him. *What the hell had just happened?* "It doesn't hurt."

Her lips formed a resolute line. "Yes, but the truth will."

BEN DISAPPEARED UPSTAIRS without a word. Quinn had to admire his resolve. It had taken her several minutes before she was composed enough to get her limbs to move. Grabbing her clothing—*or rather Josslyn's clothing*—she hurried into the guest room. Once inside, she shut and locked the door before propping her back against it. She drew in a huge lungful of air hoping it would bring her some clarity.

"You can do this," she mumbled to herself. "You just can't do *that*."

Not that there hadn't been times in her career where she had to let a man kiss her to gain the intel she needed. But those occasions usually involved administering knock-out drugs before things went too far. And every time she'd had no trouble tuning out her emotions. She'd been doing a job. Nothing more.

Clearly, she couldn't control either her emotions or her libido when it came to Ben Segar. Moments before, she'd practically admitted her heart was still his for the taking. He held all the power and he didn't even know it. She needed to get away before she did something foolish. Like tell him the truth. He wouldn't want her heart once he knew all the things she'd done.

It was a good thing she'd finally figured out where the micro card was. Her body relaxed at the knowledge and she slid to the floor. It had to be here in the lighthouse. She was sure he came here yesterday afternoon after she'd seen him at the marina in Watertown. He must have stashed the tuxedo somewhere here. It was the only scenario that made sense. Now all she had to do was find it, grab it, and disappear out of Ben's life. For good this time.

The very idea made her limbs painfully heavily.

"It's for the best," she rationalized trying in vain to ease the disappointment.

Digging deep for the stoicism that made her such a successful operative, she got to her feet and opened her suitcase. From the looks of it, the contents hadn't been disturbed. Relieved, she lifted out her clothes and pressed her thumb to a latch hidden on the side revealing a false bottom. Inside was an assortment of the tools of her trade—a burner phone, a Stingray listening device, a computer tablet, knock-out drops, and a nine-millimeter handgun. She pulled out the phone and powered it up. It had been twenty-four hours since she last checked in with her handler. Agency protocol stated she send a coded message daily. While she wouldn't be able to let him know she had located the list, at least he'd know she was still alive.

Once the phone was activated, she punched in the code that would allow her access to the secure mailboxes. The phone buzzed with an automated message.

"Access denied."

Quinn carefully reentered the code and waited.

"Access denied."

She got to her feet in an effort to shake off the wave of uneasiness washing over her. The third time she entered the code, the site kicked her out. The sound of the dial tone in her ear made her hand twitch slightly. The phone then powered off, rendering it useless.

"That's odd," she said to the empty room.

She grabbed the tablet and powered it up, then she did the same with the secure hotspot. Logging onto her photography website, she went straight to the admin page. Her handler often left coded messages in a mailbox only the two of them could access from the website. There were no new messages. In fact, there were no messages at all. It looked like the entire page had been deleted.

"Maybe there's been an internet glitch somewhere." She stoically ignored the lick of panic that ran down her spine.

Skimming the screen, she tapped in the address for a London insurance agency. She clicked on the contact tab and typed in her name to the email dashboard. The insurance agency served as a front for her real place of employment. It was here she could more easily communicate with other members of the agency. An error message popped up stating the account no longer existed.

Ominous thunder rumbled outside as the dread she was trying to hold at bay clawed at her belly. She'd been set adrift. Either because they thought she was compromised or dead. One was true, but happily, the other wasn't. How the agency had come to that conclusion so quickly was a mystery. She had one last option. A phone number she'd memorized. It was a direct line to her handler, but that always came with the risk of someone listening in. She was reluctant to utilize that option right now. Not until she had the card in her possession and could triumphantly hand it off to him. Besides, flying solo was her specialty. She didn't require the safety net of the agency to accomplish this mission. Now that she'd narrowed the search area, locating the micro card would be easy.

Except finding it meant venturing out of the room and exploring the rest of the lighthouse Ben had so beautifully restored. Given the security measures present, she assumed he did more than just think here. Clearly, there was more to the computer analyst than met the eye. But if this place was just for work, why then had he renovated it to be so elegant and pleasant? So very much like the home they'd envisioned sharing together? She pressed her fingers to her temple. It was ironic how earlier she believed the longing she felt interacting with Ben's family and friends was painful. Being back in this place brought her face-to-face with the life she'd dreamed of but could never have. And, with it, an ache so intense it nearly immobilized her.

She had to make these feelings stop. The only way to do that was to pull up her knickers and begin her search. With a resigned sigh, she set out on her task.

BEN STARED BLANKLY at the computer screen. He'd spent the past hour sifting through want-ads on the dark web, searching for anyone looking for a skilled coder who could hack into VOYEUR. Ronoff would need someone who could break through US Intelligence encryption. Most of those guys played for the wrong team, but if the money was right, an American would sell out his country in a heart-beat. So far, he hadn't found an ad with that particular description or the right price tag. He hoped that meant Ronoff didn't know what he had on the card. Because the alternative was that he already had someone with the math chops to break the code. In anticipation, he touched base with the operatives who monitored the cryptocurrency markets, but no one had heard anything about a run yet.

Now all he had to do was sit and wait. Too bad he wasn't good at waiting. Especially when the world's most exasperating woman was two floors below. A woman his body was still primed and ready for. A woman who made no sense. And that was the part that frustrated him more.

For starters, she was freakishly accurate with a gun. Not only that, but Ronoff, a guy she'd been associated with two days ago, had trashed his boat, stolen VOYEUR, and was now trying to kill him. His head was pounding just trying to fit the pieces of the puzzle together. Except they didn't fit at all.

He was swallowing two ibuprofen when his computer beeped with a FaceTime call. He tapped the button and Secretary Lyle appeared on the screen. Hopefully, she had some answers.

"You were injured?" She was never one for small talk.

"It's just a scrape," he lied. "I've had paper cuts that were worse."

She actually rolled her eyes. "The woman is still with

you?"

Quinn wasn't exactly with him in the way his body wanted, but he thought it better not to let his boss know that particular detail. "Yeah, she's here."

"Were the two men dead when you arrived?"

Ben sat up a little straighter in his chair. "No."

"I'm assuming it was you who put the bullets through their heads?"

Suddenly, he was very uncomfortable. He didn't like that his natural reaction was to protect Quinn. Especially since he had no idea what he was protecting her from.

"No."

"She shot them, then?"

"She shot the first guy while he was trying to strangle me."

Her expression matched the awe in his voice before she sighed in exasperation.

Ben's head was pounding now. "Would you mind telling me what's going on, ma'am?"

"When I notified the consulate of her death, I promptly got a call from the ambassador. It seems the woman you pulled out of the Chesapeake Bay is with British Intelligence. MI6 to be precise."

The breath caught in his lungs and he slumped back against his chair. Awe didn't even come close to the maelstrom of emotions he was feeling right now, chief among them an unexplained feeling of relief. "That explains a lot."

Except it didn't explain everything.

"I'm going to have to call their director and tell him she's alive. Especially since she killed two men on US soil."

No! He jumped from his chair. It felt suspiciously like the director had tricked him. "Tell them I shot them, damn it."

"It's not that simple, Agent Segar. There's a protocol here. Besides, if the scenario were reversed, the US intelligence community would want the same courtesy of knowing one of their own was alive."

"Then give me twenty-four hours. She's our only link to Ronoff. I'd really like to know why the hell the guy is trying to off me. Not to mention how he knew about VOYEUR." *And he tried to kill Quinn.* "Besides, she's safer with him believing she's dead. Right now, the only shot at getting my AI back might be from intel she has."

"Relax. I wasn't planning on marching her up to the embassy tonight. I agree you should find out what she knows about Ronoff. Work together. I'm assuming you can handle teaming up with her?"

Ben's mouth went dry just thinking about all the ways he'd like to team up with Quinn.

"Do what you have to in order to retrieve VOYEUR. And don't forget about the Phoenix. I'm still chasing down leads here, but perhaps our British friend knows something. There's a potential traitor out there somewhere and I want him or her exposed."

He exhaled a sigh of relief. "Thank you, ma'am."

"Contact me as soon as you have something," she ordered before signing off.

Ben dropped back into his chair. He wasn't sure whether to laugh or howl. For the past twenty-four hours, his gut had been telling him there was more to Quinn than met the eye. Most of the puzzle pieces had finally fallen into place. Except for the most important one. How did he fit into the mystery?

There was only one way to find out. It was time for her to tell the truth. He headed downstairs determined to ferret it out of her, one way or another.

CHAPTER ELEVEN

QUINN SEARCHED THROUGH all the closets on the first floor, even the pantry, with no sign of the tux. In fact, aside from the few staples Rich had supplied them with and a rogue beer in the fridge, there were no signs that anyone frequented the lighthouse at all. It was almost as if the gorgeous home was for show only. The place lacked any photos or personal effects. If she didn't know better, she'd think she'd stepped into an operative's cover house. She should know. She'd lived in enough of them.

"James Bond, indeed," she mumbled to herself.

Ben had been secluded upstairs for more than an hour. During that time, there hadn't been a sound from above. No shower running. No television droning on. No footsteps thumping on the floor. She was beginning to wonder if he was asleep.

Or dead.

Her heart stuttered at the thought. He might need help. She should definitely go up and check on him. It was as likely of an excuse as any if he caught her snooping.

She ventured over to the spiral staircase leading up to the top floor. When she looked up, she realized the steps led all the way to the torch room. She thought back to when Ben had first brought her here. There'd been a bedroom and a loo, along with a chart room, on the second floor. He could be in either place.

Using great care to keep her steps quiet, she climbed the stairs, thankful that at least the metal didn't squeak. When she reached the second floor, muffled sounds came from the torch room. There was a heavy metal door separating it from the rest of the lighthouse. If she was lucky, that was where Ben had been hiding all this time.

She glanced into the chart room. It was outfitted with a couple of upholstered chairs situated in front of a picture window overlooking the bay side of the peninsula the lighthouse was built upon. The storm had moved out to sea leaving behind a cotton candy sky of puffy clouds tinted pink by the setting sun. The room and its view were so inviting, Quinn had a hard time redirecting her attention to the bedroom across the hall.

But when she did, the sight greeting her stole her breath. If the rest of the place was gorgeous, this room was stunning. A wall of windows served as a headboard for the king-sized platform bed dominating the space. Darkness had already descended on the Atlantic and the room was in shadows, but she could easily tell the room's décor was a mixture of grays and blues—the soothing colors of the ocean.

Best of all, unlike the rest of the lighthouse, this room looked lived in. A towel hung from the knob of the toilet door. A pair of gym shorts were in a heap on the floor next to the bed. And, if she wasn't mistaken, right beside them was a crumpled tuxedo. Her heart was racing when she dropped to her knees beside it.

"Come to mummy," she whispered.

Very carefully, she dug through the pockets of the jacket. The micro card was the size of a thumbnail so it would be simple to drop into the pocket without being noticed. But it would also be easy to overlook. And even easier to lose in the dark room.

The first pocket was empty. Not even a trace of lint. Her heart was pounding now. It had to be in the other pocket.

It just had to be.

Except it wasn't.

Breathing hard, she reached back into the first pocket to double-check. When she grabbed at the pants, she froze. On the floor, six inches from her fingers, was a pair of worn boat shoes. Unfortunately, they were attached to the denim clad legs of Ben Segar.

"Looking for something?"

Heart in her throat, she rocked back onto her heels. How had she not heard him coming? The circumstances of this case were affecting her well-honed skills. A mistake like that could have gotten her killed. Thankfully, he looked more amused than murderous with his shoulder propped against the doorframe and his arms crossed over his chest.

"I didn't hear anything from up here and I thought to come up and check on you. You weren't around so I was just tidying up," she fibbed.

The man actually laughed at her. And not just a polite

chuckle, either. It was a full-on belly laugh.

Quinn got to her feet. "What's so damn funny?"

"You are." He wiped his eyes with his fingers. "You have no idea how easy you are to read. I always know when you're lying."

"I wasn't lying," she argued.

"That right there," he pointed at her mouth. "You lick your bottom lip every time you lie. It's been your tell since you were seventeen and it's still your tell now."

Damn. She had just swiped her tongue over her lip.

Still, she wasn't going down without a fight. "Two men tried to kill you today, you idiot. Obviously, I would want to check on you."

He stepped deeper into the room. "About that. Why don't you tell me everything you know about Alexi Ronoff, Agent Darby of MI6."

A powerful tingling raced from the tips of her fingers up her arms and into her lungs where it seemed to freeze her breath. How did he figure that out?

Ben took another step closer stopping a few inches away from her numb limbs. He had the nerve to cock an eyebrow at her.

"I—" She tried to find words among her scattered wits.

"Don't!" he commanded before wrapping his fingers around her elbows and yanking her body flush with his. "No more lies. No more games, Quinn. People are dying and time is running out. Ronoff has something that belongs to the US government and you're going to help me figure out how to get it back."

Anger warmed her numb body giving her the strength to jerk her arms from his grip and take a giant step away from him. "He doesn't have it," she shouted. "Why do you think I've been looking all over for it?"

He wore a perplexed expression. "What do you mean he doesn't have it? He took it from the *Seas the Day* last night."

"What? It *was* on the boat? Are you an imbecile!" She was beginning to feel light-headed. How had she missed it? "If you knew what it was, how could you leave something like that just sitting out?"

"Hey," he snapped. "I didn't know a group of Russian thugs was going to storm my boat. Perhaps you can share with the class why they targeted me in the first place?"

Alexi has the list.

She sank down onto the bed to stop her head from spinning as the enormity of the situation settled into her stomach like a rock. "I need to get word to my handler. To my parents. This is a catastrophe."

The mattress dipped as Ben plopped down beside her. "Your parents? Why would they care about some Russian stealing my micro card?"

"*Your* micro card?" She glared at him. "For such a smart man, you really are a dolt. The information on that card could cost my parents their lives! Don't you get that?"

Unexpected tears burned the back of her eyes. Not only did she not have the list, but it seemed her legendary composure had disappeared as well. She'd failed not only her government, but her family. And to make matters worse, Ben was scrutinizing her wearing a genuinely baffled look on his face.

"No," he replied. "I don't get it."

His ignorance ignited a firestorm inside of her. She shoved at his shoulder. "How could you let this happen!"

Jumping to her feet, she recklessly swiped at his head with her fist. Before she could connect, however, he grabbed her arm, yanked her flat onto the bed and pinned her there with his body. She pounded his chest in an effort to push him off.

"Ow!" he protested when her fist met his wounded shoulder. "Can you just relax and listen for one damn minute?"

He grabbed her wrists and placed her hands above her head. Her belly quivered remembering when he'd had her hands above her head earlier. *Damn body.* How could it so easily forget she was angry?

"I mean it, Quinn. I'm not the enemy here. Ronoff is."

He was right, of course. But that didn't mean she couldn't make Ben suffer a bit longer. As usual, he had other ideas. He touched his forehead to hers. Their noses brushed together and their heavy breaths mingled between their lips. It was the worst kind of torture he could deliver. Her body thrummed with desire and she couldn't douse it. She held herself still beneath his warm weight to keep from exploding with want.

"Look at me," he coaxed.

She lifted her lashes to meet his steady gaze. There was so much honor in the depths of those hazel eyes it made her throat tight.

"You said I was the only one who ever knew you," he whispered. "Well that goes both ways. Nothing has changed. I'm still the same guy you knew before."

She wanted to argue. He had changed in many ways. Starting with the sexy sculpted body currently wrapped around hers. But her emotions were too conflicted right now to find words.

"I need you to trust me, Brit. Can you do that? Can you trust me?"

If he only knew. When it came to people she trusted in this world, Ben Segar had always been at the top of that list. Even if she was a bit peeved with him right now, that would never change.

"Good girl," he said with a smile when she nodded. "This micro card you're talking about, is it the list of operatives for the Phoenix?"

"Of course, it is!" Why must he torture her by being so obtuse?

"Your parents are on that list?"

She slammed her eyelids shut. A lick of fear ran up her spine. He was questioning her as if he didn't know what information Alexi was buying. Could he be using her? *Damn it!* Yet again she was losing her head because her body couldn't control itself. She lifted her lashes only to be pinned by his steadfast gaze.

"You trust me, remember?" he reminded her.

"My mother." The words came out her mouth as though he were some sort of snake charmer.

He blinked. Twice. Then the corners of his mouth turned up in a slow smile of wonder. "Well, I'll be damned. Kick-ass women run in the family."

"Yes, well." She grunted as she struggled unsuccessfully to shove him off her heavily aroused body. "If I don't warn them, kick-ass or not, I won't have any family left."

He groaned when she nudged his shoulder again. "Could you please hold still?" He breathed the words against her ear. "Ronoff is not going to kill your parents."

She stilled beneath him. "How can you be so sure?"

"Because I said so." His lips began to trace the column of her neck.

Her head reflexively lolled to the side to give him better access. "That's not enough to reassure me. What makes you so omnipotent?"

He nibbled along her jaw until he reached the corner of her lips which he proceeded to tease with his tongue. She thrust her hips up in aggravation when he didn't answer the question. Bad idea. He pressed into her body more deeply, his impressive arousal making itself known to her tense body.

"Answer the question, Ben. Who are you?" she demanded using a voice now shaky with pent-up frustration.

"I'm just a guy who's about to make you blissfully happy," he murmured against her eyelids. "Multiple times."

This was wrong on so many counts. Despite the fact her body was reacting to every touch like it was the Sahara Desert and he was water, she had no right thinking about sex. Not while her parents were in grave danger.

"Ben," she pleaded.

"Ronoff doesn't have it," he said before nipping at her lip.

"But you said—"

"I said Ronoff took *a* micro card. I didn't realize there was another one."

As his words sank in, relief surged through her stiff limbs and she relaxed against the mattress. Taking advantage, he delved into her mouth with a deep, drugging kiss that almost wiped her mind clean.

Almost.

"What other card?" she asked.

Her question came out as more of a sigh when his fingers somehow sneaked their way beneath her shirt and began teasing her nipples with the same expert finesse that nearly had her orgasming earlier.

His teeth grazed her collarbone when his mouth began traveling south. "The one containing my AI I've been working on for over ten years. It was on a micro card in my cabin. I still can't figure out how he knew it was there. Only four people knew it existed until the night I used it at the White House."

She bit back a moan when his teeth grazed her nipple through her clothing. "That might have been my fault."

He stopped what he was doing and slowly lifted his gaze to meet hers. His expression demanded the truth. "How so?"

"It was an accident really." She exhaled wearily. "Someone was supposed to hand off the card to Alexi just as we arrived at the White House dinner. I was there to intercept it. Except the lights went out."

"Tsk, tsk, Brit. Only a poor spy blames the elements," he teased.

She tugged at his hair. He flicked a nipple with his thumb in retaliation. Her back arched at the pain and pleasure of it.

"You thought I had it."

His quietly uttered words felt chilly against her flushed skin. She could only imagine the assumptions he was jumping to.

"You were right beside us when the power went out."

"So, yesterday when you came to the marina, it wasn't to talk things out. You were looking for the micro card."

Her belly quivered for a different reason now. Ben didn't bother hiding the disappointment from his words.

"Yes," she whispered. "I didn't realize Alexi would put things together so quickly. I thought I could grab it and disappear."

"Disappear?" He dipped his chin and rested his head on her belly.

They were quiet for several long heartbeats before she gently threaded her fingers through his hair and began massaging his scalp.

"I had to protect you. I didn't want to hurt you any more than I already have," she whispered. "I'm sorry he stole your AI."

He jerked his head up. His face contorted with anger. "Sorry he stole my AI?! He tried to kill you, Quinn. Throw you away like you were garbage." He pushed up with his good arm and loomed over her. "Do you have any idea what it was like to almost lose you a second time? Can you even conceive what it did to me?"

"Ben—"

"No!" he said. "Don't say another word. It doesn't matter how I felt. Because all the time, you were going to grab the damn card and vanish. Again."

With a grunt, he rolled onto his back and stared at the ceiling.

"That's not fair." She pushed the words out past the lump in her throat shame had lodged there. "I had no control the first time. My mother had to move quickly to avoid being discovered with the evidence against Alexi's father. She wasn't expecting to get her hands on it for another week. I would have stayed if I could have. I wanted nothing more than to go to prom with you. And if you don't believe that, then you don't really know me as well as I thought you did."

She studied his profile as he seemed to ponder her words. One of the things she loved most about him was his fairness and his ability to see all sides of an equation.

"That doesn't explain this time." His jaw was clenched so tightly, she was surprised he could get the words out.

"I didn't want you to find out who I am," she admitted quietly. "What I've become."

He angled his face toward hers so they were nose to nose again but with their cheeks resting on the mattress. "Are you serious?" Reaching over he intertwined his fingers with hers. "Quinn Darby, I hate to tell you this, but I'm a little bit in awe of who you are. What you've become is a badass British secret agent."

The tightness in her chest eased. Of course he would see the good in her. In what she was. It wasn't in his nature to be judgmental. Yet another thing she cherished about Ben. The list of reasons why she adored him was growing longer and longer.

Her lips relaxed into a sly smile. "Just a little bit in awe, Mr. Bond?"

With a mischievous grin of his own, he rolled back on top of her and settled his hips between her legs. "Yeah. Did I mention I also find it very sexy?"

She wrapped her arms around his waist. "You haven't seen the depths of my talents," she teased.

His nostrils flared. "Perhaps a demonstration is in order." He planted a chaste kiss on her mouth. "Because I'm going to need those talents if we're going to get my AI back. Are you in?"

"Are you kidding? I need to pay Alexi back for trying to drown me. And I still need to find that list."

"Mmm." He was back to nuzzling her neck again, much to her delight. "I can help with that problem, too. I know exactly where the list is."

"You do?" She wasn't sure if the burst of pleasure was from his admission or the sensuous way his mouth grazed her flushed skin.

"The tux is Adam's. When I put the micro card containing my AI in the pocket after the fiasco at the White

House, I found your card. I figured it was his. Although, come to think of it, what would a sniper be doing with one?" He shook his head. "Hell, Adam would freak out if he knew you were as good a shot as he was."

Her pride wanted her to argue that she was likely a better shot, but she was more concerned with the whereabouts of the particular card she'd been searching for.

"The other one? Where is it?" she demanded.

"I left it in my desk at work because I didn't want it to get damaged at the dry cleaners."

Only Ben would be so thoughtful. Quinn wanted to laugh with relief but she leaned up and captured his mouth in a kiss instead. "I don't know how to thank you."

He wiggled his eyebrows. "Don't worry, Brit. I do."

BEN EXPECTED QUINN to demand they return to Washington immediately to retrieve the card. But once again, she confounded him by doing the unexpected. Not that his body was complaining. He relished the feel of her fingers beneath his shirt dancing along the skin on his back. The warmth of her toned thighs wrapped around his ass was drawing all the blood from one head to the other. Of course, he'd be enjoying all of this fondling a hell of a lot more if they were both naked.

Apparently she was thinking the same thing. "Does this thank-you of which you speak involve nudity?" she asked before grazing her teeth along his jaw.

"Total nudity," he murmured against her forehead. "The kind where you're fully exposed to me. All of you."

He tilted her head so their eyes met. Green eyes, shadowed with lust, were scrutinizing him carefully. *Pondering.* Her hands stilled along with his breath. But he needed her to know he wanted the real Quinn Darby. Not the cover she hid behind to do her job. It was all or nothing.

Just when his baser instincts were about to give in and take what she might offer, honest or not, she unleashed a slow, generous smile. Much like the glory of dawn spreading out over the ocean, it made his heart skip.

"I meant what I said before," she whispered. "You're the only one who's ever known me. All of me. That will never change, Ben. Ever."

Swallowing was suddenly difficult as he tried to reconcile the emotions coursing through him. She was finally back where she belonged. With him. Here in this place that had meant so much to them once.

And she's never leaving him again.

He didn't realize he'd growled that last part out loud until she responded in a shaky voice.

"Not willingly. Never."

And suddenly they were a tangle of tongues and limbs and clothing as they tried to get as close to each other as was humanly possible. Ben grimaced when he attempted to shrug out of his shirt. Quinn pushed him up onto his heels as she sat up in front of him.

"Let me."

Gently, she lifted the shirt up his torso, over his shoulder and his head, leaving an erotic trail of kisses on his skin at each stop.

"Your turn," he demanded when she flung his shirt to the floor.

This time his fingers got tangled in her bra, making her laugh. The happy sound was nearly his undoing. He desperately ripped at her clothing trying to get it off her body.

"Pants," he commanded with a ragged breath. The pain of his erection pushing against his zipper was becoming damn near unbearable.

She unwrapped her legs from around his waist and scooted back. They both reached for his fly at the same time. Brushing his hands away, she took her sweet time lowering the zipper. Her gaze dipped to his belly while her warm fingers teased the skin at his waistband.

"Quinn," he uttered in frustration.

He thought she chuckled before she pushed the two sides of denim away and he finally sprang free. Releasing a breathy sigh, she wrapped her fingers around him, slowly stroking from tip to bottom as if in a trance.

He was pleading now. "Pants. I need them off. I need yours off."

Her eyes were dazed when she finally looked up, but she didn't release him. Instead she donned a wicked smile and began to stroke him harder. Faster.

"Are you trying to end this before we get started, woman?"

His body protested strongly when he yanked her fingers

away. But he wasn't getting off in her hand. No way. Not after waiting thirteen long years to be inside her again. He shoved at her shoulders indicating she should finish undressing.

"Mmm," she said, before climbing off the bed and shimmying out of her pants.

Ben froze in the midst of shoving his jeans down his thighs, reveling in the sight of her in nothing but a black pair of panties. *Of course they are black.* Aware she had his attention, she took her time sliding the silky fabric down her long legs before kicking them off. He swore savagely when he jostled his shoulder trying to shuck his jeans. Her laughter didn't help.

"Lie back," she ordered with a grin. "That way I can pull them off."

After a brief hesitation where he reminded himself that he wanted to get to the main event by any means possible, he did as she asked. The position left him vulnerable, but the view of a naked Quinn more than made up for it.

She reached up and tugged his jeans off his legs, wearing nothing but a cat-ate-the-canary grin. He watched through half-closed eyes as she slowly crawled up his body, stopping here and there to plant a kiss on his fevered skin. When she was face-to-face with his arousal, he shuddered at the carnal image. But he didn't want her to linger there. He wanted her beneath him.

Now.

"Come here," he commanded while giving her hair a gentle tug.

She remained where she was. "I like the view right here," she replied before blowing a soft breath over the tip of him.

He bucked beneath her and that seemed to be all the encouragement she needed. Without hesitation, she drew the shaft into her mouth, suckling tightly around him. Every molecule of sense left in his brain evaporated instantly. His fingers tangled in her hair allowing him to guide her head for maximum pleasure. The soft sighs somehow managing to escape her mouth grew more urgent as the climax built inside him.

"No!" he yelled grabbing her head with his palms.

Her lips were swollen and her eyes unfocused when she looked up at him.

"Not until I'm inside you," he explained.

She nodded, still appearing to be disoriented. But then she crawled up his legs until she was poised above his erection. Ben tugged at her hips.

"Not yet."

Now she was beginning to look annoyed. He knew exactly how to wipe that expression off her face, however.

"Ladies first," he said as he dug his fingers into her fine ass and brought her forward toward his lips.

"Not necessary."

But her body wasn't protesting as much as her mouth was. Her palms hit the glass with a slap when she came up on her knees above him. He inhaled the musky smell of her, wet and ready for him. It was all he could do to keep his own body from climaxing. He needed to hurry this along but he wanted her to enjoy this time more than she had their first go around. He wanted her to want more. Lots more.

He nipped at the inside of her thigh. She responded with an aroused sigh and thrust of her hips. It was all the invitation he needed. He slipped his tongue inside to the sounds of her delighted cries when he began to suck on the aroused nub. She called out his name pleading with him to hurry, but that wasn't in the game plan. Twice he brought her to the brink without taking her over the edge. Her thighs clamped around his head in frustration. He chuckled as he cupped her luscious ass. Quinn let out a very unlady-like string of expletives. Then she proceeded to tell him how she planned to torture him next. A sheen of perspiration broke on his body just listening to her erotic words. Suddenly he couldn't make her come fast enough. Her release had her pounding on the window in front of her and declaring Ben a god. Feeling a bit smug, he bit the inside of her other thigh just for parity.

This time she let out a very satisfied sigh before scooching back onto his belly. She flipped her head back to clear the curtain of hair from her face. When she looked down at him, her effervescent smile was another boost to his ego.

"Turn over," he commanded.

She shook her head, gesturing to his shoulder. "You're not functioning at a hundred percent."

He growled with impatience. "You don't need to worry about me, Brit. I'd have to be dead to not function at a hundred percent during sex."

The damn woman actually rolled her eyes. He bucked beneath her, but all that did was bring his erection in contact with that sweet ass of hers. With a frustrated groan that sounded like a snarl even to his own ears, he reached into the side table and pulled out a condom. She snatched it from his fingers and tore it open with less than steady hands. Ben took the opportunity to fondle her breasts. One way or another, he'd wear her down and get what he wanted.

She took her time rolling the condom over him, meting out her torture with a broad smile. Once she finished, she came forward on her knees to press a tender kiss at each side of his mouth. Ben didn't want gentle. He gripped her head between his palms and brought her lips down for a punishing kiss. One she met with the same abandon.

Several long moments later, he was still on the bottom and she breathlessly lowered herself onto him. He gripped her hips with his fingers as he guided her down. A hiss escaped his mouth when she was fully seated. She was still breathing heavily when she started to move, but he wasn't ready to relinquish all the power. He let her do the work until she let out a frustrated groan.

He skimmed his fingers up her sides to capture her breasts in his hands where he returned the torture. When he began to move slowly beneath her, she threw her head back with a sigh.

"Yes," she breathed. "Please."

Her soft pleas and erotic movements were wearing down the tight leash he had on his body. They began to move in a rhythm, perfect in its synchronicity. Just as he always dreamed it would be between them. His release was building inside him. She closed her eyes dropped her chin as she rode him harder.

"Hurry, Ben," she begged.

But he wouldn't, not until she'd come again. He reached between their slick bodies and brushed his thumb against her sweet spot, feeling the tension build within. She cried out with joy at his touch. With his other hand, he rolled her nipple between his fingers until her entire body spasmed with release.

She was beautiful in her climax. And Ben wanted nothing more than to watch her come all night, but his body had other ideas. Unable to wait for her to return to earth, he thrust deeply two times before roaring at the welcome release. He was still sucking in deep breaths when she slumped down on top of him. The beat of her heart echoed his. She buried her face in his neck. He wrapped his arms snugly around her body. And he was never going to let go.

CHAPTER TWELVE

L ATER THAT EVENING, sitting on one of the barstools surrounding the island in the kitchen, Quinn shamelessly admired Ben's sleek back. Dressed in nothing but a pair of board shorts slung low on his hips, his tanned feet bare against the wood floor and his hair still a tousled mess from her fingers, he looked more appetizing than the dinner he was preparing. His muscles rippled and flexed as he carefully piled shaved roast beef on thick slices of French bread. Having just spent the last couple of hours exploring those same muscles with her hands and mouth, she could attest that his boast of being able to perform at a hundred percent in spite of a stab wound was entirely accurate. Not only that, but he'd also lived up to his promise to make her happy—multiple times. So happy, she'd blurted out a crazy promise never to leave him. A promise she desperately wished she could keep.

As if he could read her steamy thoughts, he turned and shot her a cocky smile promising he could rock her world yet again with just one touch. Her body suddenly hummed with renewed arousal making her skin tingle beneath the T-shirt she'd appropriated from the pile of his discarded clothes on the bedroom floor. She shoved a handful of

Teddy Grahams in her mouth to keep from pressing her lips to his exposed skin. He winked before returning his attention to building their sandwiches.

"I still can't get over what you've done to this place," she said in an attempt to distract her libido. "It's perfect for entertaining. Your friends and family must love hanging out here."

He didn't respond immediately, letting the silence stretch until she began to feel uncomfortable. Tossing down the knife, he stalked over to the fridge and grabbed the lone beer.

"They don't," he replied, his back still to her.

His clipped response stunned her.

"You've got to be kidding? That game room alone would give Adam and Griffin a testosterone high every time they walk in there. And this kitchen." She waved her arms. "Just look at it. Marin would be in her element. There's no way she wouldn't love it."

When he turned around, his face was closed off. Something in his expression made her shiver slightly.

"They don't come here. They never have. Period."

Nothing he was saying made sense.

"But your family? Your sister and her kids? They live so close."

"Nope," he said before popping the top on the beer and taking a long pull. He extended the bottle to her. She shook her head.

"I don't understand. Then why did you restore it? What do you do here?"

He studied her for a long moment before answering, his face still hard and his eyes unreadable. "I come here to think. That's why it's called the Think Tank."

"You *think*? Here?" She bit back a laugh when he didn't so much as move a facial muscle. Clearly, he wasn't joking. "All by yourself?" Her heart ached at the thought. "Don't you get lonely?" she asked before thinking better of it.

"It's my job."

The pieces began to click together in Quinn's mind. This place. His connections. She'd sensed he was more than he said he was. But what exactly? And why?

"Who are you?" she demanded, her heart beginning to race for a very different reason now.

He heaved a sigh before picking up the plate of sandwiches. "It's probably easier to show you."

Her curiosity piqued, Quinn slipped off the barstool, grabbed the wedding cake samples Marin had given her, and followed Ben upstairs. He hesitated in front of the steel door leading to the torch room, seeming to have a silent argument with himself.

"Ben," she coaxed. "You know all my secrets. The least you could do is share this one with me."

A slow, wolfish grin spread over his lips as his face finally relaxed. "I doubt I know all your secrets, Brit." He leaned in closer. "But I do know the one about you preferring to be on top."

His huskily uttered words brought a flush to her cheeks. He was right, though; he didn't know all her secrets. Because if he did, there was no possible way he'd be staring at her with desire in his eyes.

"I don't have to be on top every time. And stop trying to change the subject."

He donned an if-you-say-so look as he punched a code into the keypad beside the door before leaning in to have his retina scanned. The door lock clicked open. Ben glanced at her warily, but he still didn't reach for the door handle.

"Are we going to stand here all night?"

He shook his head but the move seemed to be more of an answer to the inner voices he was battling than to her question.

"The secretary had better be right about your credentials," he mumbled.

Quinn didn't have time to ponder that little tidbit because Ben opened the door and gestured for her to enter first. A wall of thick windows circled the tower. The night stars shimmered off the ocean while the moon played peekaboo behind the wispy clouds, its beams providing the room with its only light. The image would make a spectacular photograph. Her fingers itched for her camera.

As she moved deeper inside, she heard the hum of computer monitors tucked behind a low wall where a worn leather desk chair sat empty in front of them. A futon and a tray table that looked like it had been salvaged from a college dorm were the only other pieces of furniture occupying the space. She set the cake on the small table and wandered over to the bank of computers.

"It looks like you do more than think up here."

"Mmm," was all he said before slumping down on the futon.

"And there's as much security in this lighthouse as we have at Secret Intelligence Service headquarters in Vauxhall Cross." She traced her fingers along windows that had to be six inches thick. "These are one-way glass with reflective mirrors if I had to guess."

"Exactly what one would expect for a lighthouse."

"Or the studio of a cyber-spy," she countered.

He arched an eyebrow, but he didn't seem too surprised at her conclusion. "I prefer the term provocateur."

She snorted as she sat on the futon beside him.

"I repeat my question. Who are you? And, more importantly, how did you discover who I work for?"

Ben handed her a sandwich. "I have a close relationship with the Secretary of Homeland. She might have mentioned it."

A wave of sharp, unbidden jealousy washed over her at his nonchalant reply. Secretary Sabrina Lyle was a stunning, raven-haired, Latina woman with the intelligence and backbone to match her appearance. Both men and women were intimidated by her. But even more men wanted to possess her. Women coveted her steely spine.

The secretary had come up through the ranks of US Intelligence and she was well-respected within the world's covert community. A widow for more than a decade, there were frequent rumors of her taking handsome young agents "under her wing." Quinn was suddenly picturing all the ways the secretary might have "mentioned it" to Ben.

"You should see your face right now," he said with a laugh. "It's not that kind of relationship. Although I am a little flattered by your jealous scowl."

"I am not scowling," she protested, huffing in frustration when the tip of her tongue darted out to swipe at her lip.

He chuckled again before taking a bite of his sandwich. She did the same fearing if her mouth wasn't full, she'd give away more of herself to him than she already had. The past few hours had been a bit of a revelation. It was liberating to be with someone who so totally got her. A man who knew her secrets and wanted her anyway. Something warm was beginning to blossom inside of her. It felt a lot like hope. Hope that maybe she could get out of the game and have a normal life. A life with Ben.

But the funny thing about hope was it could be extinguished just as quickly as it grew. Ben said he didn't care about her past transgressions. Except he'd need a pair of rose-colored glasses as thick as the torch room windows to find something redeeming in who she had become. Her throat grew tight just thinking about the many ways he could reject her once he found out all of her secrets.

"You know you're not the only one who has stepped over the line in defense of their country."

There he went again, reading her mind. His remarkable intuition and empathy were among the attributes she cherished about him. But she doubted a man who designed artificial intelligence and surfed the web all day could relate to the things she'd had to do throughout the course of her career. Chewing quietly, she kept her opinions to herself. He took another pull from the beer.

"I've single-handedly destroyed families, tribes, and economies of small countries," he continued. "All with a couple of keystrokes. Don't think I don't feel a good measure of guilt and remorse for the acts I've committed. Just like you, they live with me every day. But I can't let them haunt me. Neither should you."

This was the Ben she knew and loved, being sweet to her. Trying to put her at ease. The guy who always found the silver lining, who saw the best in people. If only she could see her life in the same way.

"Is this the part where we compare battle scars and body counts?"

"Jesus, Quinn. You didn't ruthlessly set out to murder anyone today. You saved my life. Both our lives." Leaning in, he toyed with a piece of her hair. "Your job isn't who you are. Just like mine isn't who I am."

That was what he thought. That was all his glass-half-full optimism would ever allow him to think. But if they stood any kind of a chance for a happily ever after, she had no choice but to tell him the truth.

"You aren't getting it, Ben," she whispered. "My job is all I've ever been. Even when I was here in Watertown."

His fingers stilled against her hair. She swallowed roughly waiting for his sharp mind to connect the dots.

"That not possible. You were in high school."

"Which made me all the more invisible to the people we were investigating. I befriended their kids. It gave me full access to their homes, their boathouses, their cars." She shrugged. "Without Blaine Simpson's father providing evidence against Ronoff in exchange for protection, my mother never would have been able to accomplish her mission."

"You mean you only hung out with that dick to take down his father?"

His astonished smile made her laugh. "Yep. He was only ever a job to me."

Just as quickly, his expression shifted and he swore violently. "Your parents had no right to force you into espionage like you were a family of damn grifters."

"They didn't force me," she argued. "And grifter is a bit of an extreme comparison. But this is my family business. I was born into it. I could have opted out but that would have meant being left behind in Wales with some great-aunt I'd never met. My parents are the only family I have. I didn't want to be separated from them."

His eyes softened and he gently tugged her closer so he could brush a kiss across her forehead. She reveled in his embrace, the isolation she'd cloaked herself in for so long beginning to seep away.

"You're not going to get separated from them now. I promise. The list is safe."

"But that doesn't mean there won't be another list. Alexi won't stop looking for it. He has something to prove to his father." She snuggled in closer trying to soak up some of his confidence. "Alexi's father never gives him a chance. Even when he was in prison, he held the reins to the business tightly. Alexi believes if he can terminate those agents who set his father up, it will prove he is ready to take over the syndicate."

"The Secretary of Homeland doesn't believe a list even exists. She is adamant that the roster of operatives died with the Phoenix."

"No offense to your friend the secretary, but I can't afford to buy into her theory. Not with my mother at risk. Besides, Alexi believes the Phoenix is still alive and willing to betray the US."

His hold on her stiffened. "Does he have proof?"

"If he does, he didn't share that information. He was given proof the list was genuine, though."

"What kind of proof?"

"I'm not sure exactly. But I do know he was communicating on the dark web with my nemesis of the past three years, the Mariner."

A sharp breath sawed through his lungs. "Your nemesis?"

"Yes. The arsehole fancies himself an internet broker for secrets and violent crimes. He'll do anything for the right price. I've had to intercept or retrieve many of the items he's sold. Fortunately, we are always able to take down the buyers. But the Mariner is very slippery. No one has been able to track him down. *Yet*. But I will get my hands on him. Just you wait." She grinned at him. "And when I do, he'll be one sorry twit."

Ben jumped off the futon and began pacing the small room, his ire building with every stride. "*You* were the agent sent in to intercede?"

Taken aback by his tone, she stiffened her spine. "What's that supposed to mean?"

His eyes were wild with a mixture of anger and incredulity when he turned to face her. "For crying out loud, Quinn, those people are the worst form of scum." He squeezed his head with his fingers. "They are terrorists who wouldn't think twice in abusing and torturing you or killing you."

"I am more than capable of taking care of myself. Or do you need another demonstration similar to today's?"

He swore violently before gripping her shoulders and pulling her up to face him. "Damn it, Quinn. Just the thought of you getting within an inch of any of those bastards makes me homicidal. They have no morals. I don't even want to think about how they would have dealt with you if you got caught."

"Well, then, isn't it a good thing I don't get caught?"

Ben snorted. "You came damn close in Tunisia six months ago!"

The breath stilled in her lungs. "How do you know that?"

His fingers relaxed on her arms before he rested his forehead against hers. She could feel his fierce pulse still hammering his temple.

"You said you couldn't wait to get your hands on the Mariner. Well, sweetheart, you've not only had your hands all over him, but your mouth, too." His tone indicated he was just as shocked by the turn of events as she was.

"I don't understand," she managed to stammer.

Except she did. This place. His skills. The close contact with the Secretary of Homeland. She had sensed he was more than he appeared to be and she'd been right. The Mariner was a provocateur. And a very good one. She'd never once picked up a clue he was one of the good guys.

"We've been working together," she whispered in amazement. "All this time and we never knew it."

He brushed his lips across her hairline. "Yeah."

Another realization dawned on her. She stepped out of his embrace.

"Then you've already seen the list."

Ben shook his head. "I haven't. And I've never been asked about it. Not by Ronoff or anyone else."

"Someone is pretending to be you."

His expression grew steely. "No, someone is pretending to be the Mariner. No one but you and the Secretary know we are one and the same."

A warm feeling of pleasure surged within her at the thought of knowing his most guarded secret. He eased them back down onto the futon.

"It's probably the same person who is selling the list," she said. "We need to find out who that is."

He lifted her chin with his fingers. His honest hazel eyes bored into hers and the pleasant feeling grew stronger.

"I like that you used the term 'we,'" he remarked, his voice husky. "I need you to know you're not alone, Quinn. Not anymore. We're in this together now. Trust me."

She traced her fingers along his arm. "I haven't trusted

anyone in a long, long time. Not since you."

He shifted her so she was straddling his lap. Her hair formed a curtain around them when she pressed her forehead to his.

"Was it real back then?" His whispered words fanned her cheek. "Us? Was what we had real? Or was it just a role you were playing?"

It took everything she had to meet his eyes. The apprehension she saw within them stole her breath.

She cupped his cheek firmly. "I wasn't playing a role." She pushed the words out through her tight throat. "Never with you. What we had was real. I told you before, you are the only thing that was ever real in my life."

A fission of unease crept up her spine as she watched his eyelids slam shut. Desperate for him to believe her, she anxiously willed him to say he did. With a sudden clarity she realized just how important his trust meant. How much she needed him. And not just to get out of this mess with Alexi. Even if she survived that, she was pretty sure she wouldn't survive the rest of her life without Ben being a part of it. A major part.

Just as she was about to beg him to say something, his fingers gripped her head and pulled her in for a demanding kiss. She welcomed the invasion, answering with greedy kisses of her own. His hands found their way beneath the T-shirt she wore, branding her skin with his fingernails. Releasing a soft cry, she nipped at his jaw.

"This is as real as it gets." He panted against her ear. "You and me."

"Yes," she breathed before sealing her lips over the pulse point on his neck.

"We already know we make a great team," he murmured as his lips traced her collarbone. "Secretary Lyle practically ordered us to put our heads together to flush out the traitor, get my AI back, and destroy Ronoff for good."

A lusty laugh escaped her throat. Leaning back on her haunches, she stripped the T-shirt over her head. "Given that we are after the same person, I guess I can get behind that assignment. As long as we put more than our heads together."

His answering grin was a bit wicked. "I was hoping you'd say that."

They proceeded to work out the details of their partnership with their hands and their mouths until both of them were slick with exertion and sated with pleasure.

QUINN'S SOFT BREATHING fanned Ben's chest, her body covering his like a favorite blanket. Unlike the night before, her sleep was peaceful and deep.

The sign of a well-satisfied woman.

He, on the other hand, couldn't seem to get his brain to shut down. Not that he wasn't feeling very fulfilled himself, because he was. And it was more than that. He finally felt complete again after so many years of trying to put together the pieces of his shattered heart. Quinn was back where she belonged. With him.

Better yet, wrapped around him.

But he wasn't foolish enough to think they could sail off into the sunset and have the happily ever after they'd planned all those years ago. Not yet anyway. She was a strong, independent woman who let her career define her. He had a sneaking suspicion she didn't believe she was deserving of his love. The very idea nearly broke him. He gently stroked his fingertips along her spine, so steely yet so vulnerable. Protecting her had just become his number one priority.

And that meant finding the damn traitor. He was more convinced now that Secretary Lyle was correct. Whoever was selling the list of names had to be masquerading as the Phoenix. Worse, the asshole was impersonating his alter ego, as well. All scenarios pointed to the person behind the sale of the supposed list of names being an integral player in the US counter-intelligence community. And there was no telling what information they would attempt to sell next.

His deep sigh caused her to stir, but not wake. He slipped out from beneath her warm, languid limbs, carefully resting her body against the back of the futon. After covering her with a blanket, he pulled on his board shorts and padded over to his bank of computers. He sank into the leather chair he'd used to pilot his mission as the Mariner for the past several years and simply stared at the blank screens.

It was over. Just like Quinn, the Mariner had somehow been compromised. Someone out there had burned his alias and was likely tracing every single one of his keystrokes. He couldn't risk trying to track down whoever it was from these computers. Not until he'd done a bit of reprogramming. And that would have to be taken care of back at headquarters.

He was surprised he wasn't angrier at the situation. The alter ego had become his refuge. In the past few months, he'd welcomed the assignments allowing him to camp out here. It gave him an excuse to escape all the damn wedding planning his buddies were cheerfully enduring. Not that he begrudged his two best friends their happiness—he could honestly say he loved Marin and Josslyn like sisters. But lately, he'd begun to feel left out. No matter what they said to him or how they included him, Ben had become the fifth wheel. The truth was, he'd rather bury himself in his work than spend time pondering his lonely future.

Quinn sighed as she shifted on the futon. He glanced over at her sleeping form and his chest actually swelled. Suddenly, the future didn't seem as bleak. He'd enjoyed seeing the lighthouse through her artistic eyes today. And she was right, his friends and family would love the place. He wanted to share it with them. But mostly, he wanted to share it with her.

If he could convince her to stay.

Despite her enthusiastic lovemaking earlier, he sensed she was still skittish about letting him in completely. Her entire life has been a lie. He got that. Now all he had to do was make her understand it didn't matter. Not to him. He saw the real Quinn. And he wanted her, warts and all. He had a freaking genius IQ. Surely, he could figure something out to convince her of that.

Reaching over to snag the container with the cake samples, he began to chow down. He always thought better on a full stomach. The sugar stimulated his brain. At least that was what he'd convinced his mom and countless other women over the years. Leaning back in his chair, he studied the night sky while pondering his next steps.

Priority number one was to find the traitor. Then he could secure the list so Quinn and her parents could live in peace. As grand gestures went, that was certainly a good one.

Getting his AI back from that asshole, Ronoff, was also on his list. Not to mention giving the Russian a little payback for his attempted murder of Quinn. Not that he wasn't grateful to the dick, because had it not been for him, she wouldn't be lying naked and sated in his lighthouse right now.

He jerked upright. That was it. Ronoff was the key to everything. All he had to do was use the Russian to flush out the traitor. And he had just the way to do it while retrieving his AI in the process. His adrenaline was pumping again as he powered up the monitors in the room. The Mariner was going surfing one last time on the dark web. With a great deal of finesse and a little luck, he could trick all the players into revealing themselves. After inhaling the last piece of cake, he let his fingers dance over the keyboard.

CHAPTER THIRTEEN

QUINN WOKE TO the feel of warm sunshine on her face and a hard body wrapped around her. They were still in the torch room, their legs intertwined and Ben's arm securing her to the narrow futon. He was beautiful in his sleep, with long lashes fanned out against his cheeks and his forehead for once relaxed while his overactive brain recharged. Even the stab wound on his shoulder looked less angry.

She wanted to pinch herself to make sure she wasn't dreaming. Even after finding out who and what she was, he still wanted her. Better yet, he seemed to trust her. After everything she'd put him through, no less. He said it didn't matter to him and she desperately wanted to believe him. Could she be the original Quinn Darby? According to Ben, she could. The reality of it all was heady.

Not only that, but she had opened up to him about things she'd never been able to divulge to anyone else in her life. And, damn, if it didn't feel good to have someone else to share the burden of not only her mission, but her life. He had her back. She knew that.

He had her heart, too. She was pretty sure he always had.

Of course, she'd feel a whole lot better if she had that list in her possession. She didn't doubt it was safe where it was, but she'd been out of the game for over thirty-six hours. The idea she was losing headway on beating Alexi to it gnawed at her. As blissful as her current situation felt, she couldn't abandon her mission. They needed to get back to Washington. Which meant waking the man sleeping beside her. Biting back a self-satisfied smile brought on by the realization she was now a "they," she playfully reached out a finger to trace along his jaw. But before she made contact, he was growling seductively and rolling her beneath him.

"Hey." She laughed. "Not fair. I thought you were asleep."

"Thought you'd have your way with me, huh?" he murmured against the curve of her shoulder.

She sighed deeply as the evidence of just how awake he was pressed against her belly.

He shifted above her. "I think it's about time I get to be in the driver seat. You just lay back and enjoy the ride."

"You've learned a few things over the years." She groaned when his teeth nipped at her collarbone.

"So have you."

A nervous laugh escaped her. "Yeah, like how to kill a man with my bare hands."

His body stiffened and his expression grew clouded making her immediately regret her words.

"You don't need your bare hands. You damn near killed me once when you disappeared."

A painful lump formed in her throat. Why had she

gone there? He accepted who and what she was. Why did she feel the need to constantly remind him?

His face softened as he stared down at her. "I've dreamed of waking up with you this way for thirteen years," he whispered. "And the reality is so much better than the dream."

His admission made her heart flutter. Words were beyond her capability. So she sought out his lips instead, kissing him tenderly with the hope of conveying all the things she couldn't manage to say. He responded with a deep searching kiss in return, his body bearing down on hers. She swiped her tongue against his.

And tasted cake.

Yanking her mouth away, she tilted her head toward the little TV table. "You ate the cake? All of it?"

"Uh. . ." His pupils widened with that deer-caught-in-headlights look. "Yesss?"

"How could you? I was saving that for my breakfast. Don't you know you never eat a woman's cake?"

His lips turned up in a wicked smile. "I don't think I've heard it put quite that way before."

Quinn swatted his uninjured shoulder. "I'm serious here. There are food items that are sacred to women and you should never, *ever*, eat the last of them."

"And those would be?" He was obviously struggling to keep a straight face, which did nothing to temper her rising ire.

"Fudge brownie ice cream, cookies, chocolate of any kind, and *cake!*"

"But not pizza," he teased.

"Ohh." She shoved at his chest.

But it was no use. He wouldn't budge. Which was exactly why she preferred to be on top.

"Relax." He brushed his lips over her forehead. "Marin is always making a cake. In fact, if you ask her nicely enough, she'll make an entire cake just for you." He punctuated the last three words with three kisses to the tip of her nose.

She deflated beneath him. "I doubt that. Marin hates me."

"Marin doesn't hate you. She doesn't know you. Give it time. You two will be borrowing each other's shoes before you know it."

Give it time.

His words held the promise of a relationship with his friends in the future. A relationship with him. There went her breath again. The very idea of being the same person—the real Quinn Darby—for the rest of her life was pretty damn tantalizing. Especially if most mornings started out like this one.

"Now, where were we?" he asked before taking the lobe of her ear between his teeth.

Any worry she had about her future—their future—evaporated quickly, replaced with potent, urgent desire.

THEY TRAVELED BACK to DC in the sheriff's Blazer belonging to Ben's brother-in-law.

"Rich is sailing the *Seas the Day* back," Ben explained when they parked the SUV in a marina in Old Town Alexandria. "Just in case your Russian friend is still keeping tabs on me."

"I didn't realize you Secret Service types were so skilled at covert activities," she teased.

"I'm skilled in a lot of things, if you recall," he reminded her with a wink.

"Yeah, well, I might need a few more demonstrations before I score you on RateMyLover dot com." She bit back a laugh at his hungry look. "But for now, can we just go get the card?"

He guided her toward a Metro station. "Tell me there isn't really a RateMyLover dot com."

"Don't worry, Cyber Stud. Your performance was commensurate with your ranking on the site."

This time she did laugh at his expression. Tucking her arm through his, they made their way down the escalator and into the station. She was well aware their bantering was just a way of dealing with the tension brought on by their return to the city. Real life and her mission seemed so far away at the lighthouse. Shortly, she'd finally have her hands on the intel she'd been tasked to retrieve. But what if the Secretary of Homeland was right and it was all just a red herring? Where did that leave her? Or her parents?

As if sensing her unease, he wrapped an arm around her shoulders and pulled her in close so he could brush his lips over the top of her head.

"Easy, Brit. It's all going to work out," he tried to reassure her.

With no choice but to believe him, she relaxed into his embrace and allowed herself to simply enjoy the ease of his company all the way downtown.

To say that the Secret Service headquarters building was nondescript was an understatement. She nearly plowed into the back of Ben when he steered them off the sidewalk in the middle of H Street and into the darkened glass doors of a brown brick building with no identifying signage. It was early afternoon on a Sunday in June and the streets were teeming with tourists. Someone among them could be working for Alexi. She glanced back warily at the passersby, but no one seemed to take notice of either of them.

It was a whole different story once they made their way inside.

"Well, hello there, Agent Segar," a woman's voice called from the reception desk. "What's a handsome guy like you doing here on a beautiful summer afternoon?"

He sauntered over to the desk and bussed the receptionist on the cheek.

"Hello, yourself, Dorothy. You know I can't keep away from you."

The woman's cheeks grew rosy. "Then what are you doing with a girl young enough to be my daughter on your arm? You better not have come here to tell me you're ditching me as your plus-one for that White House wedding and taking her instead."

"You don't need me as your date to the wedding. I

know for a fact Adam has saved you a front row seat." He motioned for Quinn to step closer. "Dorothy Bergs, I'd like you to meet Quinn Darby."

"Nice to meet you," Quinn said, feeling a tad uncomfortable he was announcing her presence when she was supposed to be playing dead.

They were looking for a potential traitor. One who could tell Alexi she was still alive. She shot him a warning look but he was too busy charming the receptionist.

"And this must be the secretary's niece." As if reading her mind, Dorothy's voice had gone up a decibel or two.

He didn't miss a beat. "Yep. The secretary wanted me to show her around."

Dorothy pulled out a visitor badge and handed it to Quinn.

"Normally, visitors, including family, have to wait in the reception area." She indicated a sunny atrium room off to the side. "But the secretary has made an exception for you to visit the cyber lab. You must be very special to her."

She took the badge from the receptionist. "Um, yes. She's my favorite aunt."

"I figured." Dorothy pinned Ben with a serious look. "She wanted me to remind you to have her niece back to the residence in time for tea."

"Got it." He linked his fingers through Quinn's and tugged her toward the security station. "We won't forget."

Quinn planted her feet. Before they left the lighthouse, she'd tucked her handgun into her bag just in case they ran into any trouble along the way. There was no way she could go through security without setting off alarm bells.

He gave her a quizzical look.

"I didn't think things through." She motioned to her camera bag.

Rolling his eyes, he looked over at Dorothy for assistance. The receptionist, who was clearly more than that, jumped right to the rescue.

"I can hold that heavy camera bag here at the desk."

Dorothy reached for the bag, but Quinn held tight. Relinquishing it likely meant losing the last of her firearms.

"Do you want the list or not?" he murmured softly.

"That's playing dirty."

He arched an eyebrow at her.

With a resigned sigh, she handed the bag to Dorothy. "The secretary will be peeved if anything is disturbed in there."

Dorothy smiled admiringly as she took the bag. Quinn wasn't sure but she thought the woman mumbled "well played" beneath her breath. Once they'd made it through security, he latched onto her arm and propelled her toward the lift.

"Thanks for not trusting me to protect you," he said once the doors had closed them in.

She rolled her eyes. "It's not like you're going to beat the bad guys over the head with a hard drive. One of us should be armed."

"You're perfectly safe in this building."

"Can I trust Mrs. Moneypenny not to take my last gun?"

Her James Bond reference had his face relaxing. "If Secretary Lyle wants you to have it, you will."

"I'm really beginning to dislike your beloved secretary."

The doors opened to the sun-filled center atrium. Catwalks linked the rows of offices behind glass walls giving the workspace a vibe of relentless energy. The building's airy, open interior could not have been more different from its bland exterior. Quinn was busy admiring the architecture when two men rounded the corner. Before she knew it, Ben had her pressed up against his body and his lips locked with hers. Not that she put up much resistance, eagerly returning the kiss with a sigh.

"What was that for?" she asked when he pulled away too quickly.

"I thought you didn't want to be seen."

"And I thought you said I was perfectly safe here?"

Grinning foolishly, he led her down the hall lined with candid photos of agents protecting various presidents. "You caught me. You are safe here. I just wanted to kiss you."

She had the sense she wasn't the only one punchy over what they would find on the micro card. He stopped in front of a set of sliding glass doors. A sign beside them read, Cyber Security Lab. Dr. Bennett Segar, Director.

"Doctor? You have your PhD?"

"Mmm," he mumbled as he punched a code into a keypad.

"No retina scans?" she quipped. "I have to say I'm disappointed."

The doors slid open admitting them into a low-lit corridor with a series of cubicles housing everything from laboratory equipment to sophisticated printers. At the end of the hall, he punched a code into another keypad and the glass door in front of them unlocked. He gestured for her to precede him into his office. And suddenly she understood why Ben's bedrooms looked so pristine. He confined the mess to his office. Multicolored Post-it Notes were scattered about the desk, the multiple computer monitors, and just about every available surface. Two white boards were decorated with lines, symbols, and numbers that made absolutely no sense to Quinn. Although, upon further examination, the chaos surrounding her looked to be organized. Evidence of a brilliant mind at work. A stab of pride shot through her. How could she have ever thought him just some boring computer analyst? How had she not seen he was clearly at the top of his field?

"So, this is where the magic happens."

"Sort of." He moved a pile of periodicals off the sofa so she could sit down.

"I can see why you like the lighthouse. This place can be confining compared to the vastness of the views the torch room provides you. You always did think better near the water."

He brushed a kiss over her lips. "Nobody else gets that. Nobody but you."

"You'll be able to find it in this mess?" she teased.

"Very funny."

Pulling open the top drawer of his desk, he rummaged around until he lifted out the tiny micro card. He studied it carefully before gingerly handing it to her.

"Crazy how something so small can bring on such chaos," he said.

She let out a long sigh of relief as she cradled it in her palm. Suddenly, she was desperate to see whether or not the file was real. Reaching around him, she tried to plug the thin card into the drive on his desktop.

"Hey!" He grabbed her wrist. "What are you doing?"

"I need to see the file."

"Yeah, but not before I make sure it isn't booby-trapped." He took it from her fingers and walked over to a file cabinet on the other side of the office.

Once there, he pulled a laptop out of one of the drawers. Sitting beside her on the sofa he powered up the machine.

"Do you know anything about computers?"

She chalked up his condescending comment to the tension in the room. "I know how to boot one up."

He let out a frustrated sigh. "That's not the same as knowing how one works. This thing could contain a virus that would shut down the whole agency if we uploaded it onto my desktop computer. They're all connected by a network," he explained. "But if we use this one and anything goes wrong, all I have to do is replace the hard drive."

"I use a computer every day to edit my images," she added, feeling like she had to defend herself. "But I'm not as familiar with the inner workings of one, no. I never would have considered the virus angle. I leave that to the geniuses like you."

"Sorry," he said sheepishly. "I'm just—"

"Edgy," she finished for him. "So am I." Placing her hand on his thigh, she moved in closer once the computer screen blinked on.

"Here goes nothing," he said before slipping the card into a drive no larger than a sliver on the side of the keyboard.

Quinn held her breath, half expecting the laptop to spew smoke any minute. A line of numbers scrolled across the screen before it went black.

"No," she cried.

"Hold on," he reassured her while he punched a few keys on the keyboard.

The screen came to life again with a Phoenix rising from the ashes. When the image disappeared, a single file name remained. Phoenix Operatives. He glanced over at her, his finger hovering over the enter key.

"You ready?"

All she could do was nod, but her fingers gripped his thigh with a bit more force. He pressed the key and the short list of names appeared on the screen. They weren't in any particular order and it took her a moment to find her mother's name. She gasped when she saw it.

His hand quickly found hers. "Shit," he said.

Reading the list again, her eyes darted to a name at the bottom. One she never expected to see. The room began to spin.

"Ben!" she cried.

His grip on her hand squeezed tighter. "Yeah, I see it. We need to get out of here."

CHAPTER FOURTEEN

"LET ME SEE if I can get this straight."

Ben tried not to wince at President Manning's sharp tone. The president and his chief of staff were both pacing the West Sitting Room of the residence. Secretary Lyle was serving tea to Quinn as if she was the Queen of England. Dorothy and Josslyn played the roles of ladies in waiting, hovering behind the sofa where the other two women sat.

As for Quinn, she remained remarkably stoic. Withdrawn even. Seeing her own name on the list had clearly shocked her. He wanted to take her in his arms and reassure her that neither Ronoff nor anyone else was ever going to hurt her.

Not on his watch.

But duty dictated he report to Secretary Lyle first. Dorothy's cryptic message about tea had been clear as glass to Ben. They were to proceed to the White House as soon as they had the card. Whoever the traitor was, he or she potentially had access to extremely classified information. The list could be just the tip of the iceberg. Finding the asshole was priority one.

"Someone we've yet to identify is impersonating our

operatives and selling highly sensitive information to the son of a Russian crime lord who, coincidently, stole a very valuable artificial intelligence program developed and owned by the US government." The president directed a pointed look at Ben. "And this young lady is an agent with British Intelligence who the same son of a Russian crime lord attempted to kill two nights ago. Can someone tell me why the British ambassador isn't in on this discussion?"

"Because until we know who the black hat is, we believe it is in Agent Darby's best interest for everyone to assume she did in fact die at the hands of Alexi Ronoff," the secretary explained.

"Have you been able to verify with the CIA director if the names on that list actually were operatives working for the Phoenix?" the chief of staff asked.

Secretary Lyle shook her head. "He reiterated that only the Phoenix knew the names on the list, so verification via the agency would be impossible." She patted Quinn's hand. "Whoever composed this list did have a good working knowledge of the Phoenix Project, however. Agent Darby wasn't technically in the employ of MI6 at the time despite providing valuable assistance with the project. Only an insider would know that fact."

The president's tone softened. "Well, if Ronoff's intent is to assassinate everyone on that list then I agree Agent Darby should remain in hiding. Not to mention everyone else named."

"The CIA director has already put the protection procedures into motion," the secretary replied. "But until we find out who is leaking the intelligence and what their role is, even in protective custody, the whereabouts of those on the list could still be jeopardized."

Quinn trembled slightly. Secretary Lyle comforted her by stroking her palm down Quinn's back. Ben was astounded to see his boss acting so tenderly toward another human being. In all the years he'd worked for the woman, she'd been tough as nails, never showing any empathy to anyone. He was secretly delighted she'd decided to loosen up and show some compassion toward the woman he loved.

The woman he loved.

The realization wasn't exactly a surprise but it did hit him square in the chest. Hard. He sucked in a breath to keep from laughing in astonishment. This must be what Griff and Adam felt like when they suddenly realized they wanted to surrender complete control of their heart to the whims of a woman.

The Quinn of his past had changed into something different. But, then again, so had he. She was his future. He needed her to know that. They'd lost too much time together already. The way forward was to find whoever was behind this mess and make her safe. The irony that they'd been unknowingly working as a team for so long already wasn't lost on him. They'd tackle this next part as a team, as well. One that was united.

"Now what, Madame Secretary?" the president demanded interrupting Ben's thoughts. "I gather from your message earlier you have a plan to unmask this traitor."

"Actually, Agent Segar has already set the wheels in motion." The secretary nodded at Ben.

"I did some phishing on the dark web last," he began.

The president groaned. "Not the dark web again."

"Agent Segar is one of the top provocateurs within the counter-intelligence community." The secretary jumped in to defend him. "He's used the dark web to unmask a multitude of terrorists and others intending to do harm to the United States. I have every confidence his efforts will pay off here, as well."

"Sometimes it's as simple as turning one player against the other," Ben added.

"And, in this case, it's better to go through outside channels so we don't alert our traitor that we are on to them," the secretary continued.

The president nodded. "Makes sense. Agent Segar you have the floor."

But just as he opened his mouth to detail his strategy, the president's chief of staff held up his hand. One of his underlings had just entered the room and was whispering something to him.

"Sir, we have a message from the Situation Room," he said.

The president moved toward the staircase.

"No, Mr. President." The chief of staff sounded flabbergasted. "The message is for Agent Segar."

All eyes turned to Ben. Secretary Lyle rose from the sofa.

"That was fast."

"Do you mind telling me what is going on here, Sabrina?" the president demanded.

"Part one of Agent Segar's plan." She motioned for the president to lead the way. "He believes he can flush out the traitor and get his AI back by making a deal with Ronoff."

"We don't make deals, Sabrina," the president said as they made their way over to the West Wing. "You know that."

"Of course I do," she said with a sly grin. "But Alexi Ronoff doesn't."

Ben snagged Quinn's hand. Threading his fingers through hers, he gave them a gentle squeeze. He hated how her eyes were shuttered when she lifted her gaze. She had her game face on. And, judging by the looks of it, she still believed she was playing solo.

"We're in this together, remember?" he murmured against her ear.

She didn't respond, but at least she kept her hand firmly in his. He'd take that as a win. No doubt she was peeved he hadn't confided in her about his plan. Despite how well they worked together between the sheets, it was going to take some time for her to fully accept being part of a team. She wore her bravado like a suit of armor and he wasn't going to pierce that armor in one day. It would take time. Not too much, he hoped, because he was ready to move on from teammates to being a couple. Losing her a second time was not an option.

The Secret Service agents on both the president's and secretary's details fanned off once they reached the Situation Room. Caracas arched an eyebrow when Ben followed Secretary Lyle inside, but for once, the idiot kept his snide remarks to himself. He had no doubt there would be chatter among the agents later as many of them wondered about his role. But it didn't matter. After tonight, the Mariner would no longer exist.

"Wow. Is that the guy who tried to murder you? I expected him to be a bit more sinister looking." Josslyn took a step closer to the screen. "He's more GQ than Terminator."

Josslyn's words drew Ben's attention to the giant screen on the wall where Alexi Ronoff's ugly mug was staring back at him.

Quinn inhaled a sharp breath and jumped behind him.

"Relax," he reassured her quietly. "It's just a video. He won't know you're alive."

"I'm sorry, Doctor Benoit," the secretary was saying. "As this is a sensitive matter dealing with national security, I'm going to have to ask you leave us."

Josslyn shot a questioning look at her brother-in-law. The president nodded and pointed toward the door.

She huffed dramatically before wrapping her arms around Quinn. "You're safe now. We're all friends here. Trust Ben and his team. They won't let anyone harm you or your parents." She gave Quinn's arm a squeeze. "I'll be upstairs if you need me."

He wasn't sure if Quinn was more stunned by seeing Ronoff's face three feet high on the wall or Josslyn's gesture of friendship and support. From what he'd surmised,

Quinn hadn't had a lot of that in her life. He leaned over and brushed a kiss on his friend's cheek before she could make her way past him.

"Thank you," he murmured.

"Yeah, well, you better watch your back with that guy. I'm calling Adam before you run off and do something stupid," Josslyn warned before flouncing out of the room.

No doubt she would, but this was Ben's score to settle. He didn't need his buddies riding shotgun. With any luck, the whole thing would be resolved tonight.

The secretary pressed a button on the wall. "Roll the video."

Quinn sidled up next to him, their bodies not exactly touching. He intertwined his fingers with hers once again. The video began to play. Alexi Ronoff's tone was smug as he tossed the micro card presumably containing VOYEUR into the air and caught it again.

"Hello there, Special Agent Ben Segar. Or should I call you by your code name, Mariner?"

Ben blew out a breath. He underestimated how shedding his alter ego would affect him. And that made him despise the Russian on the screen even more than he already did.

"I enjoyed my little visit to your boat the other evening. What a fine vessel she is. Trading information on the dark web does have its perks, does it not? Especially for one trying to make a living on a measly government salary."

Ben couldn't stop the snort that escaped.

"Your reputation as an honorable dealer in, shall we

say, strategic information precedes you. And it seems we have mutual interests," Ronoff continued. "Well, aside from a beautiful photographer whom we both seemed to share a love for. Such a pity about her early departure from this earth."

This time Ben actually snarled at the screen.

Ronoff held the card between two fingers to scrutinize it. "I believe this belongs to you. I'll admit, I'm a little curious about what exactly all those formulas mean, especially since you are so eager to get it back. But I find I cannot be bothered with this jumble of numbers." The Russian's face grew hard. "You are trying to sell something that belongs to me. Something I've already paid for." His lips formed a sly smile. "I propose we make a trade. I'll be in touch with the logistics."

"What?" Quinn shouted, practically launching herself at the screen.

"Easy." Ben wrapped his arms around her waist and hauled her back against his body.

But she refused to remain still, instead turning and hitting him with the same fury she'd just directed at Ronoff.

"How could you?" she hissed. "You promised me Ronoff would never see that list." She punctuated each word with a fist to his chest.

"Hey!" He gripped her by the wrists. "Stop it, Quinn. The list *is* safe. You're safe. And so are your parents. This is just a ruse to get my AI back."

"Oh, yes, your ever-important artificial intelligence." She actually rolled her damn eyes. "Forgive me if I don't see a computer program as comparable to that of seventeen human lives." She shook off his hands. "For such a smart man, you really are a dolt. You can't program a solution to this, Ben. So, you and Alexi bond as black hats and he gives you back your AI and you give him a fake list. Then what? In the meantime, someone with access to the *real* list is still floating around out there and my mother's life hangs in the balance!"

It took everything Ben had to keep his composure. "I agree."

Her jaw dropped. "Then what the hell are you doing?"

"The traitor has been posing as the Phoenix on the dark web," he explained as patiently as he could. "And we know he's been posing as other identities as well, including mine. From what I found last night, Ronoff hasn't paid up for the list. All I have to do is have the Mariner do a little boasting about the trade and the traitor will surface for the rest of their money. In the meantime, I meet with Ronoff, arrest him for your attempted murder as well as a bevy of other charges the Treasury Department has been building against him."

She was silent for a long moment.

Too bad it wasn't long enough.

"That's the stupidest plan I've ever heard!" She pivoted on her heel to face the others in the room. "Mr. President, I demand to speak to the British ambassador. Better yet, the prime minister."

"Well, hell, why stop there?" Ben taunted her. "How about we call the Queen?"

She whirled around. He was expecting her to be wearing a look that would have his balls shriveling to raisins, but, once again, he'd misread her signals. Her face was so pale it was nearly translucent. And her green eyes were wide and unfocused.

Damn it.

Quinn was frightened out of her mind. He was an ass for provoking her. The sting of her distrust faded a bit while his chest tightened at her obvious distress.

He wrapped his fingers around her wrist and tugged her toward the door. "Will you excuse us a minute, Mr. President?"

Ben didn't wait for an answer. Instead, he towed her past the marine guards and down the hall to the first empty office he could find. Pulling her inside, he slammed the door shut behind them.

"What the hell was that back there?" he demanded.

She crossed her arms mulishly. "Call the Queen? Really?"

He clenched his fingers into a fist to keep from reaching for her. She was as prickly as a stray cat right now. There was no way she would tolerate any tenderness.

"Okay, yeah, that took things too far. My bad," he apologized. "I know you're a little freaked out about your name being on that list, but what happened to us working together? We're supposed to be partners on this mission, Quinn. This is a damn good plan. One I've played out hundreds of times."

"Well that's too bad. Because I'm not playing any longer. You can piss off, Ben Segar. Go back to the safety of your keyboard. I'll take care of this myself. I've been doing it for years."

His chest began to ache at the thought of her drifting back into the shadows. No doubt she could do it easily and he'd never find her again. And as much as he wanted to give her everything her heart desired, he wasn't going to let her have her way. Not without giving her the facts.

"I don't know how many times I can tell you I've got your back before you'll believe me. Better yet, trust me." He sighed heavily. "But no matter how angry you make me, I won't give up on you. On us. I won't let anyone hurt you, Quinn Darby. Ever. You want to know why?"

She remained silent, her only response a peeved glare.

"Because I love you," he confessed. "I always have and I always will."

Quinn sucked in a heavy breath that sounded almost like a sob.

Not exactly the reaction he expected, but he pressed on anyway. "I hope that deep down you love me, too. But, right now, I'll just settle for your trust," he continued softly. "You told me you trusted me last night. Was that just a lie?"

The air in the room grew thick as he waited for her to say something. Anything. Slowly, she shook her head from side to side.

"No, it wasn't a lie?" he prodded. "Or no, you don't trust me?"

Her eyes shimmered with moisture when she finally

raised her gaze to meet his. "No, it wasn't a lie."

"Good. I can work with that."

"I hope so," she whispered. "Because I'm new to this."

"Clearly."

"It's just—"

"No," he said. "There aren't any qualifiers, Quinn. This is an all or nothing proposition."

She nodded resolutely. "All. I want all of it."

A slow smile threatened to spread over his lips, but he bit it back. Her admission had cost her, he could tell. She'd been a one-woman show for so long, trusting wasn't going to come easy at first.

"Good, because I want all of it, too."

"You have it all wrong, though," she whispered.

"Come again?"

"I'm not freaked out about my name being on the list," she explained. "I mean, I am, but I'm more freaked out about you meeting with Alexi face-to-face. He agreed too readily. It's him I don't trust."

Understanding dawned. Her outburst from a moment ago was driven by fear. Fear for him, in particular. It was a heady feeling to have proof she actually cared for him.

"I don't trust him either," he reassured her. "That's why I'll have a handpicked team backing me up."

"But the traitor. It could be someone you know."

He shook his head. "I sincerely doubt that."

She started to say more but then closed her mouth.

"I know you're frightened for your parents, but I've used the ploy multiple times, always with success. It's all going to work out. All you have to do is—"

"Trust you," she interjected. "I know. And I do."

She was suddenly in his arms kissing him with the fervor of a woman clinging to a lifeline. For his part, he let her have her way with his mouth, sighing with encouragement while he dragged his fingers up and down her back to soothe her. If this was her way of unleashing all of her pent-up emotions, he sure as hell wasn't going to complain.

He was going to complain about the loud knocking on the door, however.

Except it was his boss.

"Agent Segar," the secretary called. "We need to strategize a response to Ronoff."

Quinn shivered at the mention of the Russian's name, but her eyes were focused and her cheeks flushed when she pulled away from him. Even more encouraging, there was a ghost of a smile on her lips.

"She's right," Quinn whispered. "I'm sorry for being such a twit."

He lifted her chin with his fingers. "If being a twit always ends with you kissing me senseless, then I think I can put up with it every now and then." He kissed the tip of her nose and reached for the doorknob.

"Ben." She wrapped her fingers around his arm. "Whatever happens, I need you to know that I love you too."

His heart stuttered to a stop before beginning to pound again. This time he didn't bother hiding his smile.

She grinned shyly back. "I loved you thirteen years

ago," she admitted. "And I never stopped. I never will."

Words failed him. He leaned in to brush a swift kiss across her mouth instead.

"Agent Segar!" The secretary's tone was becoming a lot more urgent.

Swearing in aggravation, Ben linked his fingers through Quinn's and pulled open the door. The secretary wore an annoyed expression while the president looked bemused.

"We need to talk about this before Ronoff reaches out again," the secretary stated.

He began to follow her back to the Situation Room when Quinn tugged on his hand.

"I think I'll leave this to you Yanks," she said. "I'm too emotionally involved to be objective." She stretched up and kissed him on the cheek. "I'll go find Josslyn. Maybe there's some cake left upstairs."

Reluctantly, he let her fingers slide from his. There was no doubt she wasn't objective. And he would definitely think more clearly without her there. But he still felt bereft when she walked away from him. As if he were not completely whole. The feeling should have scared the hell out of him.

Except it didn't.

Quinn practically curtsied to the secretary. "Ma'am. If you'll excuse me."

"I'll have someone escort you upstairs."

Caracas hustled forward. "I'd be happy to." He aimed his smarmy smile at Quinn. "It just so happens I love cake. It would be my pleasure to help you hunt for some."

Ben growled low as he took a step toward the other agent, but the secretary already had her hand up to stop him as though she had eyes in the back of her head.

"Stand down, Agent Caracas," she ordered. "Fortunately, you're not the only one here who enjoys a slice of cake. I happen to know Dorothy does, too."

Dorothy firmly placed her hand on Quinn's back and was steering her toward the residence before Caracas knew what hit him. Quinn glanced over her shoulder, shooting an amused grin in Ben's direction. He relaxed a bit seeing her smile.

She loved him.

He'd waited years to hear her say the words. And now she had. It was like a weight had been lifted from his heart. The jury was still out on whether or not she fully trusted him, but he figured they had a lifetime to work on that.

"Agent Segar," the secretary prompted.

With one last peek at Quinn before she disappeared down the long hall, he made his way back into the Situation Room. He had a fish to catch. A big one.

QUINN DID HER best to appear calm on the outside. But on the inside, she was a maelstrom of conflicting emotions. Beginning with her feelings about Ben.

He loves me.

His love was a gift she never expected to receive. Especially after the way she treated him thirteen years ago. Last night, he'd been a caring partner. She'd expect nothing less from him. But it had been too much to hope that their love-making meant as much to him as it did to her. Except it apparently did. She was so giddy, she wanted to dance and laugh and shout about it to the heavens.

Except she couldn't. Not when he was putting himself in so much danger. He didn't know Alexi Ronoff like she did. While she didn't doubt Ben's ability to outsmart his opponents, there was still the wildcard of the unknown traitor to deal with.

Trust no one, her handler had warned her.

Despite her little outburst moments ago, she trusted Ben. But that didn't mean she was happy about him taking on so much danger to protect her and her parents. Keeping her parents safe was something she needed to take care of herself. And she needed to do it quickly. She fingered the burner phone she'd nicked from his desk earlier. It was aptly named because she suddenly felt like it was burning a hole in her pocket.

Dorothy led them up a flight of stairs to the first-floor lobby of the West Wing. The offices were mostly empty as the older woman steered them toward the Cabinet Room, then past the press offices. The rose garden was on their right, offering a sanctuary from all the chaos of the week-end. A marine guard held the door for them as they crossed into the residence via the Palm Room.

"Is there a loo on this level, by chance, Dorothy?" she asked as soon as they entered the Center Hall.

"In the Map Room." Dorothy led the way to a room

decorated in Chippendale furniture and the aforementioned maps. "I'll be right here waiting."

Quinn was relieved the other woman didn't follow her into the toilet. Still, she only had a few minutes to accomplish her mission before she was sure Dorothy would come in after her. Once inside, she powered up the burner phone. Her hands shook as she dialed her mother's number. Before it even connected, a voice came on and informed her the phone didn't have international service.

It was worth a shot.

She weighed her options. Calling the British embassy was too risky. Not until they knew who the traitor was. Her only recourse was to reach out to her handler on the nonsecure line and have him get a message to her parents. Punching in the number she'd committed to memory years ago, she texted him telling him she was very much alive, Alexi didn't have the list, but her parents were still in grave danger. She asked him to please make sure every precaution was taken to ensure their safety. That would have to do for now.

Just as she was about to power off the phone, however, an incoming text came in, surprising her. Her handler wanted to meet. It was urgent, he insisted. Impossible, she nearly typed back before considering the possibilities. What did he mean by urgent? Had her parents' safety already been compromised? Or had the traitor been located? Could there be a way of keeping Ben from confronting Alexi?

Ben would never agree to her leaving the White House to meet with her handler. The idea of sneaking out and betraying their still-fragile trust of one another made her stomach turn. But if she could get some information that would protect him—and her parents—it was a risk she would just have to take. A plan was already beginning to hatch in her head. She said a silent prayer that he would forgive her—especially if she could give him information on the traitor.

She named a location close to the White House. A public place where they could both exchange a few words without being noticed. And one she could get to quickly. Her handler agreed to meet her there in thirty minutes. Turning the phone off, she shoved it in one of the cabinets. It was too risky to keep with her. Dorothy might appear to be motherly, but she had the clairvoyance of a Highland witch.

"You're back," Josslyn cried when Quinn and Dorothy returned to the sitting area in the residence.

Agent Groesch looked up from the seating chart she was helping organize. The little terrier yapped a few welcome barks.

"Yes." She sighed as she dropped onto the sofa next to Ben's friend. "I found it was all too much for me. My anxiety about my parents was causing me to distract Ben."

The dog trotted over from its bed and began to dance around Quinn's feet.

"Fergus, leave her alone," Josslyn commanded.

"It's okay." Quinn reached down and played with Fergus's soft ears. "I need something to divert me."

"Well you've come to the right place." Agent Groesch

indicated the place cards spread on the table in front of them. "Welcome to wedding central."

"I heard there might be cake samples somewhere," Dorothy said, sounding hopeful.

"In the kitchen." Agent Groesch stood and led the other woman in the direction of the family kitchen. "I'll get us each a piece."

Josslyn patted her stomach. "None for me. If I sample any more cake, I won't fit into my dress."

"I was thinking about the flower arrangements," Quinn began. "Would it be okay if I snapped a few pictures of the sample the florist created? And I had some more ideas to pass along to her regarding flowers that will accent the roses already in the garden outside." She was careful not to oversell her plan. "Having something else to focus on will help calm me down a bit."

"Oh, absolutely," Josslyn agreed. "Just let me finish with this and we can head downstairs."

"Take your time," Quinn replied, trying to keep her foot from tapping in agitation as she felt an imaginary clock ticking.

"You should eat something," Dorothy suggested when she emerged from the kitchen.

She waved a paper plate with a generous piece of cake in front of Quinn's nose. Despite looking delicious, she doubted she could get anything past her thick throat.

"Actually, I was going to go down to the florist shop to take some photos first," she said. "Then I thought we might check out the rose garden. Perhaps we can have some tea and cake there?"

"That sounds perfect. That way you don't have to sit around waiting for Agent Groesch and me to finish," Josslyn said. "Can you take her down to the florist shop, Dorothy?"

The older woman eyed Quinn sagely. "Of course."

"I'll meet you there shortly," Josslyn added.

"How about if we meet you in the rose garden?" Quinn suggested. "We'll bring Marilyn with us and that way I can explain my ideas to both of you at the same time."

Josslyn's face lit up. "You're so sweet to do this when you've got so many other things on your mind."

"It's a distraction, remember?" Quinn replied with a forced smile.

She hated herself for taking advantage of Ben's friends. But it was for his own protection. Surely, they would want him kept safe. With luck, none of the women in the room would pick up on the fact she was executing more of a diversion than a distraction.

The floral shop was quiet when she and Dorothy made their way down there. Too quiet. Her heart sank to the soles of her feet. If Marilyn had left already, then there went her ride. But the florist's keys were still where they'd hung the day before. Quinn sucked in a breath.

"Hullo?" she called.

A moment later, Marilyn appeared from the back of the shop. A broad smile spread over her face when she recognized Quinn.

"Well, hello there," Marilyn said. "I was hoping you'd

find your way back down here. I wanted to pick your brain about the flowers for the service. You have a natural eye for color and nature. If Miss Josslyn can't go to Africa to get married, I want to bring a little bit of Africa here."

Quinn's heart stuttered. What would it be like to have someone care for her so much they'd do anything to make her wedding perfect? To come in from their retirement and work tirelessly to ensure her wedding matched her dream? This lovely woman was indeed the national treasure Josslyn made her out to be.

Too bad Quinn was going to use that kindheartedness against her.

She'd taken advantage of people like Marilyn countless times in her career. Benevolent individuals were typically the easiest marks out there. But this was the first time she felt a wave of guilt while doing so.

The end justifies the means. She would do anything, betray anyone, to keep Ben from harm.

"I'm happy to share my ideas," Quinn said. "In fact, I had a few thoughts when we passed by the rose garden earlier. Josslyn is going to meet us out there shortly. But first, I wanted to take a few photos of the sample centerpiece." She made a show of looking around for the camera bag she'd deliberately left upstairs. "Oh, blast. I must have left my camera in the sitting room."

She looked expectantly at Dorothy. This was the tricky part. If the other woman didn't bite, she'd have to resort to something a bit more drastic. And she wasn't sure she could explain away locking the two women in the florist shop's walk-in fridge.

"I can go get it," Dorothy surprised her by saying.

"Perfect." Quinn's heart was beating out of her chest. "We'll walk down to the rose garden and meet you there. Maybe you could bring down some cake for Marilyn and we can all enjoy a leisurely chat?"

She was pushing it, she could tell by Dorothy's dubious expression, but she needed to do whatever she could to buy herself time.

"Oh, cake would be lovely," Marilyn helped her out by saying. "Especially if Chef Marin made it."

Dorothy hesitated a long moment. Quinn held her breath.

"Cake it is," she finally said. She gave Quinn a pointed look. "We'll see you in the rose garden."

Quinn waved a jaunty salute then waited patiently until the other woman's footsteps faded. She quickly turned to the florist.

"Marilyn," she whispered. "Wouldn't it be keen if we could get some El-Nino flowers for the rose garden? It would make the wedding feel a lot more like the Serengeti. And the colors would complement the roses perfectly."

"That would be lovely," the florist agreed. "But how could we get some here in time?"

"The florist at the botanic gardens is a friend of mine," she lied. "I spoke to him earlier and he's willing to let you borrow theirs."

Marilyn's smile lit up the room. "That's so kind of you."

"Anything for Josslyn. But I need your help pulling it off. I need to pick them out before they deliver them. Can you stall them in the rose garden while I dash out? I won't be more than thirty minutes."

"Well. . ." Marilyn looked a bit skittish now.

"Imagine how thrilled Josslyn will be? And you'll be the heroine of the wedding. Everyone will be talking about your arrangements."

"She will be so happy," the florist agreed. "Okay, I'll do my best."

"Remember, if anyone asks, you don't know where I've gone. It will ruin the surprise."

Marilyn pantomimed zipping her lips shut and throwing away the key. With a quick hug, Quinn shooed her out the door. She didn't bother mentioning she was going to commandeer the woman's car to do her dirty work. Instead, she simply grabbed the keys and raced out into the courtyard. Once inside the car, she pulled on the big sunglasses Marilyn left in the console. She tucked her hair inside a baseball cap she found in the back seat. All she had to do was remember to drive on the right side of the road and she just might pull this off.

She breathed a sigh of relief when an alarm didn't sound as she approached the gate. Recognizing Marilyn's car, the guard gave her a quick wave and, just like that, she was home free. Until it was time to return. But she'd worry about that after she met with her contact.

CHAPTER FIFTEEN

QUINN HASTILY WIPED her sweaty palms on the cool metal of the bench she was sitting on. The sound of the water trickling through the fountain should have calmed her racing heart. It didn't. Her contact was late.

Gazing at the tourists milling about the lush greenery housed in the stone and glass conservatory of the US Botanic Gardens, she wrestled with guilt consuming her from sneaking out. Ben had given his word. He loved her. Of course he'd make sure her parents weren't harmed. Of course he could handle confronting Alexi. But if she could find a way to give Ben an advantage, she had to do so.

She'd been absent from the White House for nearly thirty minutes. It was only a matter of time before Marilyn spilled the beans and revealed where she'd gone. Ben would be angry. And hurt. Her heart ached at the thought. She silently willed her handler to hurry.

"What a pleasant surprise it is to find you alive, my dear."

The familiar voice startled her. He had come, after all. They were sitting facing opposite directions on the backless bench. She chose to meet in one of the less populated rooms within the conservatory, a stone's throw from the

Capitol building in the heart of Washington, DC. Fortunately, the tourists were more interested in watching the staff harvest the pods of chocolate from the giant cocoa trees in the main gallery. No one was paying attention to the two supposed strangers in the orchid room.

"Trust me, it's even more pleasant to be alive. But no one must know," she murmured.

"The director must be notified."

"No!"

Her vehement objection caused more than one head to turn in their direction.

"You texted that Alexi doesn't have the list. You are sure of this?"

"Yes. The Americans have the list."

A soft whistle escaped his lips. "This is good news."

"Not really. They're going to trade it to Ronoff."

His body stiffened behind hers. "Why?"

"It's all a bluff to flush out the traitor," she explained. "But if it doesn't work, my parents and the others on that list will never be safe as long as the seller remains at large."

He said nothing. But she took comfort in the smell of his signature cologne and the feel of the heat from his body radiating beside her.

"I must get word to my parents to go underground until this mess is cleared up," she continued. "Can you do that for me?"

"Yes, of course," he reassured her.

She hadn't realized how much she needed to hear the soothing kindness and stability of his voice until she felt the knots in her muscles begin to uncoil.

"Is there any news on the identity of the traitor?"

"No," he responded. "Let's hope the Yanks have better luck."

She did her best not to wilt with disappointment. Ben would have to confront Alexi, after all.

"When are the Americans making this supposed trade with Ronoff?" he asked.

"Tonight some time," she replied. "I'm not exactly sure of the actual plan. But they have assured me he won't get his hands on the list." She heaved a sigh. "But, as we know, nothing is foolproof."

"This will be over shortly, my dear. But I worry about you. You'd be well advised to seek asylum at the embassy."

"I can't. Not until I know the traitor has been eliminated and the list is destroyed."

"Don't be brash," he argued. "Let the Americans handle this. Do what you do best. Disappear until this all blows over. Otherwise, I won't be able to help you any longer."

With those ominous words, he rose from behind her on the bench. She listened carefully for his retreating footsteps before slowly releasing the breath she was holding.

Do what you do best. Disappear.

The words stung. Mainly because they were true. Disappearing was what she was best at. Retrieving intelligence and then fading into the shadows and shedding her alias so she wouldn't be linked to the take down. How many times had she done that over the past decade? But she didn't want that life any longer. Instead, she was going back to the White House. To Ben. And his friends.

If they would have her.

With any luck, this would all be over quickly and she could photograph Josslyn's wedding. Then she and Ben could get on with that future they'd planned so long ago. No doubt he was furious with her disappearance. But she had some ideas of how to smooth things over. She smiled just thinking about them.

First things first, however, there was the matter of the El-Nino flowers to iron out. After all, the plants were her alibi, not to mention her pass to get back inside sixteen hundred Pennsylvania Avenue.

"I'D FEEL BETTER if we involved the rest of our national security team," the president said.

Secretary Lyle exchanged a look with the chief of staff, who heaved a resigned sigh.

"She's right to run this op solo, sir," he said. "Until we discover who's doling out classified intel, we don't know who we can trust."

"For heaven's sake, you don't think someone on my national security team is involved?"

"No, Mr. President," the secretary said. "I don't think it's someone high up at all."

Ben studied his boss carefully. Since she'd glanced at the list of names earlier, her demeanor had gone from intense to practically melancholy. He had the niggling feeling she knew more than she was saying.

"I want this taken care of tonight," the president insisted. "Or I bring in the rest of the team." He stood and glanced at his chief of staff. "I take it this is one of those situations where the less I know, the better. Just make sure no civilians are hurt."

"Keep me updated, Sabrina," the chief of staff ordered before following the president out of the room.

"Are you positive the only two aliases the traitor has used are the Phoenix and the Mariner?" she asked as soon as the two men had left.

"So far, yes."

The secretary dropped her head into her hands. "I'm not so sure our traitor is interested in money."

"Ma'am?"

"Well, at least that may only be part of their motive."

"I'm afraid I'm going to need more if you want me to make sense of what you're saying."

She scrubbed her fingers through her dark, shoulder length hair. "This is about revenge."

"Revenge?"

"Yes. This is personal. The Phoenix and the Mariner are the only two aliases that can be traced back to me."

His mind was whirling with questions, but he didn't dare interrupt her. Not when he sensed a huge revelation on the horizon. She rose from her chair and began to walk toward the screen where Ronoff still stared back at them mutely.

"You asked me if I was sure the Phoenix was dead."

"And you said you were positive."

"Knowing your bionic brain, my word isn't enough evidence for you to be fully convinced."

Ben wasn't sure if he was meant to answer, but the words were out before he could stop them. "There are rumors—"

"And they're exactly that. Rumors. I am sure of this because the Phoenix's real name was Ethan Lyle."

Holy shit. "Your late husband?"

She didn't immediately respond, seemingly lost in her thoughts.

He leaned back in his chair. "How many people are aware of that fact?"

"Aside from the president, the members of the national security team and British Intelligence? Apparently one other." She turned around. Her eyes were steely. "Ethan would never have used an untrained young woman as an asset. Never. Which means someone else did. And that person is our traitor. A traitor who is going to great lengths to link me to their crime. And before you ask, Ethan never shared the names with me. I knew enough never to ask."

He was still trying to wrap his head around what she'd just revealed when Dorothy strode into the room.

"She's gone," Dorothy announced.

"Who's gone?" he asked, even though he had a bad feeling who had disappeared.

"How long?" the secretary demanded.

"Best I can tell, thirty minutes."

"Thirty minutes!" Ben was out of his seat and racing to the door. "How could you let this happen?"

"She let it happen per my orders, Agent Segar."

He stopped in his tracks and turned to face the secretary. "Are you crazy? Have you forgotten that Ronoff wants her dead?"

"And have you forgotten that Ronoff believes she *is* already dead?"

His breath felt like it was traveling through a straw, he could barely get enough air into his lungs. Dorothy handed the secretary a burner phone.

"She used this," Dorothy said.

"Hmm." The secretary examined the phone before waving it in front of Ben. "One of ours."

No! It couldn't be. He opened his mouth to argue but the only sound that emerged from his throat was a pathetic wheeze. Both women gave him a pitying look.

"Haven't you heard the expression if you love someone set them free? If they come back to you, it was meant to be. If not—" The secretary glanced over to Dorothy as if the other woman would complete the sentence. Dorothy shrugged.

The straw was getting smaller because now he was feeling light-headed.

"Relax," the secretary added. "I'm sure of all the women you've been involved with, Agent Darby is the most capable of taking care of herself. You didn't really expect her to trust us to ensure her parents' safety, did you? Besides, I needed to get word to MI6 she is alive. This was the best way to do it without Ronoff finding out."

Dots began to swim before his eyes. Hell, yes, he expected her to trust him. Hadn't they just settled that argument? And still Quinn had slipped away again. He blinked several times trying to focus on the coldhearted, mercenary woman who had practically held the front door open for her. A roaring began in his ears. And then he did something completely out of character. He lunged at the Secretary of Homeland. Fortunately for his career, a pair of strong arms yanked him back.

"Bennett!" Adam shook him. "That's not how to handle this."

The damn woman was made of steel because she didn't even flinch.

"Let me remind you, Agent Segar, that our primary mission tonight is to retrieve the very valuable AI program you lost and to catch a traitor before they sign the death warrant for seventeen people. I'm not here to play matchmaker," the secretary said matter-of-factly.

He flung off Adam's hold and tried to regain what little composure he had left.

"Agent Segar," one of the marine guards said.

"What?" Ben snapped.

"There's someone at the north gate asking for you."

His heart leapt into his throat. The secretary had the nerve to raise a delicate eyebrow in an I-told-you-so manner.

"Well, don't just stand here. Go and get her." She gestured to the foyer. "We're going to need all hands on deck if we're going to pull this off."

He was jogging down the drive before he realized he had an entourage following him. Adam and Joss were hand-in-hand while Christine shadowed their steps. Dorothy did her best to keep up. Ben stopped suddenly when he spied Quinn chatting up the Uniformed Division officer manning the gate looking as if she had just returned from a walk in the park.

And holding a damn *potted plant* in her arms.

"What the hell?"

She turned her head at his words. Apparently she and Secretary Lyle were graduates of the same damn spy school for girls because she wore an identical haughty expression as his boss.

"Is that what I think it is?" a stunned-sounding Josslyn asked.

Quinn's face broke out in a rapturous smile. "No Serengeti wedding is complete without one. Or in your case, four."

Josslyn actually squealed beside him. Before she could hug Quinn, however, Ben grabbed the damn plant from her arms and shoved it at Adam.

"Ben," Quinn objected.

"Not. Here." He glared at Dorothy. "Sign her in."

Wrapping his fingers around her wrist, he marched her up the drive and into the West Wing. The marine guard was stoic as they passed him by. He led her down the hall and outside to a narrow path snaking between the Kennedy Rose Garden and the Oval Office. The agents stationed outside the president's office gave him a wide berth as he towed her toward the private pool area on the White House lawn.

"Ben," she said again.

"No."

He maneuvered them around to the corner of the cabana. Once he was sure they were out of range of the surveillance cameras, he pinned her against the wall with his body. She blinked her long lashes several times, but wisely remained quiet, because he was the one who was going to do all the talking. Not talking. *Yelling.* Demanding answers. Commanding her to never disappear again.

Except when he stared into her luminous eyes, the words seemed to get trapped in his throat. Taming Quinn was going to take some compromise. On both their parts. She smiled up at him serenely before snaking a hand between their bodies and caressing his cheek with her warm palm.

"I'm here," she whispered, seemingly reading his mind. "And I'm not going anywhere. I'm done disappearing. There's nowhere else I'd rather be than with you."

Her lips found his and he was instantly lost. He kissed her back trying his best to convey all the things he wanted to say. Needed to say. At the same time, she was communicating with her body all the things he needed to hear.

Someone cleared their throat behind them.

Pulling out of the kiss, Ben rested his forehead on the wall behind her.

"What is it now?" he demanded.

"Ronoff has sent another message," Dorothy replied. "The secretary wants you both in the Sit Room immediately."

Quinn patted his chest with her palms. "Let's go take down the black hats. Then I want to go on a long sail on that fabulous boat of yours."

He grinned foolishly. "It's a date."

Hand in hand, they followed Dorothy back to the West Wing.

"You're not going to like this," Adam said when they entered the Situation Room to find another video of Ronoff frozen on the screen.

"Let me guess," Ben responded. "He picked a public place."

Adam nodded. "With only one way in or out."

The secretary nodded and the video began to roll. This time, Ronoff was sitting aboard a yacht, a drink in hand and the Jefferson Memorial in the background.

"Hello, my friend. It is a beautiful day for a sail, no?" the Russian asked. "I find I am very impatient to retrieve what is mine. You will meet me tonight at ten p.m. in the VIP gondola of the Ferris wheel in the National Harbor. Come alone. Bring my list and I will return your numbers to you."

The video ended abruptly.

Ben swore violently.

"My thoughts exactly," Adam said. "The damn thing sits at the end of a pier crowded with tourists. The wheel is a hundred and eighty feet at the highest point. There won't be a place for me to get a clear shot. Not only that, but I don't like the idea of you spending twelve minutes trapped alone in a gondola with that douchebag."

Neither did Ben. But not because he didn't trust Ronoff. The Russian was the one who needed to worry. After what he had done to Quinn, Ben wasn't sure if he'd be able to keep from strangling the man before he retrieved his AI.

"Alexi doesn't like to get his hands dirty. If he's suggesting a face-to-face meeting, he himself won't do anything to harm Ben," Quinn chimed in. "His only interest is that list. By now, he must be getting desperate. Earning his father's respect is vital to him. Since his release from prison, the older Ronoff has been restructuring his criminal corporation. Alexi wants a seat at that table. He'll do anything to get it." She turned to Ben. "If Alexi believed you weren't the black hat you purport to be, he'd never risk even two minutes alone with you. Congratulations. Your alias is airtight."

They shared a smile and he couldn't help the burst of pride he felt at her compliment. He'd never be able to share all the details of how he'd been serving his country these past few years with anyone else, but at least Quinn knew. And that was all that mattered.

"So how are we to proceed?" the secretary asked.

"There is another way in," Ben said. "He just showed it to us. That's probably the same yacht he used in Watertown. He'll anchor it upriver and come into the harbor on Jet Skis like they rode in on the other night."

"It's an ostentatious yacht complete with a heliport,

registered in the US Virgin Islands," Quinn supplied. "Her name is *Darina*, after Alexi's mother. He had her berthed in New York the last time I checked."

The door behind them opened and Griffin slipped in.

"Nice of you to join us Agent Keller," the secretary said. "I believe Alexi Ronoff is a person of interest with the Department of Treasury."

"A person of great interest," Griff replied.

"Good. Then I'm handing his arrest off to your team. Once he's returned Agent Segar's AI, I want that yacht of his commandeered and him locked up for the attempted murder of Agent Darby, espionage, and whatever else you've got on him. That ought to hold him for starters." She punched a message into her Blackberry. "I've coordinated with the coast guard. They will await your orders, Agent Keller."

Griff nodded before giving Quinn's shoulder a gentle squeeze.

"It's all going to work out," he told her.

She smiled up at him before turning to Ben. "I know."

He and Griff exchanged fist pumps and then his friend headed out to prepare for his role in the op.

"Ben will need cover when he exits the gondola," Quinn said.

All eyes turned to look at her.

She shrugged. "I said Alexi doesn't like to get his hands dirty. That doesn't mean he won't have one of his men try something once he's left."

The secretary nodded. "That's where we come in,

Agent Darby."

Ben shot from his chair. "Like hell!"

"Stand down, Agent Segar," the secretary commanded. "She's a highly trained asset with the element of surprise in her favor. Ronoff won't be looking for her. Neither will his men. But she'll be able to identify them."

He didn't like it. Not one bit. Quinn, on the other hand, was smiling like a woman who'd just been given free rein in a shoe store.

"I agree," she said. "Adam won't be able to cover you with his sniper's rifle because of the crowd and the distance. But I know these men. I can handle them discreetly before they try to lay a finger on you."

He tried another tact. "Madame Secretary, I don't think it's appropriate for you to be involved in this."

She rose from her chair. "Why not? The president ordered me to handle this tonight. And I am. Unless you don't think we women are capable of taking down the black hats."

Adam made a choking sound behind him. Quinn arched a curious eyebrow. *Damn it.* How had this become the battle of the sexes? Quinn had already demonstrated how capable she was with a gun, but this was about keeping her safe. His boss, on the other hand, he was happy to throw to the wolves.

"Besides." The secretary's voice had a hard edge to it. "Agent Darby and I each have a score to settle with this traitor. And I, for one, would prefer to do it face-to-face." She turned to Adam. "Agent Lockett, have the CAT team secure the marina as best you can. We'll reconvene here at nineteen hundred hours. We can coordinate our efforts with Treasury before heading over to the marina. Now, if you'll excuse me, I'm going home to change into something a bit more touristy."

"I'll go and get my team ready," Adam said before leaving them alone in the Situation Room.

"I don't like you involved in this," he said.

"I know." She stood and laced her fingers through his. "And you have no idea how wonderful it makes me feel to have someone worrying about me. About what happens to me."

He tugged her body against his. "I'm never going to stop."

She stretched up on her toes and brushed a kiss over his lips. "I promise to make it easier on you."

"No more stunts like today?"

"Nope," she murmured against his mouth.

"What the hell was that you were carrying anyway?"

"Oh, my gosh!" She scooted out of his embrace. "They're El-Nino flowers. For Josslyn's wedding. Come on." She grabbed his hand. "Let's take a break from this. I'm dying to see how they look in the rose garden."

A shiver danced up his spine at her choice of words, but she was right, they could use a distraction right now. Even if it involved plants. And weddings. Glancing over his shoulder at Ronoff's face splashed on the giant screen, he made a silent vow that, after tonight, Quinn would be safe from danger for good.

CHAPTER SIXTEEN

T HE EL-NINO FLOWERS looked lovely in the rose garden just as Quinn knew they would. Even Marin was gushing over them by the time the three couples sat down to an early dinner in the family dining room later that day.

"And," Josslyn announced to the group, "Quinn is going to stay and photograph the entire wedding!"

Quinn waited for the familiar dread that making plans for the future used to bring, but none came. Instead, she felt a burst of pure joy bubbling inside her. She actually had a future to look forward to. A future with Ben. One that wouldn't force her into hiding every few months. One where she could be who she wanted to be right out in the open. One where her parents could abandon their false identities and live their lives freely. It was so perfect. She almost didn't dare believe it. As if sensing her tumultuous emotions, Ben covered her hand with his and gave it a gentle squeeze in a silent show of reassurance.

"I'm still trying to wrap my head around Ben being a spy, too," Marin said.

"Why don't you say it a little louder," Adam teased. "I don't think they heard you in Georgetown."

Marin's face fell. "It isn't a secret any more, is it?"

"No," Ben reassured her. "But I'd rather not broadcast it too widely. I'm sure I made a few enemies during my days as the Mariner."

"Freaking brilliant if you ask me." Adam raised his glass. "Congratulations, Bennett, on your excellent service to your country. And on finding your dream girl again. I never doubted for a minute she was real."

Griffin coughed into his napkin.

Adam ignored him and continued. "Here's to a long, happy future for you two."

Everyone raised their glasses. Quinn's heart squeezed when Ben smiled over the rim of his glass at her.

"To the future," she added. "I'm so honored to be a part of your family of friends."

"Ahh," Josslyn said. "I like that. We are a family of friends. And you'll always have a home with us."

Griffin's phone vibrated on the table. "The coast guard is calling. Excuse me. I have to take this. I'll meet you in the Woodshed at seven."

"I should probably get changed," Quinn said.

"I had Terrie put your stuff in the room you used the other night," Josslyn announced. "Do you remember how to get there?"

"You mean I don't have to have an escort?"

Agent Groesch snorted behind them. "As if that would keep you where you're supposed to be."

Ben grinned as he helped Quinn from her chair. "I'll show you the way."

"Just don't get lost up there, you two," Adam called after them. "I want to run the tactical by you both before I leave for the harbor."

Ben led the way through the West sitting area to the Center Hall and up the stairs.

"Marilyn didn't get in too much trouble because of me, did she?"

"Nah. But I doubt she'll leave her car keys lying around any longer."

She made a mental note to apologize to the florist the next time she visited.

"The architecture in this house is so lovely," she remarked as they strolled beneath the skylight illuminating the third-floor Center Hall. "I wish I had time to explore more of it."

He lifted her fingers to his lips and kissed them. "There will be plenty of time after tonight. Trust me, Marin will be thrilled to regale you in the art history surrounding the White House."

They reached her bedroom where Ben proceeded to lay down on the bed, propping his hands behind his head and crossing his feet at the ankles. She opened up her case and began sorting through her clothes.

"You're awfully calm for someone who's about to come face-to-face with a nasty criminal."

She hated the fact he was put in this position because of her. And she found herself worrying about all the ways tonight could go wrong. Alexi was a ruthless man, not to mention unpredictable. Clearly, Ben had more training than she gave him credit for. She just hoped his ample brain was enough to outwit Alexi and flush out a traitor. If not, she'd be there to finish the Russian and the traitor off one way or another.

"I'm trying not to think about it." He donned a wolfish grin. "I'd rather think about you naked."

She tossed a shoe at him. "I'll just be glad when this is all over with."

"Mmm," he murmured as his eyes drifted closed.

"Secretary Lyle seems very sure the traitor will show tonight."

"Actually, I think she has an idea of who it might be."

Quinn paused in her search for the right pair of shorts. "What?"

His eyelids popped open. "Did you ever meet the Phoenix?"

"No." She shook her head. "I don't even know if my mother met him—or her—face-to-face."

"The secretary seems to believe your name being on the list is an important clue to the traitor's identity."

Her neck began to tingle. "As far as I know, my mother never told anyone I was working with her."

"You're sure?"

She crawled up on the bed. "I think so. But I guess I really don't know."

They lay beside one another, each of them quietly pondering the possibilities before she spoke again.

"The Phoenix—"

"Is well and truly dead," he answered before she could

finish her question. He turned his head so he was facing her. "He was the secretary's husband."

"Wow. Then this is personal for her, too."

He rolled over her body, bracing himself on his uninjured arm as he gazed down at her. "I thought you came up here to change?"

"I did." She swatted at his chest. "But you distracted me."

"Then the least I can do is help you out of your clothes." He snagged the shoulder of her shirt with his teeth.

She laughed at his antics. "I'm pretty sure that will be even more distracting."

"Good." He glanced at the clock on the bedside table. "We've got a half hour before we need to get ready for this op. I think we should distract each other until then."

Quinn wanted to object. She really did. But his hands and his mouth were doing such a marvelous job removing her clothing, she decided it was better to just let herself be distracted.

The cadence of their lovemaking was different than it had been the night before. Despite the looming confrontation with Alexi and the potential unmasking of the traitor, the urgency between them was replaced by a more profound coupling. Earlier, they had both confessed their love to one another. Now, they were letting their bodies express that love.

This is home. This was who the real Quinn Darby was. The woman Ben Segar loved. The woman made better by his love. Now that he'd found that woman, he was never letting her go.

ADAM HANDED QUINN a Glock.

"How comfortable are you with this type of handgun?" he asked.

Across the room, Ben's chest swelled with pride. "Comfortable enough to fire a perfect kill shot twice yesterday."

"You took those guys down?" The awe in his friend's voice was unmistakable.

"Ben was occupied in both instances."

He appreciated how she tried to downplay the incident.

"In that case," Adam laid a cache of guns on the table. "Choose your poison."

"Hey, Bennett, are you paying attention over here?" Griffin demanded.

"Yeah, sorry." He inserted the earwig into his ear.

"This device functions similarly to a standard-issue Secret Service comm," Griffin explained. "But it's undetectable. You'll be able to hear us, but you won't have the advantage of an attached microphone, but that's what this little beauty is for."

He slid what looked like a button cover over the second button on Ben's golf shirt.

"This will record your conversation with Ronoff. We'll know the instant anything goes south. See if you can get him to talk about his other illegal enterprises. Specifically, the money laundering and the cryptocurrency schemes. Whatever you can get will bolster our case."

"It's probably better if I play dumb and let him do the talking. The more pointed questions I ask, the more likely he is to catch on to what I'm really doing."

"Huh." Griffin donned an impressed look. "I forgot you're more in touch with your covert side than either of us are. Do what you do best, Boy Genius, and the rest of us will listen in with awe."

"Too bad Kevlar would be noticeable beneath his shirt," Adam said. "I'd feel a lot better if he wore a vest."

Ben shook his head. "Too risky. But the secretary needs to be wrapped in it."

Secretary Lyle chose that moment to enter the room with Dorothy in tow. "Thank you for the confidence, Agent Segar."

Dorothy shot Ben a withering look.

"I'll be taking my detail in with us," the secretary announced. "Agent Lockett, will you please fill the two agents in before you make your way to the harbor?"

She rounded the conference table to where Quinn was inspecting the weapons.

"I guess we should make your boyfriend happy." She handed Quinn a vest. "But make sure you can fit it under your blouse. I don't want the tourists to get jumpy."

"Yes, ma'am." Quinn shot him a saucy look and mouthed the word "boyfriend" as she took the vest and headed into the restroom to put it on.

"Ronoff will expect you to arrive via your boat," the

secretary continued.

"We've already got that covered." Griff pulled up video of the National Harbor on the screen. "Once Ronoff's yacht drops anchor, Ben will sail in."

"I'm headed to Fort McNair now to wait on Agent Keller's signal."

The secretary gestured to his shoulder. "Are you okay to sail with your injury?"

"It's just a scrape."

She arched an eyebrow but said nothing.

"Agent Lockett is assigning one of the tactical team to me," Ben conceded. "He'll be aboard as backup."

"Good. Agent Darby and my detail will make our way to the harbor." She slipped an earwig into her ear. "I want to be in constant communication."

Quinn emerged from the bathroom with her hair tucked beneath a Washington Nationals baseball cap. Her denim blouse was tied in a bow at her waist just above a pair of white cut-offs. No doubt her Glock was hidden in the fanny pack at her side, but Ben was more concerned with the attention her endless tanned legs would attract. There was no way she would be inconspicuous in that outfit.

Griffin handed her a cell phone and a pair of aviator sunglasses. "There's a camera imbedded in the lens. It will be transmitting back to us in the van. The phone is your comm. With everyone having a cell phone glued to their ear, no one will even suspect."

"Got it." After shoving the phone in her back pocket,

she carefully adjusted the sunglass above the bill of the baseball cap and then made her way over to Ben. "Are you sure your shoulder is up to this?" she asked quietly.

"I didn't hear any complaints about my shoulder a half hour ago," he murmured.

She blushed. "That's because I was concentrating on other parts of your physique."

"Hey, if you two are done whispering over there," Adam called from across the room. "I'd like to get this show on the road."

The secretary grabbed her vest. "Get your team in place, Agent Lockett. The rest of us will make our way down to the harbor via different routes."

Quinn squeezed his hand. "Thank you," she whispered.

"For what?"

"For doing this. For still loving me. For everything."

"Stay safe," he managed to grind out through his tight throat.

"Coming, Agent Darby?" the secretary called.

It irked Ben how she made it sound like the two women were going to a day spa rather than a covert op. "Keep her safe, too," he said, gesturing to his boss.

Quinn nodded. Ignoring the rest of the room, she pressed a kiss to his lips. "I'll see you later."

For the first time since she had catapulted back into this life, Ben watched her leave the room without experiencing an overwhelming premonition he wouldn't ever see her again. Her promise of the future hung in the air and Ben suddenly couldn't wait to get this evening over with.

"You're sure you're good with this?" Griff asked for what felt like the hundredth time during the ten-minute drive from the White House to Fort McNair.

They were seated in the gray van with the logo from a cable company on the sides disguising a sophisticated command center on the iinterior. Ben was surprised at just how good he was. He double-checked his weapon and replaced it in its holder. Leaning down, he secured the knife at his ankle.

"Yeah, just make sure nothing happens to Quinn, okay?"

"Something tells me she can take care of herself. I'm really sorry about all that shit that went down yesterday. We just didn't know what to make of her. She hurt you in the past, yet you seemed very protective of her."

Was that only yesterday? So much had happened since then. The revelation of her true identity. The fragile restoration of their trust. And the rekindling of their love. The past seventy-two hours felt surreal. If he was dreaming, he sure as hell didn't want to wake up.

His buddy elbowed him in the ribs. "You're grinning like an idiot."

"Sorry." Ben tried and failed to wipe the smile from his lips. "None of us knew what to make of Quinn when she arrived. Least of all, me. I would have filled you in had I known what to tell you."

"Just like you filled us in on your alter ego?"

Ben shrugged. "It started out as a lark and then became something challenging and rewarding. I wasn't sure you guys would understand since most of my captures took place within a computer."

"I get that. But I still don't know why you had to keep it so hush-hush. Adam kept his dad a secret all those years and now this. I feel kind of boring having a life that's an open book."

"That's the stupidest thing I've ever heard. This isn't a contest."

"Actually, come to think of it, I do have a secret." Griff fidgeted next to him.

"Let me guess. You have jock itch?" Ben teased.

"No, asshole, my wife is pregnant."

He announced it so loudly the rest of the team in the van broke out in applause.

Ben laughed. "And that's why you don't have any secrets. You're supposed to keep 'em, you know, secret." He slapped his friend on the shoulder. "Congratulations, bro. That's awesome news."

Griff beamed. "Yeah, it is pretty cool, isn't it?"

Both men sobered up when the van came to a stop at the marina. They shared a silent fist bump before Ben climbed out of the van.

"Ben," Griff called after him. "We got your six, man."

"Yeah, all for one and one for all." He gave his buddy a salute before heading to his sailboat.

CHAPTER SEVENTEEN

T HEY LEFT THE White House in a small Mercedes SUV with one of the secretary's agents at the wheel. The other agent rode shotgun.

"This is my private vehicle, Caracas. Don't you dare get a scratch on it," the secretary ordered.

"Yes, ma'am."

"We'll pose as mother and daughter," she explained to Quinn. "The agents will act as our companions."

Caracas grinned at Quinn through the rearview mirror.

"There will be no PDA. Not even hand-holding."

The agent's grin faded at the secretary's words.

"Do you mind if we listen to the baseball game, ma'am?" the other agent asked.

"Of course I don't. We've got a thirty-minute drive ahead of us. We might as well be entertained."

Quinn was glad she didn't have to make small talk. Her thoughts were already so scattered she needed to get them refocused before they arrived at the harbor. She settled back against the seat hoping to do just that.

Unfortunately, the secretary had other plans.

"How is your mother these days?"

The question caught her off guard. It took her a few

seconds to recover.

"Well, I hope. My work doesn't allow me to see my parents as often as I would like. I take it you've met her?"

"Years ago, yes. I had just joined the agency. I was based in London and your mother was responsible for some of our training." The other woman smiled. "You were just a toddler at the time. Oh, how your mother loved to show off pictures of you."

Quinn was taken aback. The mum she remembered growing up always seemed to want her kept in the shadows, an ornament to be trotted out whenever her alias required it.

"You were the center of her world."

"Somehow I doubt that," Quinn said without thinking. "My father was the one she doted on. They have a unique kind of love. He was and always will be her primary focus." *There wasn't always room for curious little girl in their orbit.*

Secretary Lyle's expression grew melancholy. "That's because she almost lost him."

"What?" Quinn turned toward the other woman.

"It was around the same time I was there. You were too young to remember." The secretary turned to look out the window. "We all run the risk of taking our work home with us. In this case, an agent from the other side was able to track your mother down. Only it was your father who was caught in the cross fire."

Quinn felt light-headed. She couldn't imagine life without her sweet, jovial father. Or how her mum would have suffered losing her best friend and soul mate.

"As you well know, this life isn't conducive to long-term relationships."

She looked up from her trembling hands to see the other woman studying her.

"Sacrifices are made for the good of our career. Of our country. After the incident, your mother didn't want to make that sacrifice any longer. She wanted to give it all up. For your father. And for you."

"That doesn't make sense. She didn't give it up."

"No. Because your father loved her enough to know what clipping her wings would do to her. She needed the game as much as it needed her. She was brilliant at it. Everyone knew that. Even your father. So they made it work."

The secretary's revelations stunned her.

"I get the sense you are a lot like her."

Quinn snorted. "Hardly. Mum and Dad wanted to leave me with an aunt when they were out in the field. But I would always pitch a horrid fit until they took me. She could barely relate to me until I joined the game."

"My guess is she was afraid to get too close to you. That way if something did happen it wouldn't hurt too much." She locked eyes with Quinn. "Sound familiar? I'm sure we are all guilty of that MO in this profession."

Unable to stand the other woman's scrutiny any longer, Quinn turned her face toward the window. They were crossing the Woodrow Wilson Bridge. She stared off into the water, wondering if she really knew anything about anything. There had never been any doubt her parents loved her. They just didn't do it in the all-consuming way parents did these days. She'd been given little guidance on how to navigate life. Most of it she figured out on her own. No doubt, that was what made her a successful spy. But it also made her a serial loner. A trait she desperately wanted to change.

Her attention was suddenly refocused when a large boat in the water caught her eye.

"There it is. Alexi's yacht," she said.

The secretary already had her phone to ear. The yacht slowly crawled toward the shore where hotels, glass sculptures, and the Capitol Ferris wheel decorated the landscape. Crowded among the landmarks were hundreds of people all enjoying a summer Sunday evening. She sucked in a breath when a surge of uneasiness coursed through her body.

"I know," the secretary said, seeming to sense Quinn's thoughts. "We'll need to be extra cautious. But whatever happens, the traitor must be apprehended tonight."

Quinn turned to meet her fierce gaze. "Agreed."

A few minutes later, Agent Caracas left the car with the valet at the Gaylord Hotel. The four of them wandered through the hotel's expansive atrium featuring a silent disco, a decorative fountain, and a miniature colonial village, all of it overshadowed by a stunning nineteen-story wall of metal and glass overlooking the Potomac River. With so much going on, it was difficult to focus on the faces in the crowd. Quinn kept her eyes peeled for anyone looking familiar, but her pulse raced at the feeling of being trapped despite the enormous picture window in front of them.

She felt better once they emerged onto Water Street and made their way toward the river. All around them, families were battling dripping ices, while couples strolled hand-in-hand window shopping. She was glad the secretary issued her warning to her detail because Agent Caracas hovered beside Quinn, seeming to pay more attention to her than the woman he was charged to protect.

"What are we looking for?" he asked.

Quinn didn't take her eyes off the crowd. "I'll let you know when I see it."

"So what gives between you and Inspector Gadget?"

She jerked her head around to glare at him. "Inspector Gadget?"

"Segar. The Boy Genius. The guy plays with computers all day. I mean, how sexy is that?"

As much as she wanted to shoot the Neanderthal in the bullocks, she needed him in case things went south later on.

"Very sexy," she replied before returning to scouring the faces among the pedestrians.

He was blessedly silent for several moments before he spoke again. "You're not the secretary's niece, are you?"

She grinned slyly rather than confirm or deny his question. The two women might not be related, but Quinn felt a remarkable kinship with Secretary Lyle. Maybe it was the similar life experiences or the passion for their jobs they shared. Quinn suddenly realized she had tremendous respect for the other woman and what she must have gone through to get where she was today. What she had given up. Not only that, she was grateful for the insight into her mother's past. The awareness made her even more determined to secure her mother's future.

"We have an hour to kill before we meet our friends. Let's go get tickets for the Capitol Wheel. I'd love to get a view from up top." The secretary led the way toward the pier.

The sun was setting, turning the night sky into a kaleidoscope of purples and pinks. Children holding glow sticks ran along the shoreline in front of a giant sculpture of a man awakening from being buried in the sand. A row of beached Jet Skis formed a jagged line between the pier and the sandy shore. Quinn pulled the phone from her pocket and snapped a few photos. Then, while Caracas purchased four tickets for them to ride the Ferris wheel, she carefully used the viewfinder to take in every aspect of their surroundings.

"Segar has a berth at the end of the second row," the secretary relayed to her. "He's a few minutes out."

"No sign of Alexi?"

"Not yet."

She relaxed when the ticket handler exchanged a knowing nod with the secretary as they boarded their gondola. The idea of leaving Ben alone on the ground was unnerving, but she felt better knowing Adam's team had managed to fan out within the harbor. The door closed behind Agent Caracas preventing any other passengers from joining them. They spread out among the two bench seats.

The secretary immediately got on the phone. "Talk to me, Agent Lockett."

The Ferris wheel began to creep up toward the now dark sky. Quinn did her best to scope out the pier, but with night descending, it was nearly impossible to decipher the white hats from the black hats.

"Relax," the secretary advised. "Ronoff hasn't even left his yacht yet. We have a few minutes to assess the landscape and figure out the best place to wait. There's a bar adjacent to the pier. It's probably best if I watch from there. You and Agent Caracas can take a moonlight stroll along the docks when Ronoff gets close."

Quinn nodded.

"I'm not sure I'm comfortable leaving you with just one agent," Caracas argued. "It's against protocol, ma'am."

"I appreciate your devotion to duties, Agent Caracas. But the CAT team will make sure I'm covered. Your job is to keep Agent Darby from harm."

The agent donned a dumbfounded look. "*Agent* Darby?"

"Presently with Her Majesty's Secret Intelligence Service." Biting back a smug smile, Quinn extended her hand. "A pleasure working with you this evening."

"I did not see that coming." Agent Caracas shook her hand.

Secretary Lyle chuckled quietly then took another call.

"Understood," she said before hanging up.

With the exception of the music being piped in, the gondola was quiet for the rest of their ride. Presumably, all four were pondering the logistics and potential risks. Quinn definitely was. Just as they neared the dock, she spied two tandem Jet Skis approaching from the direction of Alexi's yacht.

"There." She discretely pointed just as the cell phone in her back pocket rang.

"Hey there, gorgeous. Uncle Adam here."

Quinn smiled. "Hey yourself. Our guests are on their way."

"Looks like it. The Boy Genius would rather you're not on that part of the deck when our friend arrives."

"Copy that. I was planning to check out the boats anyway."

"Let me know if you find anything you like."

Adam clicked off before Quinn got the chance to tell him she was more worried about finding something she didn't like.

"Watch your step." Agent Caracas was all business as they exited the gondola.

Sensing his tension, she slipped her arms through his.

"Relax and be vigilant. You Secret Service agents have the best eyes in the business. Rely on your instincts now."

"Still don't want to tell me what or, better yet, who we're looking for?" he asked quietly.

"Honestly, I have no idea." She patted his arm. "But I'm confident we'll sort it out."

They strolled the docks of the marina in silence, both on the alert for anything out of the ordinary. A cool breeze blew in off the river. Strings of patio lights illuminated the wooden walkway between the boat slips. She was relieved not to see people enjoying the evening from the deck of their boats. Too many eyes and even more potential collateral damage.

As they made their way along the last wharf where the *Seas the Day* was docked, Ben emerged from the aft deck. Her stomach seized with worry. Caracas's hold tightened on her arm.

"Behave," she hissed.

Ben's step faltered slightly at the sight of them arm-in-arm. A low growl escaped his throat. She was ready to whisper a few words of encouragement to Ben when they passed, but Caracas beat her to the punch.

"I've got her six," he murmured. "Go take care of business."

With a slight nod, Ben hurried on his way.

"Thank you." She gave his arm another squeeze.

"Yeah, yeah," the agent mumbled.

They reached the end of the wharf and turned around. Her heart beat faster at the sound of Alexi's Jet Skis roaring up to the pier. She tried to hurry their steps but Agent Caracas held her back.

"You're not to be seen, remember?"

She sighed with frustration just as a familiar scent wafted under her nose. It took her a second to place it before realizing it was a men's cologne. Exactly like the distinct one worn by her handler. She glanced furiously around her, but it was no use. The smell was already gone.

THE SIGHT OF Caracas with his paws all over Quinn sent Ben's blood pressure skyrocketing north. The sight of Ronoff strolling along the pier as if he owned it nearly had his BP in orbit. He took a few deep breaths and fell into step twenty meters behind the Russian. Ronoff zigged and zagged his way around the crowds, twice bumping into people as he did so. Ben wondered if Ronoff was drunk. Or just odd. Like the guy walking beside him holding an umbrella on a clear evening.

When Ronoff arrived at the Capitol Wheel, one of his posse cut to the front. Those waiting in line for the last ride of the night began to shout at him in aggravation. Ben heard Adam's distinctive chuckle as he walked past.

"We might just solve our problem with crowd sourcing," Griffin's voice came over the comm.

"Just be alert," Adam replied. "It could be a diversion."

The CAT member operating the Ferris wheel could have won an Academy Award for his performance. No way was he going to let Ronoff just waltz on board the VIP gondola without waiting in line. Not until the Russian body guard greased the skids with a handful of bills.

"Remind me to make sure Becker deposits that in the agency's sunshine fund," Adam quipped.

Ben's face relaxed into a wry smile. No matter what went down in the next few minutes, his friends had his back. Quinn was safe with Caracas. The other agent might be a loudmouth asshole but he would put the mission first and protect her at any cost. And she could certainly protect herself against him.

"They're letting him aboard," Griff relayed.

Increasing his pace, Ben stepped around the crowd to the front of the line. Agent Becker gave him a stern look before Ronoff waved Ben into the black gondola marked with the number forty-two. One of Ronoff's henchmen tried to climb aboard as well, but Ben put his hand out to stop him.

"The agreement was we meet alone," he said.

"Make up your mind," Becker prodded from the dock. "This isn't a private trip. These people in line want their chance, too."

Ronoff shook his head at his bodyguard and Becker appeared to take great delight in shoving the door closed in his face. The gondola moved forward several feet allowing others to enter the car behind them. Ben took a moment to assess his surroundings. The glass enclosed pod was approximately six feet long, five feet wide, and five feet high. He was about to spend twelve minutes trapped in an airtight glass box suspended one hundred eighty feet in the air with a ruthless killer. Without any option for an escape route. No wonder his pulse was beating to the cadence of the "William Tell Overture."

"Sit, Agent Segar."

Ronoff indicated the three empty bucket seats. He was spread out in one closest to the outer window. Ben strategically took the one closer to the door, catty-corner from Ronoff. The Russian smirked at his choice.

"You are wise to not trust me. I am not a man who plays fair."

"Does that mean you didn't bring my program?"

The gondola moved forward again.

"I did not," he replied with a grin. "It turns out it is worth a lot more to someone else."

Fuck.

The word echoed in his ear when both Adam and Griff parodied his sentiment. The gondola shifted forward again. They'd reached nine o'clock on the wheel and the tip of the Washington Monument came into view.

"Then this little party was for nothing."

It was going to be a long twelve minutes.

"Easy, Bennett," Griffin murmured into his earwig. "See if you can get him talking. The plan was to retrieve your AI when we grab him."

The gondola crawled up to eleven o'clock. The lights on the side of the Ferris wheel were pulsing to the music, touching off a low throbbing in Ben's temple.

"Don't be such a party pooper, Agent Segar." The Russian took a small, silver flask from his pocket. He offered it to Ben who declined it with a shake of his head. "You have a very talented mathematical mind, I think. You are wasting it on artificial intelligence. Cryptocurrency is where you should be using your talents. I have big plans to manipulate the market. I think you and I could work well together."

"I don't swing that way."

Ronoff's head snapped up. The insolent lazy look he'd

been wearing was replaced by a laser-focused expression of equal parts fury and admiration. The admiration seemed to win out because he relaxed back again and grinned at Ben.

"I am very discreet. If I had to guess, our mutual friend told you."

His fingers clenched along with his gut at the Russian's reference to Quinn as a friend.

"Nothing is foolproof. Or untraceable. Not even on the dark web."

The Russian's flinch was nearly undetectable as he considered Ben's words. Ben took some solace in the idea he could intimidate the other man.

"I have to wonder why a list that was so important to you, you had to kill an innocent woman is no longer critical?" Ben continued.

"Oh, it is still very important to me. Critical, as you say, in fact." Ronoff sniffled as he waved his hand. "I have chosen to honor my deal with the original seller. I don't trust you to give me the actual list, you see. Even better, the seller is very interested in your program. I have offered it in exchange for my final payment for the list." He pulled out a handkerchief and dabbed at his watery eyes. "I don't think you understand, Agent Segar. I own you now. I can sell you out to any of the parties you have double-crossed these past few years."

Ben's knuckles were white on the arm rest. He'd calculated the risk when he'd initiated his plan, but everything depended on the traitor showing up tonight. The odds were quickly running against him.

The Russian blew his nose. "Ah, but you are angry at me for killing your friend. She was beautiful, no?"

Nausea rose up the back of Ben's throat. This man had tried to kill the woman he loved and he dared to pretend remorse. He hoped Griffin had enough to put him away forever.

"She was innocent," Ben protested. "And she didn't deserve to die."

Ronoff scoffed at the word innocent. "You loved her. And now she's gone."

Ben dug his fingers into the leather armrest in his seat, but he didn't bother answering. The gondola had reached twelve o'clock. The Jefferson Memorial, the Washington Monument, and the Capitol Dome were all lit up majestically against the inky-black sky. But Ben saw none of this.

Ronoff laughed. "You think your feelings were not obvious the other night at the White House? Or that a man like me cannot know what desire looks like on another man's face. Trust me, Agent Segar, you wore your desire for Quinn Darby very plainly."

"Trusting you is not something I plan to do. Not after tonight."

The Russian swiped at his eyes. "She had nine lives, that one. But only one of them was meant to be spent with you." He was suddenly overcome with a coughing fit.

"She was the last name on your damn list."

Ben had shocked him. Ronoff was suddenly flushed.

"You have seen the list." He coughed the words out. "She said no one else would know that name was on it. It is the Phoenix's list."

The conversation was suddenly difficult to follow.

"Who is 'she'?"

Ronoff was overcome with another coughing fit. His eyes were bloodshot and his nose still ran.

"Is this guy high?" Griff asked.

Ben didn't know or care. There was something he was missing here. His neck tingled and his pulse raced.

"What *she* are you talking about, Ronoff?" he demanded.

The wheel passed by the dock and began its assent up to the sky again.

Ronoff began to wheeze. "She knows . . . you are the Mariner," he managed to get out. "She will . . . use it . . . against you!"

Suddenly, the Russian was clutching at his chest.

"What the hell is going on in there, Bennett?" Adam barked into his earwig.

"Hell if I know."

He was just reaching over to help the other man when Ronoff began to convulse violently.

"Don't touch him!" Griffin screamed in his ear. "It might be on his clothes!"

Ben didn't have to wonder what "it" might be. He had seen enough nerve gas attacks during his days in Special Forces to know the seriousness—and the fatality—of them.

"Get this thing down!" he yelled, feeling a bit like he was trapped in a giant petri dish.

By the time they'd reached the dock, Ronoff was vomiting up blood. Ben perched himself on the back of his chair to avoid any contact. The Russian's bodyguards tried to rush the gondola but Adam's team was already in place.

"Get our man out of there," the secretary commanded. "And get a hazmat team in here immediately."

Ben didn't have to be asked twice. He leaped from the glass deathtrap and scoured the dock.

"She's safe," the secretary assured him.

Quinn emerged from the crowd. "I'm here."

He quickly pulled her into his arms and glanced around again.

"What is it?" both Quinn and the secretary asked at the same time.

"Have either of you seen a man with an umbrella?"

CHAPTER EIGHTEEN

"R ONOFF'S DEAD."

Adam delivered the news to the group assembled on the back deck of the *Seas the Day*. Thirty minutes had passed since they'd pulled Ben from the gondola. He'd been checked by the EMTs and the military team summoned by the secretary, but thankfully there were no traces of whatever killed Alexi.

Quinn wasn't sure how to feel about Adam's announcement. She was glad the Russian could do no harm to her mother or anyone else on the list. But she was frustrated they had lost their only connection to the traitor. A traitor who could now sell out Ben to the many enemies he'd made throughout his tenure as the Mariner.

"Cause of death?" the secretary demanded.

"They're running with cardiac arrest for now," Adam replied.

"Did they check for puncture wounds?" Ben paused in his pacing of the deck where he was still looking for some mysterious man with an umbrella.

The secretary pulled her phone to her ear. "Have the body sent to the medical examiner at Walter Reed. I'll let them know to suit up." She nodded at Ben. "And to follow up on your theory, Agent Segar."

"You're certain this man poisoned Alexi?" she asked him.

"No." He dragged his fingers through his hair. "We can't be sure until we figure out the exact cause of death. But it had all the earmarks of a poisonous chemical attack. And since no one else is affected, we have to assume he ingested it somehow. Or someone injected him with it."

She reached for his hand and gave it a squeeze. The small act seemed to refocus him. He ceased his pacing and pulled her into his arms.

"I'm sorry," he murmured against her hair. "I honestly thought this would work. We'll find the traitor. I promise."

Leaning into his chest she took some solace in the strong heartbeat beneath her ear. They were both still alive and together. But for how long? Even if she spent the rest of her life pretending to be dead, Ben's future was now in grave danger.

"I want to listen to that audio again," the secretary insisted.

Ben stepped out of their embrace. "Me, too. I'm sure Ronoff used the word *she* when he referred to the traitor."

"Dude, it was hard to understand anything he said those last few minutes." Adam pulled up the audio on a tablet and handed the secretary a pair of earbuds.

Several minutes later, she shook her head and handed the earbuds to Ben. He swore as he listened.

"It's all garbled because he was gasping for air." His face was resolute, however, when he turned back to his boss. "I swear I heard what I heard."

The secretary's nod wasn't exactly patronizing, but she didn't give the impression she fully believed his account of what Ronoff said in the gondola. Or his fixation on a man carrying an umbrella.

"The president wants a briefing back at the White House," she announced.

Ben groaned quietly.

"Relax, Agent Segar," she said. "I'll take the heat on this one. No one was injured. Property wasn't damaged and we prevented a likely cryptocurrency attack. All in all, the night wasn't a total loss."

Since they hadn't accomplished their primary goal of outing the traitor, Quinn was reluctant to agree with the other woman.

"I want to see you first thing tomorrow." The secretary looked directly at her. "Both of you."

Agent Caracas handed her on to the dock. He glanced back at Quinn. "Pleasure working with you, Agent Darby," he said. "If Inspector Gadget here fails to treat you right, you let me know."

Ben flipped the other agent off. Agent Caracas's laugh rang out through the marina.

"What next?" Griffin asked once the secretary's footsteps faded. "I know you've got something going on in that mastermind brain of yours."

"I'm afraid this one has me stumped." Ben sank down onto one of the bench seats.

Quinn sat beside him. "What about the *Seas the Day*?

She can't stay here."

"I'll sail her back to Alexandria first thing tomorrow." He threaded his fingers through hers. "I want you to go back with Adam to the Crown."

"Absolutely not." She gripped his hand firmly. "We're a team now, remember? If I'm not allowed to be out of your sight, then the same goes for you."

"Good, then you're both coming back to the Crown," Griffin insisted.

Ben grinned before shaking his head. "I'm not leaving my boat."

"And I'm not leaving you." She leaned over and kissed him.

"You're both insane," Adam argued.

"Then we're perfect for each other," Ben said with a laugh.

"Bennett, you can't stay out here all night." Griffin looked as if he wanted to haul them both over his shoulder and carry them all the way back to the White House.

"I appreciate the concern, guys." Ben stood up, pulling her along with him. "But the traitor won't show now. Not with Ronoff dead. They'll have to find another sucker to buy that list. The Mariner may have been burned, but I can still navigate the dark web using another alias."

Adam and Griffin exchanged a look.

"You're taking this a lot better than I thought you would," Adam remarked.

Quinn was also a bit uneasy about Ben's quick rebound, but she kept her feelings to herself.

"We'll head back in the morning," he told his friends. "Go home. Get some sleep. Tomorrow is a work day."

"Okay." Adam shrugged.

"If you say so." Griffin looked at Ben like he wanted to say more.

"Yeah. I say so. Now get out of here."

The three exchanged man hugs before Adam and Griffin climbed off the boat. Their reluctant footsteps echoed on the dock until they were swallowed up by the sounds of laughter and music being carried from the various hotels and restaurants within the harbor. Ben quickly spun her around toward the cabin.

"Ben—"

"Not here," he murmured. "Let's get inside."

She stepped down into the galley, but he didn't stop there. With his chest pressed to her back, he propelled her toward the forward cabin. Her shins bumped up against the bed just as his mouth found the tender skin on her neck.

"What are you doing?"

He released her and took a step back. She twirled around just in time to see him shuck his shirt. The sight of his naked chest brought goose bumps to her skin.

"We're going to do what I've dreamt of doing every time I crawled into this bunk. Take your clothes off."

The boat swayed slightly with the tide. She wanted to defy him. To discuss whatever had happened in the gondola. But apparently her fingers were on a different wavelength because they were already unfastening her shorts. He stepped out of his shoes and shoved his jeans and briefs down his legs. All it took was one glance for her to realize he was not in the mood for discussion.

He reached for the buttons of her shirt and began to undo them. At the same time, he tugged her body flush with his. She let out a soft moan at the contact. Forgetting the buttons, he pushed her shorts and her panties past her hips. This time her moan sounded a bit more impatient. His chuckle held a ruthless edge when he eased her down onto the mattress.

She struggled to free herself from her clothes, but Ben was no help. Instead, he rained kisses on her with an urgency that had her stomach fluttering with multiple emotions.

"It's okay," she breathed. "I'm not going anywhere. I'm here."

But her attempts at soothing him only spurred his fervor higher. He tore at her blouse, pushing the sides of her bra away to expose her breasts. Growling something obscene, he took her nipple into his mouth. She arched into him, the heat of his body searing her skin.

"Oh," she cried trying desperately to shimmy out of her shorts.

He finally took pity on her and shoved the denim and silk down to her ankles where she kicked them off. She twisted out of her bra while he rolled on a condom. He entered her with a single thrust before he stilled, hovering above her in a plank position. She gazed up into his stormy eyes. It was costing him to rein in his lust. But he was a gentleman at heart.

"Wrap your legs around me," he ordered.

Caught up in the moment, she did as she was told. He began to move within her, all the while whispering naughty, erotic things in her ear. The sway of the boat and the feel of his teeth grazing her skin added to the sensual bombardment. It wasn't long before she was soaring toward the edge.

"I—"

"Let go," he growled.

And she did. A thousand pinpricks of light danced before her eyes while her body convulsed around him. It was as if all the pent-up emotion of the day had formed a vapor that now drifted out of the cabin. A moment later, he threw his head back with a grunt before collapsing on top of her. The beat of his heart pounded against her ribs. Noise from the nightspots in the harbor wafted through the windows. The bed continued to rock gently beneath them lulling her into a semiconscious state. She ran her fingers over his back, surprised to feel the tension still bunched there.

"What is it?" she asked softly.

He didn't bother lifting his head, leaving his cheek resting against the fevered skin of her breast. "We have to disappear."

His words made her heart stutter. "You can't be serious?"

This time he did turn to face her. His expression was resigned. "I'll do whatever it takes to keep you safe. And if that means going dark until we find this traitor, then that's what we'll do. I have enough provisions and bona fides at the Think Tank to sail away for a couple of years."

"You keep false identity papers?"

"I had to be prepared for something like this to happen. No doubt you have multiple sets of your own."

She did. But then going dark was a common practice for her. She was adapted to it. No, born to it. Used to the isolation and loneliness that went along with weeks or months living in the shadows.

Ben, however, was not.

"I don't think you've thought this entirely through," she cautioned him. "If we did that, you wouldn't be able to see or communicate with your family. Rebecca, Rich, and the kids would miss you. So would your mum. Even your crazy aunt Marnie. Adam and Josslyn are getting married in a week's time. You have to be there for that."

He had much more to lose than she ever did. And he was so cavalier about leaving it all behind. Except she now knew the value of all the things Ben would be giving up. She wasn't sure if her heartache was for him or for all the things she'd missed over the years by not having a large family and a circle of friends. Either way, she was determined he would not walk away from his happy life.

Not even for her.

"My family and friends will understand. The only important thing is that we're together." He rolled off her and went to dispose of the condom. A moment later, he wandered back with a box of Teddy Grahams.

"I hate to break it to you, but those things are only found in America," she teased, trying to lighten the mood when he slipped back into the bed.

"Then I better enjoy them while I can."

"Ben—"

He shook his head then draped an arm around her shoulder pulling her close. "This isn't up for debate. I won't lose you again."

She swallowed painfully. He was choosing her over everyone else in his life. The very idea was overwhelming. Tears formed at the back of her eyes. As much as she treasured the gesture, they'd never be able to fully appreciate their love for one another as long as the traitor threatened. There had to be an answer.

Two hours later, Ben was face down on the mattress in a deep slumber following another bout of zealous lovemaking. Sleep evaded Quinn, however. She was still trying to figure a way out of their dilemma. There was something she was missing. A vital clue she couldn't quite put her finger on. The musky scent of sex permeated the cabin as she kept replaying the evening over and over again in her mind.

That's it!

Her handler had been on the pier this evening. She was sure of it. With all the hullaballoo surrounding Alexi's death, she'd forgotten completely about catching a whiff of his distinctive cologne. What had he wanted? How had he found her? She needed to contact him. Especially if she and Ben were going dark as he planned.

After carefully untangling her limbs from his, she edged out of the bed and gathered up her scattered clothing. Her blouse was a goner so she nicked a T-shirt from one of the drawers instead. She quietly slipped into the loo and got dressed. There had been a burner phone near the boat's navigation station earlier. She said a silent hallelujah when it was still right where she'd seen it. So as not to chance waking Ben, she decided to sneak out to the aft deck to make her call. Her senses must have been teasing her, because as she opened the cabin door, she swore she smelled the cologne yet again.

Quinn stopped dead in her tracks at the sight that greeted her. A man with a trench coat and an umbrella was seated on one of the benches, his posture so relaxed it was as if he owned the boat. But it was the gun in his hand that had her drawing in a shocked breath. Particularly since it was pointed at the Secretary of Homeland.

"Hullo, my dear. I've been waiting for you."

For the first time ever, her skin crawled at the sound of her handler's voice.

BEN SHOT UP out of the bed. He wasn't sure what had awakened him, but the empty space beside him had his heart racing. She wouldn't leave him again.

Not willingly. She'd promised as much the night before. His heart beat faster. The sound of hushed voices from the deck had him yanking on his jeans. He didn't bother with shoes, but grabbed his Glock instead. As silently as he could, he crept toward the stairs. His gut did a somersault when he recognized Quinn's voice above. But it was the other voices that had him clicking the safety off his weapon.

With as much stealth as he could muster, he opened the cabin door.

"Stay back," Quinn and the secretary shouted at the same time.

As if he was going to listen to either one of them. Not when there was a man with a gun pointed at his boss's chest sitting on his aft deck. Even worse, he had an umbrella trained in Quinn's direction. He rounded out his ensemble with a trench coat and a bowler hat. All that was missing was a monocle and he could have been the guy from Monopoly.

"I told you the guy was real."

Ben casually strolled onto the deck, hoping to ease some of the tension with a little levity. Out of the corner of his eye, he caught sight of one of the secretary's detail face down in a pool of blood on the dock. Caracas was nowhere to be found. He couldn't decide if that was good or bad. But he didn't have time to puzzle that out right now. One agent was down and he was not going to lose the secretary or Quinn. Time to figure out what game this cat was playing.

"Ah, welcome, Agent Segar. Or should I say the Mariner? I'm glad we are finally all here," Mr. Monopoly said, his words dripping with a very British accent. "Place your weapon on the floor and kick it over to me or they both die."

He reluctantly did as he was told before risking a peek at Quinn. Her lips were drawn tight with disgust.

"You know this guy?" he asked her.

"Unfortunately." Her tone was brittle and she looked poised for battle. "This is all my fault. I never should have sought him out earlier. All this time I thought he could be trusted."

So this was who she'd met at the botanic gardens. A rendezvous Secretary Lyle had sanctioned. There were pieces to this puzzle he wasn't privy to and right now he was pissed off at his boss for letting Quinn get swept up in this mess. Ben edged closer to her.

Mr. Monopoly jabbed his umbrella in her direction. "Stay where you are!"

Cautious of what might be inside the tip of that thing, he did as the guy asked and froze.

"But we're not all here, Sir Rodney," the secretary drawled, cool as a cucumber despite having a gun pointed at her heart from four feet away. "We're missing one important person. Where is she?"

Ben's ears perked up at her question. There was a "she" and damn if the secretary didn't know it all along. Mr. Monopoly remained quiet, his only tell that he was annoyed, a slight snarl of his upper lip.

"Ah, so you don't know where she is, do you?" the secretary taunted. "Is that what this is all about? You expected her to show up here tonight, as well."

Mr. Monopoly cocked the gun. Quinn tensed for flight. Ben rocked forward on his toes preparing to stop her. It was his job to take a bullet for the secretary, not hers.

"But I keep asking myself, why kill Ronoff?" the secretary continued as if she was trying to outwit the man at a game of backgammon, not life or death. "How does he fit into all of this?"

Sir Rodney remained stoic. There wasn't a tremor in either hand. Clearly, he was professionally trained.

"I'd rather know how this *she* fits into the all of this," Ben tossed out.

"It's a long and sordid story," Secretary Lyle replied. "But I might as well explain while we're waiting. The *she* we speak of is Lady Eugenie, Sir Rodney's very wicked daughter."

The revelation exposed a slight chink in the guy's armor. His hands weren't so steady at the mention of his daughter. Ben hoped the secretary knew what she was doing.

"The British Service and the CIA have an exchange program and Lady Eugenie was assigned to headquarters at Langley. Specifically, to work for the Phoenix."

The secretary's tone grew sharper. Ben had an idea where all this was headed. And he didn't like it. Not one bit. For her part, Quinn was taking it all in as if it were a production at the Kennedy Center.

"Except she wanted more than to just work for the Phoenix, she wanted to seduce him."

Quinn gasped softly. Sir Rodney's sigh was more re-signed.

"Eugenie has always been impetuous," he said. "I've apologized every way I know how, Sabrina. You have to know Ethan only had eyes for you."

"Which made your daughter not only impetuous, but dangerous," the secretary snapped.

"You still can't blame her for his death," Sir Rodney exclaimed.

Holy shit.

"The proof is out there and I'll find it. But let's get back to the issue at hand, why kill Alexi Ronoff?"

Sir Rodney's British reserve was slipping. "Because he was the only one who would benefit from the information Eugenie had to sell. With him out of the picture, she'd have to cease this ridiculous nonsense."

"And by nonsense, you mean the constant threats to my career and reputation?" the secretary clarified.

"Yes!" Sir Rodney glared at Ben. "That was until this dolt decided to reveal his true self. What a stupid risk you took. Now she has something else to hold over Sabrina's head. Don't think she won't sell you out in a heartbeat. If she hasn't already."

Ben refused to be cowed by a caricature of a spy wield-ing a poison umbrella. "And you thought my plan was idiotic," he blurted out. "This guy is trying to flush out his own daughter with a damn poison umbrella tip!"

"He's right, Daddy. You do look a tad ridiculous."

Four heads turned toward the dock where a woman

stood holding a Lugar equipped with a silencer. It was aimed directly for the secretary's jugular.

Double shit!

Several beads of sweat began to form on the back of Ben's neck. His brain was working overtime to figure a way out of this mess. Out of the corner of his eye, he spied Caracas hunkered down behind a Chris-Craft cruising boat. His gun was trained on Sir Rodney. The addition of another weapon made the other agent's job nearly impossible. The only thing Ben could hope for was that Caracas had called for backup and Adam was somewhere in the dark waiting for a clear shot.

"Eugenie! Don't do anything rash," her father ordered. "You've caused enough trouble."

"*I've* caused trouble?" Eugenie's laughed humorlessly. "The troublemaker is this woman. She ruined my life. Destroyed my career. All because her husband preferred a younger, more vibrant woman over a cold-hearted bitch."

Quinn flinched. Secretary Lyle didn't so much as bat an eyelash.

"And you." It was Ben's turn to flinch when Eugenie aimed her gun at Quinn. "You became the darling of MI6. You were nothing until I made you. Your mother refused to involve you until she was ordered by the Phoenix to do so."

"Ethan would never have used an untrained operative," Secretary Lyle insisted. "Especially not one as young as she was."

"Of course, he wouldn't. I needed the case solved so I

could prove to him I was worthy to stay on the project. So I acted on the Phoenix's behalf." She swerved, pointing the barrel of the gun back toward the secretary. "But you had to intercede, didn't you?"

"You bet I did."

Eugenie growled low in her throat. A boat's engine roared to life beside them.

"And for that you will pay. I'm happy to sell out your husband's assets on your behalf. And now I get to add our little sweetheart's beloved, the Mariner, to the list. I'll be rich with the bidding war he'll bring in. But perhaps it's best just to put you out of your misery right now."

"Eugenie, no!" Sir Rodney cried.

And then everything seemed to happen in a nanosecond. Caracas leaped from his hiding place just as gunshots rang out. Ben covered Quinn with this body. Sir Rodney screamed. When the dust cleared. Eugenie was climbing aboard a cigarette boat built for speed. Ben snatched up his Glock.

"You okay?" he breathed.

Quinn nodded. She gripped his face with both palms. He was grateful for the enthusiastic kiss she gave him, but the moaning beside him kept him from returning it.

"Madam Secretary!" Ben crawled away from Quinn.

"I'm unhurt," she replied. "But Agent Caracas needs medical attention. He'll bleed out without a tourniquet."

"The secretary," Caracas wheezed. "Don't leave her unprotected."

Adam and Griff suddenly jumped on board like the

cavalry. Griff gingerly hurled the umbrella into the drink while Ben pulled a first-aid kit from beneath the captain's chair.

"Nice shot," Griff said gesturing to Sir Rodney who was slumped back with a bullet hole to the head.

"Yeah, but the girl was too slippery," Adam replied.

"Don't worry," Griff said. "The coast guard will get her before she leaves the Potomac."

Ben heaved a breath of relief as he administered to the other agent's leg. "You hear that, Quinn. It's finally over."

When she didn't respond, he glanced up at his buddies. Griff darted down below. He reemerged ten seconds later, a stricken look on his face.

"Not there."

"It will never be over as long as Eugenie is alive," the secretary said ominously. "For you. Or for Quinn."

"No!"

Ben shot from the boat. He frantically searched the dock for her.

"There!" Adam pointed toward the beach area. Someone was running along the sand. They tripped over the leg from The Awakening sculpture before jumping on one of the Jet Skis and firing it up.

"We have to stop her!" Ben began to untie the lines. "Help me out here."

Adam released the starboard side as Ben fired up the engine. Luckily, he was in the end slip. It was less than a minute before he was out on the river. He could hear the roar of the cigarette boat ahead of them.

"Where is she?" he demanded.

"About a hundred meters behind it," Adam called from the bow. "But she's gaining on them quickly."

Ben gunned the engines but the big boat had too much mass to catch them. Griff barked into his cell phone.

"The coast guard is in place to intercept," he told them.

The news didn't provide the reassurance Ben needed. He urged the *Seas the Day* to move faster.

"Holy shit," Adam called from the bow. "Quinn has nearly caught up to them."

Gunfire echoed up ahead. Ben's breath got caught in his throat. The coast guard cutter flew in from nowhere. His knuckles were white on the wheel. They heard the captain of the cutter ordering both vehicles to stop. Eugenie ignored the command. A moment later, her boat exploded in a ball of fire.

"Quinn!" Ben cried.

But it was no use. The Jet Ski was gone.

CHAPTER NINETEEN

THE SUN WAS barely creeping over the horizon when Ben steered the *Seas the Day* into the slip at the Old Town Alexandria Marina. His head was throbbing and his muscles ached from trawling the water near the accident site. It had been five hours since the explosion. He, Adam, and Griffin had tirelessly searched for any sign of Quinn, until the coast guard captain overseeing the operation had unceremoniously thrown Ben's ass out of the area.

Griffin tied off one side of the stern while Adam took the bow. After killing the engine, Ben grabbed the hose from the dock and aimed it at the blood Caracas and the Monopoly Man left behind. As long as he kept himself busy he wouldn't have to think about the last few hours. His friends had other ideas, however.

"Dude, you're gonna spray a hole into the hull if you keep that up. Why don't I see if one of the guys who work here will detail it for you and we can head back home?"

Griffin's tone was equal parts wary and patronizing with a touch of pity thrown in for good measure. Ben ignored him. Instead, he welcomed the numbness that had begun to seep into his limbs. Detachment was good. It kept the sharp tentacles of anger at bay.

There was more murmuring behind him. Apparently, Marin and Josslyn had been waiting at the dock. He didn't bother acknowledging them when they climbed aboard.

"How is he doing?" Josslyn asked.

"About as bad as a guy can get when they lose the person they love," he heard Adam reply.

"For the second time," Griff added.

"It's so heartbreaking," Marin said.

Tossing down the nozzle, he swore violently.

"I'm right here, you know," he shouted. "You don't have to talk about me like I'm gonna freaking break or something!"

When he spun around to face his friends, all four of them wore identical expressions looking at him like he was going to do just that. Break. And it took every bit of fortitude he possessed not to. Not here. Not in front of them.

"No one thinks you're going to break, Ben," Griff began. "But you aren't made of steel, either. You need to process everything that has happened. If I know you, that brain of yours is demanding answers when there just might not be any. Why don't we head back to the townhouse? You can grab a shower and get some rest."

"I'll cook us breakfast," Marin added. "Whatever you want."

"What I want is to be left alone."

"Oh, Ben," Josslyn spoke softly. "We're your friends. We hate to see you hurting like this. Let us help you."

"She's right," Griff butted in. "You shouldn't be alone

right now."

As if to punctuate their clinginess, Ben's phone buzzed in his pocket. He didn't bother checking the caller ID because he knew it was his sister. She'd already called eleven times in the past hour, likely leaving eleven anguished voice mails of consolation. He wasn't ready to listen to that shit. Hell, he might never be able to listen to it. He turned the ringer off.

"Who told Rebecca?" he snapped.

Adam shot a warning glare from over his fiancée's shoulder.

"I texted her," Josslyn replied. "We all just want to—"

"Smother me?"

Both women gasped. Adam stepped in front of them.

"Bennett, I'm going to give you a free pass on that one, because I can relate to the pain you're feeling right now. And we're going to respect your wishes and give you some space. But don't even think about shutting us out," Adam cautioned. "You were a relentless prick to me last year when it came to burying my emotions. I'll be all too happy to return the favor."

Adam gestured for the women to make their way off the boat. Marin took a step toward Ben but quickly thought better of it. Good thing because he was pretty sure he wouldn't be able to tolerate any touching right now.

"You know where to find us," Griff said. "All you have to do is reach out. Day or night. And we're there."

And they would be. That was the problem. His chosen family would offer platitudes and condolences. They'd feed him and joke with him. But when they were done, they'd pair off and he'd be left alone.

Again.

And there went that anger he was trying to keep reined in, churning in his gut like lava. But, damn it, Quinn had left him. She was gone. Stupidly sacrificing her life to protect him and her parents. And no matter how many cookies Marin tried to feed or how many beers he shared with Griff and Adam, the sting wasn't going away.

Ever.

He jerked at the hose and wound it up. Griff was right about one thing; he needed answers. Minutes later, he was making his way onto the Potomac. He steered the bow of the boat toward the starboard side, careful to navigate past the part of the river where the explosion had taken place last night. The puddle pirates of the coast guard could order him out of that part of the river, but he had every right to search the rest of the Potomac for anything that would give him closure.

Ben doubted he'd ever get out of his mind the image of that ball of fire Quinn ignited when she launched her Jet Ski like a weapon into the hull of the boat. The coast guard hadn't even bothered with rescue mode. They'd gone straight into recovery. Cleaning up the river before the weekend boaters descended in four days.

His throat grew tight and he reached for the bottle of water, chugging half before pouring the rest over top of his head to keep him awake. He sailed aimlessly for an hour, venturing out into the Atlantic where his thoughts were consumed with keeping his boat upright. By the time he turned back, his muscles were exhausted and body was drenched with sweat despite it being barely nine in the morning.

Too bad none of it dulled the pain.

He was passing the buoy marking the turn to Watertown when his phone buzzed with a text. Not surprising it was Rebecca again.

Come home.

As much as he loved and appreciated his family, that was the last thing he wanted to do. But if he went back to Alexandria, Griff and Adam would be lurking around the marina within hours no matter what they'd promised. There was one place he could hide where no one would find him. Where the memories of Quinn would be the most painful because she was the only one he'd ever shared the place with. But as angry as he was at her impetuous act last night, he never wanted to forget her. He steered the *Seas the Day* in the direction of the lighthouse.

Twenty minutes later, he tied off the boat and shoved a six-pack of beers into a backpack. Not enough to get him as soused as he wanted to be, but it was a start. He trudged up the wooden steps and nearly fell back down at the sight of a woman sitting on the porch of the Think Tank.

Too bad it wasn't the woman he dreamed of seeing.

Secretary Lyle got to her feet, brushing sand off her pants as she did so. Ben was tempted to pop the top on one of those beers right now. He glanced over at her detail, both of them were unsuccessful at hiding their pitying looks.

"Caracas?" Ben asked.

"Stable, but the doctors expect him to make a full recovery."

"Be sure and congratulate him for me at the medal ceremony." He moved to go past her, but she blocked him.

Despite the years of having manners and respect drilled into him, Ben had a very difficult time suppressing the urge to shove the woman out of his way.

She cocked her head to the side. "You're angry at me for something. And I'd like to know why."

The truth rolled off his tongue before he could stop it. "It's simple. You ruthlessly sent the woman I loved to her death." He was surprised at how good it felt to get that off his chest.

"Agent Darby did what she thought was necessary."

"The coast guard would have picked Eugenie up!"

The secretary scoffed. "Eugenie was a trained professional. Assets of her caliber don't get *picked up*. She was too big of a liability to me, to you, and to Agent Darby. It was too much of a risk to chance her slipping away."

"So you sent Quinn after her! I saw the little hand signals the two of you were exchanging. What was that some secret code you were taught at spy school?"

He took a step toward her. The agents on her detail edged closer but she waved them away.

"Quinn launched herself at that boat because she believed her only purpose in this world was to serve and protect." His voice grew hoarse as he tried to press the words out past the boulder in his throat. "She also foolishly believed she wasn't deserving of anything more. Well who the hell was serving and protecting her? Not you. Instead you took advantage of that!"

The secretary sighed in exasperation. "Perhaps we should take this inside."

Hell no!

He was done talking. It was time to get a good drunk on. Preferably one that lasted six months.

"Sorry Madame Secretary, I have a strict 'no girls allowed' policy at the Think Tank."

This time he was able to dodge around her. He quickly leaned into the retinal scanner, grateful when the locks clicked open.

"You might want to rethink that policy," she murmured.

"Not gonna happen. And if you don't like it, fire my ass. Better yet, I quit."

He stormed into the lighthouse, satisfaction beginning to build inside him at the idea of slamming the door in his boss's—make that ex-boss's—face. But something inside caught his eye.

More like a someone.

His heart stopped in his chest. The backpack slid from his fingers.

"Quinn," he somehow managed to say.

"Finally," she said, her tone a bit north of snippy. "Where have you been?"

Where had he been? What the hell?

"I'll just let the two of you sort this out," he heard the secretary say. "I'll expect to see both of you in my office—"

He slammed the door in her face.

"You probably shouldn't have done that," Quinn said with a laugh.

The anger he'd been holding in check for past six hours surged to the surface. He stalked across the living room stopping inches from where she stood.

"Never mind that," he bit out. "What do you mean where have *I* been? Where the hell have *you* been?"

She had the good grace to look sheepish. "Here. Waiting for you."

He wanted to touch her. To make sure this wasn't some grief-induced hallucination. But he didn't dare. Because if it really was her standing before him, he might just strangle her.

"I tried to call you." She pulled a cell phone out of her pocket. One adorned with photos of Liam and Brianna on its case. "Multiple times. You wouldn't answer."

"That was you." His brain was having trouble keeping up.

"We didn't have a rendezvous plan. There wasn't time. I knew you'd come here eventually, but I wasn't sure how to get inside. So I went to Watertown and found Rebecca. When you didn't answer my calls, I contacted Secretary Lyle. She has an override for your retina, by the way."

It felt like the world was spinning him in concentric circles. So many thoughts were ricocheting through his mind. He homed in on the most important one.

"I thought you were dead."

"That was the point," she replied, matter-of-factly. "When I've had to do that before, letting someone know I was alive wasn't exactly a priority."

"*You've done that before!*" Ben was pretty sure his head was going to explode.

"Quite successfully, obviously."

That was it. He didn't care if they both self-combusted. No way he couldn't touch her now. He snatched her shoulders and pulled her flush against him.

She winced beneath his touch and he suddenly felt guilty as hell.

"You're hurt?"

"Just my shoulder. It took most of the force when I hit the water."

Relaxing his grip, he leaned down and nudged the strap of her tank top down with his nose before brushing his lips against the already darkening skin.

"Mmm." She arched into him.

He traced is fingers down her arm, alarmed when she jumped again once he reached her wrist.

"Just a little sprain," she whispered.

Gently, he lifted her wrist to his mouth and kissed it.

He was pretty sure the sound that came out of her throat was a purr.

"Any place else?" he asked.

She seductively trailed a finger along her jaw. He obliged her by nipping at the soft skin there.

"How come you don't smell like the Potomac?" he

murmured.

"Oh, didn't I mention I borrowed your shower?" She wrapped her arms around his neck. "It was nice, but not quite as fun as our shower together yesterday morning."

With a growl he hauled her up by the ass until she wrapped her legs around him. He carried her up the stairs.

"You better not have used all of the hot water."

"I'll keep you warm if I did."

Five minutes later, they were naked and slick beneath the twin sprays of water. With their hands and mouths, they worshiped each other, whispering promises of more to come.

"I told you I'd never leave you," she panted when he'd pinned her to the tile wall.

He chuckled. "Yes, but how many lives do you have left, Agent Darby?"

Ever so gently, she cupped his face. "It's just plain old Miss Darby from here on out. I think I'll try my hand at photography full-time. It's definitely a lot safer. And that line of work should leave enough room for me to spend quality time with the other people in my life."

Ben swallowed roughly. He liked the sound of that. Well, all of it except the "plain old Miss Darby" part. There was nothing plain about her. And he had a few suggestions about the Miss Darby moniker, as well. But that could wait. Right now, he was too busy demonstrating his own concept of quality time to her.

EPILOGUE

B EN TUGGED AT the tie of his morning suit with one hand while juggling a glass in the other.

"Is it just me, or does it feel surreal drinking shots in the White House Rose Garden?" Adam was still wearing the same bemused expression he'd been sporting since Josslyn strutted down the aisle an hour before.

Ben, Adam, and Griffin were staked out in a corner of the garden, their backs to the Oval. Each of them held a shot glass of whiskey between their fingers, the amber liquid seeming to wink back at Ben. Wedding guests milled about around them, their attention so focused on nibbling appetizers and enjoying cocktails they largely ignored the groom and his two best men. The former roommates grinned as they clinked their glasses together before downing the contents.

"I'll tell you what feels surreal," Christine announced as she sauntered up to join the trio. "Watching you sworn bachelors willingly walk down the aisle and turn yourselves into adoring saps. And I'm not the only one who feels that way. That sound you hear is the single women all over DC shedding tears of sorrow."

His buddies donned identical shit-eating grins as they

searched the grounds for their respective spouses. Josslyn wasn't hard to find. She was the center of attention in the middle of a sea of lavishly decorated tables. Holding hands with her little niece, Arabelle, the two swayed to the music being played by a string quartet. With every twirl, the hundreds of beads trimming her ivory wedding gown shimmered beneath the rays of the late afternoon sun. Marin watched from a few yards away, standing guard over the stunning three-tier wedding cake she'd crafted for the occasion.

Ben scanned the crowd looking for Quinn. He doubted he'd ever lose the feeling of apprehension that gripped him whenever they were apart. In the two weeks since the incident with Ronoff, they'd spent most of their time holed up at the Think Tank. Thirteen years of lost time was a lot to make up for. They passed the days sharing their dreams and their passion, getting to know one another again as their true selves. Quinn insisted they invite his family and friends to enjoy the lighthouse. He suspected it was her way of trying to win everyone over, but she need not have worried. Once the real Quinn Darby came out from the shadows, everyone instantly fell in love with her.

His heart ticked up a notch when he spied her over in the corner near the Palm Room. With her camera dangling from her fingertips, she was in a deep conversation with the Secretary of Homeland. The other woman was relentless as Fergus trying to get her hooks in Quinn, but until this moment Ben was able to run interference. While he believed Quinn when she said she was out of the game, he didn't trust his boss not to lure her back somehow.

He moved to take a step forward to intervene, but stopped short when the vice president sidled up next to Secretary Lyle, his hand suddenly landing possessively on her back. Ben waited to see the secretary unman the Veep, but she surprised Ben by inching closer to the man. Quinn smiled politely before escaping the two of them and heading back toward the center of the garden. Catching his gaze on her, she winked at him before putting the camera back to her face and capturing what was undoubtedly an adorable shot of Josslyn and her niece.

"Damn. Am I seeing things or does the Veep seem awfully chummy with the secretary?"

"You have been in your lab too long, Inspector Gadget," Christine teased. "Those two have been an item for a couple of months, now. I've been assigned to her detail while Caracas is out and I can report that Secretary Lyle and the vice president are very cute together."

Ben shivered. "'Cute' is not a word I'd ever associate with that woman."

Adam laughed. "The vice president is a stand-up guy. Let's hope she doesn't eat him alive."

"What is with you and ties, Ben?" Christine reached over to adjust his shirt collar and tighten the fabric around his neck. "Honestly, I don't know how you three idiots got so lucky to find women who would have you for the rest of their lives."

Her eyes were shining when she smoothed out Ben's lapels.

"But congratulations. I'm happy for you guys."

Ben brushed a kiss on his colleague's cheek. "You're next."

She swiped at her nose. "Well, if you three can do it, there's hope for me yet."

Adam pulled her in for a hug before Griff followed suit. Seconds later, Arabelle came skipping over to them.

"Uncle Adam." The little girl grabbed Adam's fingers. "It's your turn to dance with me."

Griffin laughed out loud as the normally stoic sniper allowed a six-year-old to drag him onto the dance floor with little struggle.

"Uh-oh, Griff." Christine gestured toward the wedding cake. "I think you better go get your wife before she commits a federal crime tossing her cookies in the White House rose bushes."

"Ah, shit. I thought morning sickness was supposed to only be in the morning." Griffin raced across the garden to rescue a very green Marin.

Ben shook his head with a smile. "You're right, Christine. We have become saps."

"And knowing you three, you'll excel at it. They're very lucky women." She gave his shoulder a pat and wandered over to the bar.

Quinn made her way through the maze of tables to join him. She gifted him with one of her sexy smiles that never failed to make the back of his neck tight. Ben couldn't help himself. He leaned down and pressed a firm kiss to her mouth.

"Enjoying yourself?" he asked against her lips.

"Totally. You have amazing friends."

"They're your friends now, too."

"I know. And I'm still pinching myself." Her voice was filled with wonder. "I never let myself dream of ever having a normal life that included friends."

"It's the 'normal life' part that's going to take some getting used to. Particularly for you."

"About that. . ." Her emerald eyes were solemn. "Secretary Lyle had an idea—"

"No!" The tightness in his neck wasn't so erotic any longer, more like a boa constrictor was wrapping itself around him. No way was Quinn putting herself back in danger. Not when he'd just found her again. Not when she was his future. He'd kill the secretary first.

She closed the distance between their bodies and placed her palm on his chest. His breathing seemed to steady with her touch.

"It's not what you're thinking," she explained. "She wants me to teach. At Langley. And she's asked my mum to come, too."

His vision began to clear. "Would that make you happy?"

"It would make me feel useful." She wrapped her arms around his neck. "But I only need one thing to make me happy, Ben Segar. And that's you. We're a team. Now and forever."

"I think I can get behind that mission."

From across the rose garden, Secretary Lyle watched

two of the intelligence community's best operatives exchange a passionate kiss.

"They make a nice couple," her companion remarked.

"They do," she replied with a sigh.

"Don't sound so disappointed. You did a kind thing finally putting them back together."

She hadn't done it to be kind. She'd done it for Ethan. To right a wrong. Ethan was always the more romantic one. In her line of work, happy endings were rare. It was nice to finally orchestrate one.

"Love wins out," she replied.

"As it always should."

THE END

ACKNOWLEDGEMENTS

Some books it takes a village to prop me up and keep me writing. This one would not have been possible without three people in my village. Allison Baker, thanks for always being my plot whisperer. I love that you dream about my books. Or was it a nightmare? Melanie Lanham and Anna Doll, huge thanks for volunteering to proofread the final version days before Christmas. I love you ladies!

THE MEN OF THE SECRET SERVICE SERIES

Book 1: *Recipe for Disaster*

Book 2: *Shot in the Dark*

Book 3: *Between Love and Honor*

More fantastic reads by Tracy Solheim

Smolder

Holiday at Magnolia Bay

Available now at your favorite online retailer!

ABOUT THE AUTHOR

Tracy Solheim is the international bestselling author of the Out of Bound Series for Penguin. Her books feature members of the fictitious Baltimore Blaze football team and the women who love them. In a previous life, Tracy wrote best sellers for Congress and was a freelance journalist for regional and national magazines. She's a military brat who now makes her home in Johns Creek, Georgia, with her husband, their two children, a pesky Labrador retriever puppy and a horse named after her first novel. Her fifth book for Berkley, Back To Before, will be released in January. She also has a digital holiday novella for Tule Publishing's Southern Born Books coming October 20. See what she's up to at www.tracysolheim.com. Or on facebook at Tracy Solheim Books and Twitter at @TracyKSolheim.

Thank you for reading

BETWEEN LOVE AND HONOR

If you enjoyed this book, you can find more from all our great authors at TulePublishing.com, or from your favorite online retailer.

TULE
PUBLISHING

CPSIA information can be obtained
at www.ICGtesting.com
Printed in the USA
LVHW110020010420
651840LV00005B/1351

9 781951 786373